'The Prisoner of Mount Warning: With a ⟨ 〉... a
journey from Sydney to the dope fields or Byron Bay, the private eye
novel has come a long way from Raymond Chandler ... the detective
novel's move into an era of magic mushrooms and free love.'
– Sydney Morning Herald

'National Treasure: Michael Wilding has form ... Witty and genuinely
funny ... But don't be conned. This is fiction with more truth than lies.'
– Christopher Bantick, Weekend Australian

'Thoroughly enjoyable, sometimes hilarious ... But it is not lightweight:
it is tough, well-calculated, smoothly witty.'
– Brian Matthews, Australian Book Review

'Superfluous Men: I laughed out loud quite a few times and chuckled
often. You're the funniest writer around.' – Peter Corris

'You have a way of being gloomily funny that speaks for all the early-
retired and those who cannot avoid weary contempt for the bureaucrats
both in and out of the universities.' – Frank Kermode

'Academia Nuts: Wilding at his absolute satirical best.' – David Williamson

'Very clever, in the grand tradition of Lucky Jim.' – The Guardian

'A witty campus novel? In 2004? It seemed as likely as a holiday
romance set amid the tropical delights of Guantanamo Bay ... But it is
very funny. So funny that I had to stop reading it in bed in case my roars
of laughter were disturbing the neighbours: so funny that it deserves to
be the final great campus novel. It is unlikely to be challenged. For what
Wilding's aged unreconstructed dons are playing with such absurd brio
is unmistakably the last waltz.'
– Laurie Taylor, Times Higher Educational Supplement

'Wild Amazement: What I think absorbs the reader in the deeply
revelatory unmemoir Wild Amazement is ... Michael's clear, almost
hyper real remembrance, as if experienced on a guided tour of a radiant,

countercultural Disneyland, of a way of life, and a gravely joyous
bohemia now gone, of how it was, and what a time it was, it really was,
in Sydney in the sixties and seventies, in the Newcastle and the Journos'
Club and the Push parties and the plans for a literary life.'
– Bob Ellis, *Overland*.

*'Wildest Dreams*: Deserves to be thought of as a contemporary classic.'
– Adrian Caesar. An *Australian* Book of the Year

*'Raising Spirits, Making Gold and Swapping Wives: the True Adventures of
Dr John Dee and Sir Edward Kelly*: The story of Queen Elizabeth I's necro-
mancer, John Dee, as transcribed from original documents interspersed
with Michael Wilding's own words. A piece of esoterica designed to
startle and delight the modern reader.' – Peter Porter, *The Economist*
Books of the Year

*'Living Together*: A very funny book and a perfect picture of the people,
the time, the place … Wilding's writing has a dry vitality – alert, acid,
but often grimly intelligent.' – David Marr

*'Pacific Highway*: … humorous … menacing …'
– Brian Kiernan, *Running Wild*

*'Somewhere New*: What strikes one first, apart from the impressive merits
of individual stories, is Wilding's keen sense of literary integrity …
Wilding's voice in these stories is always one to attend to: an ironic,
witty, highly educated, … passionate authorial persona who has
believed in literature as a life of principle … No one in English writes
better fiction about the process of writing than Wilding.' – Don Graham

*'This is for You*: 21st-century writing for 21st-century people.'
– J. P. Donleavy.

'Erotic, fiercely intelligent and mordantly funny.'
– Janette Turner Hospital.

'His stories subvert and transcend not only sexual and social conventions
… but story-telling itself.' – Jim Crace

# THE MAGIC
# OF IT

Michael Wilding's fiction includes *Living Together*, *The Short Story Embassy*, *The Man of Slow Feeling*, *The Paraguayan Experiment*, *Wild Amazement*, *Academia Nuts* and *Superfluous Men*. His private-eye Plant previously debuted in the pilot *National Treasure* (2007) and *The Prisoner of Mount Warning* (2010).

He has taught English and Australian Literature and creative writing at the University of Sydney, where he is now emeritus professor, and various universities internationally. He has also been a milkman, postman, apple-picker, newspaper columnist, *Cosmopolitan* Bachelor of the Month, Fellow of the Australian Academy of the Humanities, and Chair of the New South Wales Writers' Centre.

## Also by Michael Wilding

www.michael-wilding.com

# THE MAGIC OF IT

Michael Wilding

Illustrations by
Garry Shead

ARCADIA

This Project has been assisted by the Australian Government through the Australia Council, its arts funding and advisory body.

**Australian Government**

Australia Council
for the Arts

*Press On – 8*
ISSN 1836-9413

The Magic Of It

Sir Henry Parkes is quoted from 'A. G. Stephens's Bulletin Diary', ed. Leon Cantrell, in Bruce Bennett, ed., *Cross Currents: Magazines and Newspapers in Australian Literature*, Longman Cheshire, Melbourne, 1981. A couple of sentences describing the University grounds are quoted from Christina Stead, *Seven Poor Men of Sydney*, 1934.

FIRST EDITION

ISBN 978-1-921875-37-3

National Library of Australia
Cataloguing-in-publication entry:
Michael Wilding
The Magic Of It
Illustrations by Garry Shead
ISBN: 978-1-921875-37-3
I. Title.
A823.3

Design and typesetting by Art Rowlands
Set in Palatino 11.5pt
Printed by Tenderprint Australia Pty Ltd

Published in Australia by Arcadia
the general books' imprint of Australian Scholarly Publishing Pty Ltd

*To Jean Bedford and Peter Corris*

# One

The phone rang. Plant's enemy. He hated it when it rang for the trouble it invariably brought. He hated it when it failed to ring, for its failure to bring work, or joy, or diversion, or even just the reassurance that there was a world out there that cared about him. Perhaps hatred was too strong a word. Resentment, perhaps. No, resentment was not right. Hatred was bad. It was not good to hate. But it captured his feelings.

The answering machine kicked in.

'Your call could not be taken. Please leave a message after the tone.'

Plant sat there, monitoring it.

'Macabre,' said a voice. Slow, sinister, resonant, dwelling on the Rs, more Rs than the word possessed, rolling them with a skill attainable only by long practice. 'Drop round, would you.'

Plant picked up the receiver but the line was already dead, and the machine was offering bland thanks for the message.

He took his phone book from the desk. No doubt he could have had all the numbers programmed into the handset. And no doubt that way they could be accessed. And not only by himself. No doubt someone could copy his phone book too, but it would involve more trouble. He found the number and called back. Without thinking. Had he thought, he might not have called. But then what would he have done? Sat there

1

the rest of the day glowering at the silent machine.

'Macabre,' said the voice again.

'Plant,' said Plant.

'Yes.'

'You called.'

'Yes.'

'I just missed it.'

'Yes,' said the voice. 'Not the story of your life, let us hope.'

'What can I do for you?' said Plant.

'I left you a message.'

'Here I am,' said Plant.

'The message stands.'

'You want me to drop round?'

'So the message states.'

'When?'

'No time like the present.'

'I might have a few things to do.'

'Most unlikely.'

'I guess so,' said Plant. But the line had already gone dead.

'See,' he said to the phone, 'no one trusts you. No one even wants to speak to you.'

*

It could have been Mackenzie Arber himself who had exploited the connotations of his name. The alternative theory was that he had come to accept that that was how people referred to him, Macabre, and had come

2

to terms with it, using it himself so it would not seem to be something that annoyed him. He began to dress himself in black and hang peculiar looking metallic medallions on a chain round his neck, like a bishop of an unregistered religious order. These days he had shaved off his greasy and no doubt greying locks and went around bald. Plant found him unsavoury. But he found more and more people unsavoury. And they appeared to prosper, the unsavoury ones. Prosper and multiply.

The little bell rang as Plant opened the door to Mac Arber's bookshop. A tinkling little fairy bell. Somehow it always annoyed Plant. Or maybe just stepping inside the doorway upset him, some weird energy settling on him immediately and disturbing his fragile sense of wellbeing. The smell of burning incense hung heavily in the low-ceilinged room. The music of Peter Warlock accompanied it.

What am I doing here? Plant asked himself, why do I do this?

Because I have so little else to do, is that the sorry answer? So little work, and so few inner resources? It seemed so. One thing to be said for visiting Mac Arber, it made him feel he should change his ways. Perhaps that was why he called in so rarely and so reluctantly.

'Keeping busy?' said Mac Arber. He flashed an evil smile. 'Clearly not.'

He could have replied, yes, hectic, what was it you wanted, you've got a hundred and eighty seconds, spill it. But he didn't. The mistake was ever to have

3

entered Mac's shop. He was wrong-footed as soon as he stepped inside the door.

'So,' he said.

'So shall you reap,' said Mac Arber.

Sometimes, generally indeed, it was just too hard to attempt to deal with Mac. Sometimes it was best just to stand there impassively. Plant tried it for a while. Most distasteful thing I ever stood still for, as William Burroughs put it. Mac turned the pages of something on his desk. It could have been a rare folio. Or it could have been the local street paper. He moistened his thumb and forefinger, protruding a purple tongue through distended lips, before turning each page. Plant waited. Peter Warlock was succeeded by the flagellant beat of Percy Grainger.

'OK, tell me,' said Plant.

Mac Arber put a damp finger to the side of a hairy nostril.

'You still drink coffee?'

'No,' said Plant.

'A little place down the street does a nice line in tisanes.'

'Let's go.'

'So impatient,' said Mac.

Plant headed out to the pavement and the fresh, polluted, carbon-saturated streets of Glebe. Mac turned his OPEN sign round in the window. HAVING A READ. TRY AGAIN LATER, it announced.

'Shop bugged?' Plant asked.

'Who knows?'

'I'm sure you do. Taping your customers, is that it?'

'Taping them, really, you think I'm offering bondage now?'

'I think you'd offer anything if there was a percentage in it,' said Plant.

'A significant percentage,' said Mac.

'You don't come cheap,' said Plant. 'Any more.'

'A matter of what the market will bear,' said Mac.

\*

They sat in Mac's chosen dive, metal chairs and black-topped tables made from some unspeakable composite. Black-clad, metal-pierced creatures sat around. The university cast its baleful influence over the suburb but these were not students. Graduate students, maybe. Lecturers in media or gender studies. Maybe just creatures drawn to the baleful ambience. In another era they would have been succubi and incubi. Or succubuses and incubuses.

Mac ordered a long black coffee. Plant asked for the same.

'I thought you said you no longer drank coffee,' Mac said.

'Only when I thought you were threatening to make me one.'

'You don't like my coffee? Or you fear I might slip in some love philtre?'

'Something like that.'

'What I like about you,' said Mac, 'and this won't

take long, is how unforthcoming you are.'

'Takes one to spot one.'

Mac beamed.

'Can we get to the point?'

'But of course,' said Mac. He blew across the surface of his coffee.

'You called me.'

'Indeed.'

'So?'

'So here you are. You know how much I enjoy your company.'

'I guess sitting in that shop all day with nobody coming in you've got nothing better to do than practise prevaricating conversations.'

'You'd be surprised,' said Mac. 'You would be surprised how many people call in.'

'I would.'

'And what fascinating things they have to say.'

'Tell me.'

'No.'

Plant sighed and waited.

'You're still doing research assistance?'

'If I'm asked nicely.'

'And investigative reporting?'

'You know me,' said Plant.

'I had a visitor,' said Mac. 'An old acquaintance. A client from long ago and far away.'

'Back from beyond the grave?' suggested Plant.

'How right you are. From the old world.'

'Your fame has spread.'

'It has,' said Mac modestly. 'But in this case I knew him before he was translated to the further shore.'

'A he,' said Plant.

'You prefer lady clients?'

'Just establishing the first fact in this miasma of memory lane.'

'But you still prefer the ladies.'

'They can be troublesome.'

'Exactly,' said Mac. 'I think they may have been troubling my visitor.'

'Is that so?'

'I only suspect. He was not forthcoming.'

'Must have been some conversation,' said Plant. 'The two of you playing evasions.'

'He needs some assistance,' said Mac. 'Research assistance. I said I would inquire. Are you busy at the moment?'

'Always busy,' said Plant.

'So you'd be interested?'

'Could be. Who is he?'

'He is quite eminent.'

'Naturally.'

'He used to teach down the street.' Mac gestured in the direction of the university. 'Then he went off.'

'But now he's back.'

'Briefly. Distinguished visiting professor. Or British Academy travel scholarship. You know the sort of thing. Other people's money.'

'So how do you know him?'

'We go back a long time.'

'So you said. Doing what?'

'I used to look out for things for him.'

'What sort of things?'

'Books, of course.'

'Of course. What sort of books?'

'Rare books.'

'Aren't they all?'

'Some are rarer than others.'

'Those sort of books.'

'Oh no, not those sort. He wouldn't have needed to buy those. The university library has one of the finest collections of those in the world. Of the historic material, anyway. Not so hot on the contemporary. He could just have closeted himself away in the X cage if that was what he wanted.'

'If you say so,' said Plant.

'Whatever made you think I deal in that sort of thing?'

'Intuition,' said Plant.

'Of course. How could I forget? You are a researcher.'

'I am indeed,' said Plant. 'Though I am not finding out that much at this very moment.'

'Oh dear,' said Mac. 'Professional confidences, you know. The habit of caution.'

'That why you dress like a defrocked priest?' said Plant. 'The secrets of the confessional.'

'In another lifetime I would still have been wearing my frock,' said Mac.

'I hear you can still be seen in it in this one,' said Plant. 'What sort of books?'

'Pure magic,' Mac cooed.

'I'm sure. Aren't all your books?'

'You flatter me,' said Mac, 'but you speak the truth.'

'I wish you would.'

'Flatter you?'

'Speak the truth.'

'Oh, but I do,' said Mac. 'That was his interest. He became an authority. And in my little way I helped. Helped him build up his library. So he could write his learned studies.'

'What learned studies?'

'Magic,' said Mac. 'How many times must I tell you?'

'So why does he need my help if he's a magician? I'd have thought he'd be able to find out just about anything if he's any good.'

'I didn't say he was a magician,' said Mac. 'He is an academic. A historian of magic rather than a practising magus.'

'So he's not going to cast spells on me if he doesn't like me.'

Mac giggled.

'Oh, he might. But then, who could fail to like you?'

'So what does he want me to do? Track down some rare old books?'

'Oh no, I can do that,' said Mac.

'I didn't mean to tread on your toes.'

Mac smiled.

'Feel free,' he said. 'Any time.'

'And if he's an academic he must have a team of

research assistants to look things up in the library for him.'

'I don't think it is library work that he wants done.'

'So what is it?'

'I think it would be best if he tells you himself,' said Mac.

'So where do I find him?'

'Ah,' said Mac, spooning out some dregs of undissolved sugar from the bottom of his cup and gazing at them as if he were attempting divination. 'That could be a problem.'

'Don't tell me,' said Plant. 'He's invisible.'

'Oh no,' said Mac. 'No, he aims for a very high profile. Invisibility is not for him. No, he's travelling.'

'On his broomstick? Astrally?'

'Wouldn't that be lovely?' said Mac. 'How, I know not. When, I do. He is out of town till Wednesday evening. Then he addresses the Friends of the University Library. Just turn up there and make yourself known to him. He thought that might be the easiest.'

'Easiest for him, no doubt,' said Plant. 'And how did he know I would be available next Wednesday evening?'

'Not by second sight,' Mac assured him. 'We all know you're always available.'

'I might not be interested in that sort of thing.'

'How can you not be interested? With that extravagant lifestyle you have to maintain.'

'What extravagant lifestyle?'

'Just keeping that body and soul together,' said Mac. 'Don't you find it a struggle?'

# Two

Plant had never found the university library an especially friendly place. Any place that levied fines had trouble sustaining friendship. Some of the librarians were friendly. But others exuded an air of resentment, a compound of envy of the academic borrowers who did not have to keep long regular hours in the air-conditioned nightmare, and loathing of the students who had their life before them and could make better choices. He was not surprised that the assembled Friends of the Library totalled no more than a dozen. Including himself. He suspected he had been instructed to meet there in order to swell the numbers; if the addition of one person could be thought to swell anything.

He made his way down beneath the surface of the earth. The meeting was in a basement room deep in the building's bowels. The windowless walls were lined with glass-fronted wooden bookcases. Locked, all of them. He checked. The leather bindings and gold lettering proclaimed rare books. He looked through the glass at them. This was not the collection of erotica for which the library was once famed. That was kept down beneath the bowels, in the gonads.

Along with the memories of slaughtered cattle, the leather bindings attempted to exude other achievements of old-world culture. Theology. Philosophy. Voyages of Exploration and Discovery.

But locked away, they could do little to communicate any of it. They rested there immobilised in the constant-temperature recycled air, inert. Plant sat there with them.

Dr Major bustled in, bringing the assembled number to thirteen. A coven. He put his briefcase on the table in the front and proceeded to take out books. He stacked them in two piles, spines towards his audience so they could read the titles. MAJOR MAGIC the spines proclaimed. They were all the same book. All twelve of them. How had he known how many he would need to bring to sell one to everybody? Divination? Or the long experience of addressing library friends? Plant pondered and did the sums. If Major sold ten a week for fifty weeks of the year that would be five hundred copies. Six hundred if he sold twelve. A good sale for an academic book. And that would be on top of bookshop sales. Assuming there were any. And assuming he could average a bunch of library friends or amateur magicians or adult education students gathered in meet-the-writer seminars once a week. Maybe once a month was more realistic. One hundred and forty-four copies a year. With print runs of academic books down from four hundred to two hundred copies an edition, it was an acceptable total.

Dr Major was a dapper sort of fellow. None of the baggy Harris Tweed and leather-patched elbow look, no egg-stained tie and dirty scuffed shoes of the classic academic. He was more of a modern classic. Lightweight suit, hand-stitched lapels. Striped tie that no doubt blazoned some collegiate affiliation. Or regimental. Light blue pressed shirt, tonally complementing the darker blue suit. Highly polished shoes. Gold rimmed glasses, put on and off for effect. Thick gold wedding ring.

The talk was pretty dapper, too. And no less highly polished. A magisterial range as more or less befitted his name. Witch-burnings through the ages. Innocent old women scapegoated. Wise women healers persecuted by patriarchal medical establishment. Analogies with the Holocaust. Shamanism. Aboriginal men of high degree. Respect for indigenous peoples. All shiningly politically correct. Blowfish and zombies and Tonton Macoute, as seen in Graham Greene. Anglo-Saxon charms. Love philtres from former canonical texts, *Romeo and Juliet*, *A Midsummer Night's Dream*. Dr Dee and Sir Edward Kelly summoning up angels. Aleister Crowley summoning up demons. Dennis Wheatley and Harry Potter to round it all off. Witty rather than impassioned. There was no indication of whether he believed in any of it.

Plant wondered if it was carefully pitched at the sort of general interest audience Major knew from experience he was likely to encounter. Or if it was spontaneously and naturally bland. It offered anecdotal frissons, but nothing intellectually disturbing. Major could have given the talk a thousand times, and probably had. But the delivery was lively. The teeth flashed a white, welcoming smile. The range implied a global expertise. It was unclear to Plant

14

whether there was any specific scholarly depth, any individual, original research underpinning it. But then it wasn't an academic paper. More of an evening's light entertainment. Even if the audience for such occasions had waned over the years. Basically Plant wondered why bother? But he wondered that about more and more human endeavour, including much if not most of his own.

Afterwards, after the painful wait for questions and the scraping around by the retired librarian introducing the session to think of some, followed by the vote of thanks, and the presentation of a book token to the speaker, and the acclamation, the audience lined up to buy a signed copy of the new book. At a special price for the evening. Twenty per cent discount. It still seemed expensive, to Plant, but half a dozen people bought copies. Plant waited till the business was finished and then joined the dispersed queue.

Major flashed him a glittering smile and opened a book to inscribe it.

'Name,' he demanded.

'No, no,' said Plant, quickly. But not quickly enough.

'To Nono,' Major wrote, 'with best wishes, Arch Major.'

It was a practised flourish, fountain pen, gold nib, real black ink.

'No,' said Plant, 'I'm not buying a book. Or I wasn't.'

The smile went steely. It was not just without warmth, it had a positive chill.

'You asked to meet me here.'

'Meet you?' said Major. He made it sound like mincemeat.

'Mac Arber set it up.'

'Set it up? Set what up?'

'He said you needed some research done.'

'Research?' Major said. 'I do my own research, thank you very much. How do you think I write these books? By trusting irresponsible incompetents? Hands on, that's my principle.'

He put the pen back in an inside pocket and opened and shut his hands, flexing the fingers. Heavy academic menace.

'Admirable,' said Plant. 'But Mac gave me the impression this might be a different sort of research. More investigative.'

Major stopped in mid flex.

'Ah, you're that chap. Of course. That puts a different complexion on it. Well, you might as well take the book now I've inscribed it.' He looked at it before he handed it over. 'Nono,' he added. Alert to the principle of always using peoples' names when you want to do business with them.

'The name's Plant,' said Plant.

'Nono Plant,' said Major.

'Keith, actually.'

'Nono some kind of nickname?'

'Why not?' Plant agreed.

He took it as the price to pay for not paying for the book.

*

They walked through the university grounds. Beneath the crescent moon the pseudo-Gothic buildings looked suitably pseudo-Gothic. Grotesques of merino rams and kangaroos peered down at them. Huge fruit-bats circled round, passing across the silver scimitar. Possums gibbered in the trees. Low throbbings emanated from deserted buildings, evil experiments, or air-conditioning keeping evil experiments cool. Frogs croaked in the basement of the old Teachers College and in the University Oval. Faint lights gleamed, as in castles over the bog, in the Methodist and Presbyterian Colleges. A paralysed wasteland in which nothing changed, suspended in time.

'The thing is,' said Major, 'I've been getting threats.'

'What sort of threats?'

'Oh, the usual kind. Anonymous notes of the "All is discovered, flee while you can" kind.'

'What do they say?'

'"All is discovered, flee while you can."'

'Really?'

'Yes, really. Could be a try-on, of course. Sending them to everyone on spec and seeing how many run. But I haven't heard of anyone else getting them.'

'Have you asked?'

'Of course not.'

'How long has this been happening?'

'A couple of months. Since I've been in Australia.'

'Where were you before?'

'Oxford, of course.'

He said it with some irritation, as if Plant should have known.

'And you didn't receive any notes there?'

'Oxford? No.'

The effrontery of even suggesting it.

'Any idea what they're about?'

'None at all.'

'Or who might be sending them?'

'No.'

'Not even a suspicion?'

'No.'

'You used to teach here, didn't you?'

'Aeons ago.'

'Could it be a jealous former colleague?'

'Easily.'

'An ex-girlfriend?'

Major gave his flaring, toothy grin.

'The thought had passed my mind.'

'I thought you had no suspicions.'

'I don't.'

'But you concede it could be a girlfriend. Or a colleague.'

'Ex-girlfriend. Former colleague,' said Major. 'Can't help having thoughts. Even discreditable ones.'

'How long are you here for?'

'Nearly done,' said Major. 'Off to the University of Mangoland tomorrow followed by a quick trip to Mount Krakatoa Bat Caves College. After which, the Byron Bay Writers' Festival, and then back to the home of lost causes.'

'So how long?'

'Give it another couple of weeks.'

'And you've been here how long?'

'I told you. A couple of months. I had the term off. Thought I'd revisit the old place. See what I was missing. Not a lot. Not a lot at all.'

'Are you teaching here?'

'Heaven forbid.'

'So you're doing what, exactly?'

'Bit of this, bit of that. Promoting the book. The one you have there. Limbering up for the new project. Change of clime. You know.'

'Not sure I do,' said Plant, 'but I'll believe you.'

They had passed the sports oval and reached the colleges.

'Might as well come in for a drink since you're here,' Major suggested.

## Three

They climbed echoing concrete stairs to a bleak institutional room. The furnishings had the note of post Second World War austerity, a utilitarian brown pervading everything, transforming what was probably real, endangered rainforest wood into the appearance of ersatz veneer. Major dropped his briefcase onto a desk and gestured at a nasty, narrow armchair. Plant sat in it. An open door revealed a bedroom with a made bed. Single. A bookcase held a couple of dozen copies of MAJOR MAGIC standing to attention. The weekly world edition of the UK *Telegraph* protruded from the plastic bag lining a waste paper bin beneath the desk. The room looked totally impersonal, temporary home to a succession of itinerant academics who had left no individual trace. There was a pervasive chill.

Major opened a cupboard and brought out a bottle of McWilliams.

'Sherry, Nono?' he asked.

Plant tried to recall when he had last been offered a sherry. Christmas at his aunt's? Melbourne University?

'It's tolerable,' Major assured him. 'Australians should've stuck with what they knew and carried on making sherry. No point trying to beat the Frogs at what they know best.'

'What do they know best?'

'The Frogs? Wine-making, of course. Apart from revolting and collaborating. Always felt it was a bad

20

idea trying to flood the world with Australian wine. Same with Australian movies.'

'Leave it to the French?'

'I think so, don't you? Or the Californians.'

He finished inspecting the bottle and glasses and poured Plant a drink.

'No nibblies, sorry about that.'

He turned an upright chair around from the desk, and sat on it. Maybe politeness required he offered the single armchair to Plant. Maybe the upright was more comfortable. Maybe he calculated that it gave him the commanding heights.

Plant was used to being commanded. 'Tell me more about the threats,' he said.

'No more to tell, really.'

'Well fill me in on the background,' said Plant. 'You're visiting your old department?'

'Absolutely not. Miserable buggers. I wrote and offered and they said they had no budget for visitors. I told them I didn't need their filthy lucre, just a room. They replied they had no office accommodation either. They call them offices here. Rather vulgar, don't you think? They had the hide to suggest I apply for a carrel in the library stacks. Rather have a bench in the park. So I got an old mate to fix me up in college here. You can forget the department. Once you've left, they hate you. Once you've shown them you can survive without them, survive better away from them, show them there's a real world out there and you can do very nicely in it, thank you very much, they're consumed

23

with envy and resentment.'

'So that might explain the threatening notes.'

'Yes, it might. Some threat.'

'But you take it as threatening enough to ask me to look into it.'

'I haven't asked you yet.'

Plant stirred in his chair.

'Do you want me to look into it?'

'Reckon you can do anything?'

'What do you want done?'

'Find out who's been sending them for starters.'

'I can try.'

'You get paid for trying or you get paid by results?'

'I work on a retainer.'

'I feared you would.' He smiled at Plant, his white, disarming smile. 'I mean you'd have to, wouldn't you?'

'So you have no contact with the English department. Or your former colleagues.'

'Oh, I bump into them round the traps,' Major said. 'That's all I'd expect, anyway. I wasn't planning to try and pinch their piddling jobs off them. Seduce their students, or anything.'

'Could that be a possibility?'

'Could what?'

'Seducing students.'

'In this day and age? Forget it. You'd have to be suicidal.'

'In the past?'

'In the past? The past is a foreign country.'

'Could that perhaps lie behind the notes?'

'Ah. I see what you're driving at.'

Plant waited impassively.

'Have another sherry, Nono?'

'Why not?'

'Why not, indeed? The attitude that can get us all into so much trouble.'

'And has it?'

'I've no idea. That's where you come in.'

'But you think it might have.'

'Could've. No doubt could've.'

'Can I see one of these notes?'

'Didn't keep them. Tossed them out straight away.'

'In the bin?' Plant asked. He looked across at it, reluctant to get up and rummage around amongst old apple cores and expatriate English newspapers.

'Burned them, actually. That's what you do with that sort of thing. Consume the evil intent in a purifying element.'

Plant looked up.

'Just quoting,' said Major.

'Quoting what?'

'Myself, who better? My book. What to do with magic spells. Burn them.'

'Is that so?'

'According to the best authorities.'

'Of which you're one.'

'Oh, I'm just a scholar. Don't go thinking I believe in all that.'

'But you still burned the notes.'

'Can't be too careful.'

'Maybe it would be more careful to keep the next one. Give us something to go on.'

'If you say so. If there is another one.'

'You don't think there will be.'

'No idea.'

'How seriously are you taking this?' Plant asked.

Major tugged at his right ear lobe. Plant promised himself to read Major on Magic carefully to see if that was a ritual gesture for warding off something or other.

'Normally I wouldn't bother a damn,' said Major. 'I don't think they're death threats, do you?'

'It has been known.'

'I imagine it has.'

Plant waited.

'But the reason I thought I should see you, or someone like you,' he began, and tailed off. 'The thing is, it's a ticklish situation at the moment. I'm a contender for a top job.'

'I thought you had a top job.'

'Just an Oxford fellow,' said Major. 'Up to twenty hours a week teaching.'

'So there are higher things?'

'I'm in for a chair.'

'As in a professorship.'

'As in a professorship. I wouldn't want some idiotic business like this queering my pitch.'

'Why would it?'

'Depends how widely these notes are being sent.'

'Is there anything in it? From the way you describe them, they're not specific.'

'Wouldn't matter if there was or there wasn't. Send notes like this round to the committee, they'll think no smoke without fire.'

'And not just from burning evil intent in a purifying element.'

'Exactly.'

'And is there?'

'Is there what?'

'Is there anything in it?'

'Who can say? No knowing what's behind it.'

'Some big scandal you're not telling me about?'

'Of course not.'

'Some small one.'

'Not that I know of. But these chaps can blow up anything out of proportion. Tell total lies, for that matter.'

'You think it's a chap.'

'Manner of speaking.'

'Could it be a woman?'

'Could be, no doubt.'

'A sexual harassment case?'

'Why do you say that?'

'They're all the rage.'

'Can't think of anything. Nothing done without consent. Nothing done under age.'

'That's not necessarily the issue. They can allege improper influence.'

'I'm sure all sorts of things can be alleged,' said

Major, 'but my conscience is clean.'

'Hands clean too?'

Major held them out. Well-kept fingernails. No signs of heavy lifting or untoward manual endeavour. No cuts or sores from cultivating the garden. No shaking. Palms down. No chance to read them.

'Maybe you should tell me anything in your past you might think could be a problem.'

'You're joking,' said Major.

'Not at all,' said Plant.

'You think I'm going to plunge into an orgy of self-incrimination you can record on your files for anyone to see?'

'No one sees my files.'

'Anyone can see anyone's files if they're determined enough,' said Major. 'No, no, Nono, you don't catch an old bird with chaff. I plead the fifth on that one. You find out anything that might be construed as problematic, I'll fill you in on it. But I'm not going to dictate to you the record of my secret life.'

'But there is such.'

'Such what?'

'My Secret Life? My Life and Loves? Memoirs of Casanova?'

Major seemed to be torn between vainglorious boasting and protestations of innocence. It was hard for a career academic of a certain age to claim that he'd never had a bit on the side, never availed himself of the pulchritudinous offerings of the liberated years. Machismo required it. And it was hard for the sensitive

New Age survivor in the era of political correctness to admit that he'd ever tiptoed through the tulips, sauntered down the primrose path, plucked the flowers of yesteryear. Oh, how the rules had changed.

'Look, Nono, I'm just your average, decent family man, nothing more, nothing less. Just a regular guy. I don't know what's behind these notes. Probably nothing. But they need to be looked into. Could be some lunatic. But lunatics have a way of causing trouble. And right now I don't want any trouble.'

'You want this top job. This chair.'

'Of course I do. Who wouldn't?'

'Who else does?'

'What do you mean?'

'Who are your rivals for it? Could one of them be sending the notes?'

'Hard to imagine. Hardly think of them as rivals. Candidates. But I suppose they could.'

'Are any of them here?'

'In Australia? I shouldn't think so. None that I know of.'

'So since the notes began here we'd best begin looking here. And they may have nothing to do with the job. Who knows you're in for it?'

'My referees. The committee, maybe, if it's met yet. Otherwise no one. You don't go around telling people you've applied for these things. I don't think the notes necessarily have anything to do with it. It's just unfortunate timing.'

They left it at that. Or rather, Major left it at that.

'You know your way round the place, I gather.'

'I can find the gate to get out,' said Plant.

'That's always worth knowing,' said Major. 'But what I meant was, you know how the place works. You did research here.'

'I did research here.'

'Ever complete it?'

'Yes.'

'Well, that puts you in a select twenty-two per cent or less.'

Plant nodded.

Major didn't ask what the topic had been. Maybe Mac had told him. Maybe he didn't care.

'So it's over to you,' said Major. 'You want a cheque in advance?'

Plant nodded.

'As long as it's on an Australian bank.'

'Suspicious blighter, aren't you,' said Major. 'That's good, part of your job I imagine. Yes, we keep an account open here.'

He took out his Mont Blanc and his cheque book and signed one.

'Let me know if any more notes show up,' Plant said, putting it carefully in his wallet.

'Of course.'

'Let me see them before you burn them. Don't just photocopy them.'

'Will do,' said Major.

# Four

'This is a regular lunch date, is it?' Plant asked.

'I suppose you could call it that,' said Dennis.

'Like every month?'

'Well, a bit more often.'

'Once a week?'

'That sort of thing.'

'Every few days?' Plant persisted.

'A man's got to eat,' said Dennis. 'We used to come here when we had to teach. Get up steam to spend the afternoon sweating over a hot student or two. Trouble was you had to drag yourself out and get back on time. Missed them once or twice towards the end. They'd cut and run. Can't say I blamed them. Felt that way myself.' He sighed, unregretfully. 'Thankfully all that's finished with retirement. Now we can spread ourselves. The padrone's an understanding sort of bloke. Leaves us alone. Lets us sit here till they start coming in for dinner, he doesn't seem to mind. Starched tablecloths. Doesn't mark up the wine too much. What more can you want?'

Dennis had been around the university for years. He had once been one of Plant's supervisors, the one he had preferred. He had been an ideal supervisor. He never inquired how Plant was doing, never even inquired what he was doing. He just let him be, which was the perfect, non-invasive supervision relationship. If Plant wanted to see him or ask him to read a chapter, he was always available. But otherwise he left Plant to himself. Plant had kept in touch in the same detached sort of way over the years. Dennis had never shown any interest in having protégées. He had never shown any interest in having students, for that matter. He certainly had no interest in their subsequent careers. He had no ambitions in using his successful students as a stepping-stone to higher things. He had no interest in higher things. But he was always interested in having lunch. He seemed the obvious person to ask about Major.

'You don't miss the teaching?' Plant asked.

'Can't say I do. How about you, Tony?'

'What's that?' said Tony, arriving and pulling out a chair and pouring himself a glass of Vernaccia di San Gimignano and taking a swig of it. He was dressed like Dennis in blue blazer, open-necked checked shirt, light cotton trousers.

'Do you miss the teaching?'

Tony laughed.

'You will notice how he avoids self-incrimination,' Dennis pointed out to Plant.

Tony laughed again and took his spectacles from his shirt pocket and peered at the specials blackboard.

'Ah, gnocchi.'

'It's always gnocchi on a Thursday.'

'But it is reassuring to be reassured in this world of change.'

Outside on the pavement a man in a dark grey suit and crested tie tapped on the window.

'Ah, our third man,' said Dennis, raising a hand in salute. Tony turned round laboriously and nodded, in greeting or recognition or confirmation. Reassured.

If that was the third man, where did that put Plant? Out of the circle. He was not offended. He was happy enough to be allowed on the edge as an observer.

After leaving Major he had spent a lot of time puzzling over what to do next. It was what he was paid to do, puzzle. Or solve puzzles. He was not sure that it ever became easier with practice. They were rarely the same puzzles. That in itself was a relief. He was saved the monotony of repetition. But with Major he was not sure where to go. No evidence, the threatening notes burned. No indication of what the threats might refer to, with Major blandly refusing to admit to anything.

In desperation he decided to call someone who taught in the department, and thought of Dennis.

'Not any more,' said Dennis. 'Anyway, the department doesn't exist any more, either. That's all in the past. It's Hell now.'

'Wasn't it always?' Plant had asked.

'Now it's official. School of History, English, Languages, Literature. So HELL. We're all in the same boat now. Ready for a ship burial.'

'I think it's the past I'm interested in,' said Plant.

'Come and have lunch,' said Dennis. 'The past is always with us.'

'That would be nice,' said Plant. 'When suits you?'

'What about today?'

'Today?'

'Treat every day as if it were your last. There may not be many more.'

'Today, then,' Plant had agreed.

*

The third man came in and joined them. Dennis introduced him. Paul Revill. They were all in their late fifties or early sixties. Not exactly well-preserved, but nor were they obviously incapacitated. No industrial injuries.

The waiter came to the table.

'You need menus?'

'Know them by heart,' said Tony.

'You ready to order?'

They ordered.

'Another bottle of wine?'

'We'd better,' said Revill, dispersing what was left round the four glasses.

Dennis and Revill ordered a fritto misto between them. Tony ordered gnocchi Romana. Plant ordered gnocchi with pesto. The waiter brought them a plate of antipasto.

'Did we order this?' Tony asked.

'On the house,' the waiter said.

It was all very cosy.

*

'I didn't realise you'd retired,' Plant said.

'Got leaned on,' said Dennis.

Revill guffawed.

'Come lean on me,' he said. 'I didn't notice any resistance.'

'I tried to resist,' said Dennis. 'I thought if I looked resistant they might make me a better offer.'

'Did they?' Plant asked.

'Of course not. It was take it or leave it.'

'We took it,' said Tony.

'With such alacrity,' said Dennis.

'All of you?' Plant asked.

'Superfluous men,' said Tony.

'Remember my forgotten man,' Dennis sang. Sort of sang.

Plant knew what it felt like. He probably knew better than they did. At least they had had their day. Sometimes he felt that his had never dawned. He had slipped straight from graduation to superfluity. Years of research and still no job. No career. No pension plan or state superannuation like these comfortable old buffers. Comfortable not so old buffers, indeed, all determined to live another quarter of a century to get their full pension's worth and more, their last revenge on the system. He didn't blame them. But as for himself, he felt he was truly one of a lost generation. He could have told them but they wouldn't have understood. They might have expressed sympathy but their true grief was kept only for themselves, and they indulged it with delight, the last remaining pleasure.

'So you're all retired now?'

'Absolutely,' said Dennis.

'I'm not,' said Revill.

'As good as,' said Tony.

'You're still there?' Plant asked.

'Till the end of the year. Then I go.'

'I thought you were going next month,' said Dennis.

'That's leave,' said Revill.

'Paul's finagled it so that his last long lingering leave segues seamlessly into early retirement,' said Tony. 'In the past they required you to come back and work for a year after taking leave. Two years at some places. They thought it seemed unseemly to take a sabbatical and fail to return. Now they're so eager to get rid of us they bend all the rules.'

'Should I complain?' Revill asked. 'Insist on serving out the equivalent amount of time I spend away?'

'If you want to threaten them,' said Dennis.

'You think it might get me a better deal?'

'No,' said Dennis.

'No,' said Tony.

'You regret going?' Plant asked.

'Je ne regret rien,' Dennis sang.

'He's never been so happy,' Tony said. 'See how he sings. Listen even.'

'Like a bird on the wire,' Dennis sang.

'The thing about early retirement,' Tony said, 'is it formalises your sense of irrelevance. You no longer need to seem to care. Not even to yourself. The great social lies stand revealed, and you stand apart from them.'

36

# Five

'I heard one of your former colleagues speak the other night,' Plant said.

'That was rash,' said Tony.

'Not voluntarily, I hope,' said Dennis.

'Archer Major,' said Plant.

'There's a name from the past,' said Dennis. 'The good old, bad old days.'

'What days were they?' Revill asked.

'The days before sexual harassment was an issue?' Plant suggested. The source of the anonymous letters could lie there, in some unsavoury episode from the past.

'Ah, those good old, bad old days,' said Revill.

'Major was into harassment from the time he could walk,' said Tony.

'From the cradle,' agreed Dennis. 'It was called pastoral care, in those days.'

'Was there a lot of it?' Plant asked.

'No idea, really,' said Dennis. 'No one bothered to remark. Just par for the course.'

'Old men's dreams,' said Tony.

'I don't imagine Major's given it away,' said Dennis.

'I don't think he ever gave anything away,' said Revill.

'Was he sort of known for it?' Plant asked.

'Notorious,' said Dennis.

'Now that's not a bad movie,' said Tony.

Plant wondered if Tony were deliberately diverting the topic in accord with his earlier avoidance of self-incrimination. Was it such a hazardous topic? Or were they simply incapable of keeping to any topic, years of tutorials having accustomed them to seizing on any diversion rather than tramping down the same old paths again, year after year. Or, to be more charitable, perhaps having kept to the topic in hand for all those teaching years, now they were happy to relax into irrelevance. Was it now just a routine of word association and repartee, buried allusion and one-upping, to while away the empty afternoons while they hoed into the wine? Could you hoe into a liquid? It was the sort of question they might well have discussed. He didn't ask. But whatever the appropriate phrase was, they were certainly doing it.

'He seemed pretty straight up and down,' Plant said.

'Who did?'

'Archer Major.'

'Major? Couldn't lie straight in his bed,' said Revill. 'Or in anyone else's.'

'Depends on who else was in it,' said Dennis.

'He liked the girls?' Plant asked.

'I never saw any sign that he actually liked them,' said Revill.

'He preferred boys?' Plant asked.

'Not that I noticed. Wouldn't put it past him, though. Or animals.'

'When you say he didn't like them,' Plant asked,

'you mean he wasn't really into girls?'

'He was into them all right,' said Revill. 'But what he was really into was the social register.'

'The what?' Tony asked. 'What social register?'

'Class,' said Revill. 'Social-climbing. The English disease.'

'He was English?' Plant asked.

'Still is, I imagine.'

'So it was a matter of status.'

'Everything is a matter of status to the English,' said Dennis. 'Fucked his way to the top.'

'Really?'

'Rubbish,' said Revill. 'He was up there from the beginning. He would never have got that Oxford job if he hadn't been. He was just out here putting in his time. Academic jackarooing.'

'You don't think it was his bedside manner?' said Dennis.

'What bedside manner? He was about as appealing as toad in the hole.'

'And now the frog has turned into a prince,' said Tony.

'He always had connections,' said Revill. 'You don't get in there without them. Not in England.'

'Not anywhere,' said Tony.

'And Major's in there?' Plant asked.

'He's aiming there. I hear he's got his sights on an Oxford chair,' said Revill.

Dennis spluttered. 'You're joking.'

'Choking? You're the one who seems to be choking,'

said Revill. 'You know me, I never joke.'

'That's dreadful,' said Dennis.

'I thought it would cheer you up. I've been saving it.'

'Why do you always have to ruin lunch with some hideous bit of news?' Tony asked.

'To stop you getting a false sense of wellbeing. Keep you on your toes.'

Dennis drained the bottle into his glass.

'We're going to need another one after that,' he said.

'We certainly are,' said Tony.

They certainly ordered another one, whether they needed it or not.

'You see,' said Revill, 'how else would you have been able to justify another one?'

'Easily,' said Tony.

'Why do we need justification?' Dennis asked. 'That's just your unreconstructed Englishness.'

'You're English, too?' Plant asked.

'I cannot tell a lie,' said Revill.

'That's what all the English say,' said Tony.

'Just don't believe them,' said Dennis.

Plant helped them with the necessary wine. It seemed a pleasant enough way to spend the afternoon. Being a retired academic didn't seem such a bad life. Sharing malevolence about former colleagues. Eating good food in a quiet restaurant.

'It gets busy at night,' Dennis said.

But at lunch it was an enclave of peace. The padrone dozed in a chair near the entrance. The waiter dozed behind the cash register. There was no piped music. No one talked loudly into mobile phones. The life of the street passed them by, insulated by the plate glass windows, offering a library of allusion. Girls in their summer dresses. A lady with a dog. A Prelude, a Pathfinder, a Rover, an Odyssey. An advertisement on a bus proclaiming The Real Thing.

*

Plant let the conversation wind around. He did not want to give the impression of directing it. Ask these people a straight question and you would probably get no answer at all. Maybe not. Maybe you would get a full hour's lecture. Or a full fifty-minute lecture. It wasn't done to lecture the full hour. Like hour-long television programmes, you never got the full sixty minutes worth. Time off for coming and going, time off for the commercials.

He didn't want to be seen obviously to be asking about Major. Careless talk costs lives, and all that. He didn't want the word getting around and having whoever had been sending the notes alerted. Nor for that matter did he want Major to hear he had been asking about him. There was no way he was going to get anywhere without nosing around. But people could get touchy. And asking questions about the person who had hired you might cause offence. Even though it was something Plant repeatedly found himself doing. Funny that. What a world of mistrust.

It was a while before the conversation circled back to Major. But in the end it did. Dennis raised the horror of it again. The Oxford chair. Fame and glory. They argued about whether it was a Regius chair or not. And if it were, why the monarch or the prime minister would want to nominate Major.

'Because he's one of them,' said Revill.

There was an exchange of badinage about Major's sexuality.

'I don't believe it,' said Dennis. 'Why would the government want an Anglo-Saxonist as an adviser?'

'Our Germanic heritage,' said Tony. 'The House of Saxe-Coburg-Gotha. Ein Volk, ein Reich, ein Führer.'

'All those people with language skills were spooks,' said Revill. 'They used them for code-breaking.'

'Give him a couple of drinks and off he goes,' said Tony, 'finds the trace of the secret state everywhere.'

'Secret work on the Anglo-Saxon charters?' Dennis chuckled.

'In the war.'

'Which war was that?'

'World War II.'

'A bit before Major's time, I would have thought. Unless he's found a magic formula against ageing.'

'You think they closed down those units after the war?' Revill asked. 'Whatever they might have said, you can be sure they kept them going. For the real war.'

'The real war?' Plant asked.

'The Cold War.'

'Who's they and who's them?' Tony asked sceptically.

'They are the government and them's our colleagues,' said Revill.

'Former colleagues,' said Dennis.

'Classicists and Anglo-Saxonists and Asianists,' said Revill. 'The old code-breaking teams were all back here teaching when Major came. He was in with them.'

'How do you know?'

Revill shrugged. 'He used to lunch with them in the staff club. He had a nose for where the power lay and they were the only game in town.'

'The only game?'

'The great game. Not too many openings for an Anglo-Saxonist.'

'I didn't realise that's what he was,' said Plant. 'I thought his field was magic.'

'Archer Major, the would-be arch-magus,' said Revill. 'He began in Anglo-Saxon. Old English as they call it to try and make it seem relevant to modern English. Which it isn't. One of those easy options. Bugger all to know about. You could read all the surviving texts in a day. Just a matter of learning the language. No problems, there's hardly any vocabulary. Major did a thesis on the Anglo-Saxon charms. No one had really bothered much about them before. Then he moved on to medieval magic. At some point he realised the future of teaching Old English was limited, but there was a market out there for magic.

Mugged up on the Renaissance. Then he made a quick leap into popular culture. Dennis Wheatley. Vampires. Swords and sorcery. Suddenly he's poised for cultural studies. Magic in the movies. Endless possibilities in the great degradation of our times. He never looked back. Hopped from job to job and wound up in Oxford.'

'And now he's poised for a chair,' Dennis groaned. 'How can such things be?'

'Because he was a government man from the beginning,' said Revill.

'You think everyone's a government man. Or woman,' said Tony.

'And aren't they?'

'Who knows?'

'Who knows indeed? But the government's the biggest employer. All you can be sure of is you don't get to the top unless you do the state some service.'

'So you're saying he's code-breaking for the government?' Plant asked.

'I'm not saying he's doing anything.'

'Used to break codes.'

'I'm just saying he's wired. He's got connections. That's how he got back to Oxford. That's how they're considering him for that chair. Who knows whether he's doing anything or not? But he's a trusty.'

'He could be casting magic spells for the government,' said Dennis.

'He could be,' Revill agreed.

Dennis laughed.

'Your suspicions know no bounds, do they?'

'No,' said Revill.

'Maybe he's using that magic to try and hook himself a chair,' said Tony.

'Why wouldn't he?' said Revill.

'I didn't get the impression he necessarily believed in magic,' said Plant.

Revill started to say something and then checked himself.

'Major was always pretty flexible when it came to belief,' Dennis said.

Plant turned to Revill. 'You were going to say?'

'Can't remember,' said Revill. 'Nothing important.'

'Like Major's beliefs,' said Dennis.

'Was he popular?' Plant asked.

'Popular?' Tony gasped.

There was a silence.

Now I have blown it, Plant told himself. Now I have been too pushing and shown my hand. Now they know I am after something.

'Popular,' said Dennis reflectively. 'Not a word we hear that much. Never had much cause to use it, to be honest.'

Plant went for broke.

'Did he have enemies?'

'Enemies?' said Revill. 'Did he have friends?'

Tony laughed appreciatively. Dennis shook his head. Reflectively, again.

The waiter came and asked them if they wanted coffee. 'Short black, short black, long black?'

They agreed.

'And a long black for me,' said Plant. And left it at that.

He wasn't sure exactly how much he had learned. But he had learned one important thing. Or the possibility of it. If Major was wired, as Revill insisted, and was doing government work, it would mean his academic salary was supplemented. And that was a good sign. It made it more likely that he could afford to hire Plant. And not just hire, but also pay the bill. It made Plant feel more secure. Checking on his employers had started to become pretty well the first thing he did on any job. Especially checking on their ability to pay the bill. With that ascertained, he could get on with the rest of the assignment.

# *Six*

Plant went back to the library. It was as if he had never been away. Not just from the friends' meeting. That had been a mere fleabite, barely drawing blood. Though fleabites could spread noxious plagues. The last plague in Sydney had been less than a century ago. He remembered seeing the photographs. Heaps of slaughtered rats outside houses in the Rocks, and rat-catchers in rat-catcher caps and bowler hats. He thought he remembered bowler hats. Fleas he had no recollections of. No photographs of slaughtered fleas as far as he could recall. He could check at the university museum's collection of photographs of old Sydney. It was like the old days indeed, always thinking up somewhere else to go rather than the library. Some other institutional archive, of course, those were the institutionalised years. The years of graduate research. And now he was back. Research Assistance. Investigative Reporting. As his business card put it.

Nearly back. He stopped at the coffee stall just inside the university grounds, a clutter of metal and plastic chairs and tables outside a hole in the wall, dispensing soft drinks and packaged sandwiches. Anything to delay entering the library, as ever. In the past he had had a jam doughnut in the student union. Now it was a choice of blueberry or chocolate chip muffin or apricot Danish. The onward creep of bourgeois food fashion. Or American and European cultural imperialism. Globalisation. Instead of the good old Austral-British proletarian jam doughnut. British not being European. He chose the Danish and sat on a plastic chair and watched the students and the occasional academic going in and out of the campus. Would this have been the life? Scholarship. The sad contagion of the gown.

He licked his sticky fingers and wiped them as well as he could with a paper napkin and headed for the library. Once through the automatic doors the accumulated weight of the past bore down, floor upon floor of books and a floor of administration. A heavy weight to bear. He found a computer terminal and keyed in Archer Major's name. There was only one book listed. Plant went for it, up on the sixth floor. *The Charm of Charms.* A slim volume from an obscure university press. He turned to the back, to the warning pasted on the back fly leaf to return it by the due date or suffer a punitive fine. The last date anyone had returned it was 1979.

The idea had been to find all of Major's books. The copy of *Magic* listed half a dozen or so by the same author opposite its title page. So much for the interest and loyalty of colleagues and former colleagues, making sure they kept up to date with your work and ordered it for the library. Of course they might all have bought their own personal copies. Or received inscribed complimentary ones. But Plant doubted it. Doubted either possibility.

It rather spoiled his strategy. His plan had been to locate the books to see which had been recently borrowed and then, somehow, find a way to find out from the computer records who had been borrowing them. It could have been difficult. At least that was one difficulty removed. The books were not there, except for this one title. No doubt it had been published when Major had been on the staff and no doubt Major had ordered it for the library himself. Of course someone might have consulted it in the library without borrowing it, in the years since 1979. But that was no help. He had hoped to find out who was showing a current interest in Major, and there was no sign that anyone was.

*The Charm of Charms* was up amongst the runes in the 439s, Dewey system, along with shelves of Norse remains, Vikings, and Danes. It was not where he wanted to be. Even if he had begun the day with an apricot Danish. Had there been a significance in his breakfast choice beyond his ken? Weird, he reflected, to use another of those Old Norse derived words. He went back down to the reference shelves by the computer terminals and looked up Major in the British *Who's Who*. He was not listed, nor in any other directory that Plant consulted. He gazed out of the window idly, looking at the clock tower and the flag flying at half-mast. He wondered for whom it flew. Maybe they kept it permanently at half-mast. It might be a way of keeping everybody subdued and threatened.

Magic, he decided. He went back to the terminals and punched up magic and found his way to the 130s. He might find something useful browsing through the current academic state of play in the subject. If he sat there quietly, he might find some beautiful young witch, leafing through a handbook of spells, who would clasp him to her bosom and initiate him into the secrets of the occult. Libraries always had this effect on him, heady erotic fantasies of dark doings behind the shelves. It had never happened in his experience but he was always hopeful. He placed *The Charm of Charms* on an empty desk against the wall and began searching slowly along the shelves with his neck twisted round to one side to read the upright spines of the books, out-of-body experiences, the devil and all his works, witchcraft through the ages, the accumulated wisdom on spells and hexes and spirits and ESP and voodoo and zombies.

He edged his way slowly through the holdings, wondering about the forces pent up in the books. Were the spells safely inert, merely recorded in print? Or were they active, written down but not fixed, emanating their energies through the bindings so that to stand between the shelves was like standing beneath a mobile-phone mast and being zapped with dangerous energy? Plant was not a sceptic. He did not have the impermeable insulation of the implacable rationalist. Something in him wanted to believe. Wanted to believe that the lithe young priestess would trip in there and offer him a sip from the Circean cup. It was written in the literature. It was part of the cultural heritage. When would it happen to him?

And she came. Young and slim and Nordic, as upright as a rune and as bright as a fairy. The signs must have been auspicious. He had been right to select the apricot Danish.

And there she was standing beside him, reaching for the same shelves.

'That old black magic,' she said, and smiled.

'Dangerous stuff.'

'Is it?' she said. 'Are you an adept?'

'Not me,' said Plant. 'What about you?'

'No,' she said.

'Pity,' he said, 'I was hoping for someone to explain it all to me.'

'You should meet my mother,' she said.

He had never been that keen on meeting beautiful young girls' mothers. It had never seemed to be to his advantage in the past. They sensed something about him.

'Should I?'

'If you want to know about magic,' she said. 'She'll tell you everything you ever wanted to know but were afraid to ask.'

'Really?'

'And more.'

'Maybe I should meet her.'

'Maybe you should.'

'Where is she?'

'In the car. Right outside the library.'

'I didn't think you could park there any more.'

'She's in the disabled zone.'

'I'm sorry.'

'The sick shaman,' she said. 'The wound and the bow.'

'Oh,' said Plant.

'She's all right. She just twisted her ankle. That's why she sent me in to find a couple of things for her.'

'Would she talk to me?'

'Would she stop?'

# Seven

They checked out their books at the desk, the borrowings recorded on computer, the library cards scanned and validated. They went through the security screen without setting off any alarm, watched by the duty librarian who managed to combine weary impassivity with suspicion and disapproval. She led him across to an early model Astra with a MAGIC HAPPENS sticker on the dust-coated rear window. Star-dust-coated maybe.

'I've brought you a sacrificial offering,' the girl said. 'He wants to know about magic. I said you would fill him in while I go off and do a few things.'

'Did you now?' said the mother.

And she hadn't mentioned going off to do a few things.

'Get in the back,' the girl told Plant.

He didn't think they were going to kidnap him and boil him down with marinated eye of newt and sun-dried wing of bat. Or turn him loose in the hog sty. He hoped not. She drove through the university grounds, dodging the university security vehicles and the university bicycle police, and stopped at the outdoor eatery with easiest access, where people passed on their way to and from the bus stop and the footbridge, back where Plant had begun his morning. The mother struggled out with a couple of crutches and settled in the nearest chair.

'Can I get you a coffee?'

'No,' she said.

'Tea?'

'No.'

'Soft drink?' he persisted.

'Just hot water,' she said.

'Hot water.'

'Yes,' she said. She produced a tea-bag on a string.

'Herbal tea,' she said. 'I bring my own.'

Plant went off and worked the coffee machine. It dispensed hot water, if you pressed the right buttons. After a while he found them.

'Thank you for talking to me,' Plant said.

'I haven't yet.'

He smiled.

'Freya,' she said.

'Plant,' he said.

She picked up *The Charm of Charms* he had put on the metal table.

'You're interested in rune magic?' she asked.

'Not especially,' he said. 'Well, I don't know. I might be. I heard a talk by Dr Major the other night. I went to borrow his books but this was the only one they had.'

'You're not missing much.'

'He doesn't know much?'

'He doesn't say much,' she said. 'I've never known exactly what he knows.'

'You know him?'

'Knew him,' she said. 'Past tense. Before he sprouted wings.'

56

'Sprouted wings?'

'And flew. A stratospheric rise to higher realms.'

Plant figured she meant overseas. He didn't see Major as the angelic type.

'But you haven't kept in touch.'

'Certainly not in touch,' she said. 'I had quite enough of that.'

She cackled. It was the only word for it. Until then, except for the crutches, she had seemed quite presentable. An older version of the daughter but presentable. Presentable as in attractive. But the cackle was enough to freeze the marrow of his bones.

'What's your interest?' she asked. 'Magic or Major?'

She had those milky blue eyes that had gazed on other realms. Not the eyes of older policemen and customs officers, those hard looks that threatened you with violent ends if you tried to evade the truth, but eyes that looked through you and beyond and already knew the truth. Plant found them no less threatening.

'Major, really,' he said.

'Why?'

'I do a bit of journalism. Freelance. He seems like an interesting subject.'

There was no actual lie in what he said. Each component sentence was unfaultable. If put together they added up to something greater than the sum of the parts, so be it. Hopefully.

'He isn't that interesting,' she said. 'I knew him when he was starting out. He's really very ordinary. Even less than ordinary. He worked on making himself seem interesting.'

'How did he do that?'

'Magic,' she said.

'He used magic?'

She cackled again. A couple of currawongs in the bushes flew off in alarm. They sounded as if they were alarmed, anyway. Plant was not sure how skilled he was in reading the book of nature.

'That's what he would like you to think,' she said. 'But probably not. Not to begin with. Not when I knew him. He was just a rather ordinary philologist. No literary judgment. No historical sense. No taste. No flair.'

She waved her open hand out at the world and twitched her nostrils.

'The only thing he could do was conjugate old English verbs. Rote-learning. He looked around to see what hadn't been done to death. Being short of ideas he didn't want to have to struggle with things people had spent a lot of time thinking about. It would be too hard to think of anything new. So he chose the charms. Everyone else had done *Beowulf* and *The Wanderer* and *The Seafarer* and the *Chronicles*. Even the riddles. So he did the charms. He couldn't think of anything literary to say so he decided he'd mug up on rune magic. From conjugating to conjuring. That's when I took him in hand.'

'In hand,' said Plant.

'In those days I used to go to the spiritualist church,' she said. 'I took him along so he could see what a séance was like. He said he wanted to go for his research, see what summoning up spirits was all about. I think I thought I wanted to convert him. To a sense of higher things, you know. He was such a typical academic then. No doubt still is. Nineteenth-century scientific rationalist, no sense of mystery let alone the divine, and a Herbert Spencer survival of the fittest competitiveness, you know, getting to the top rather than caring about the truth. Of course, it was a few decades closer to the nineteenth-century back then. I thought I could soften him up a bit. Make him a better person.'

'And did you?'

'I think I just gave him a few hints for his career path. He was shrewd, no doubt about that. He knew he wasn't much good at the literary stuff. A cloth ear, no feeling for beauty or mystery.' She laughed, that eldritch cackle. 'No sense of the magic of it all. But he figured magic itself might be a useful topic. It wasn't that fashionable, not in academic circles, at that time. Academics sneered at it. Like they sneer at most things. Mumbo-jumbo they called it. I remember when I wanted to do my thesis, they refused the topic. But in Anglo-Saxon there wasn't a lot going on. So he mugged up on the charms and the runes and got himself a nice little untilled patch there. Later he moved into the Frances Yates stuff, Renaissance magic, went and spent sabbatical leave at the Warburg and Courtauld Institute and hung around those people. By then it was getting modish and there he was, in the right place at the right time.'

'You said he went to séances.'

'I took him along, yes.'

'So he believed in it?'

'Not necessarily. I think he just went along for the ride at first.' She cackled some more.

'What sort of séances?'

'The usual thing,' she said. 'You sit round in a circle, do a medit-ation, and then someone starts off. Something comes through.'

'Spirits of the dead?'

'Spirits of the dead, disincarnate entities, space creatures, who knows? Forces of the lower astral. It's sort of interesting to begin with. But it can be a trap. You get caught up with the voices, but in the end what they say isn't very interesting. It's one of the stages you have to get beyond.'

'For what?'

'For higher things.'

'And did Dr Major go on to higher things?'

'Hard to say. Though I doubt it, knowing him. He stuck around for a while. There were a number of different groups. Beginners. People who'd been doing it a while. And then Irene had some other thing going.'

'Irene?'

'She ran the groups.'

'She still around?'

'I imagine you'd find she's passed over to the other side. This was twenty, thirty years ago and she was an old woman then.'

Students came and went from the tables around

them, chewing away with the indefatigable appetite of the young and copying out each others' assignments. Academics settled down with their morning papers and breakfast tea. Administrative officers settled down for a smoke and a caffeine shot. Sparrows and pigeons and mynahs pecked around for crumbs amongst their feet.

'What was the other thing she had going?' Plant asked.

'Some people are better at it than others, better channels, you know. They just are. Nothing much you can do about it. Some people kept going for months and nothing much came through. Others were wide open. I think she filtered off some of the natural mediums into sub-groups. They sat around doing telepathy. Buzzing round the world and looking into strange places.'

'Was Major one of them?'

'He could have been.'

'What sort of places were they looking into?'

'I was never part of it so I can't say. That was all sort of technique, you know. I was more interested in the spiritual message. The ancient wisdom.'

'How do you mean, technique?' Plant asked.

'You're not interested in the ancient wisdom?'

'Not right now.'

'I didn't think you were,' she said.

'Give me time,' he said.

'It's not for me to give you time,' she said.

She looked at him severely. It was something he

was quite used to, Plant, being looked at severely. But she still managed to make him feel uncomfortable. He was used to that, too. But it didn't make it any more enjoyable.

'Tell me about technique,' he persisted.

'Psychic espionage is more your thing, is that it?'

'Is that what it was?'

'The sort of stuff they make television programmes about. Seeing if they could look inside military installations.'

'Is that what they were doing?'

'There used to be all these theories about Pine Gap. That the Americans were doing secret space travel from there. Flying saucers over Alice Springs. Activating the rainbow serpent beneath Ayers Rock. That sort of stuff. The base was all highly secret and fenced off and high security. Still is, I imagine. So people tried to tune into it and get in by telepathic means.'

'Is that what Major was doing?'

'Seems a bit unlikely, doesn't it? A bit too acid-crazed hippy for him, you'd think. It was just one of those things around at the time. I've no idea what they were doing, to be honest. But they were doing telepathic stuff, I remember that. They used to tape it. Or try and tape it. The trouble was the tapes never worked. They'd tune into some force or other and someone would start channelling, but it never recorded on tape.'

'Why was that?'

'Either the space creatures made sure they zapped

out the tapes, or Irene was no good with tape recorders.'

'And nothing ever came out?'

'So they said.'

'But it might have and they weren't saying.'

'Maybe. I've no idea, I wasn't part of it.'

'But Major was?'

'Could have been.'

'For how long?'

'I've no idea. We broke up. He found other playmates. In the plural.'

'He spread himself around?'

'In those days people did. And he was no exception. That was the way it was.'

'No ill feelings?'

'Why would there be?'

'So there weren't?'

'Not at all.'

'Could any of his other playmates have ill feelings?'

'Are you looking for someone to give you some dirt on him?'

'No.'

'So why do you ask?'

'Background,' he said.

'What paper did you say you write for?'

'I didn't.'

'That's right. Freelance, I think you said.'

'Yes.'

'You're not a journalist at all.'

'Yes, I am,' said Plant.

'On and off,' he added.

'When they hire me,' he tried explaining.

She looked at him with those disturbing milky blue eyes.

'You're trying to get something on Archer.'

'Not at all.'

'You've been getting me to talk under false pretences.'

'Well, maybe,' said Plant, impaled by the eyes. 'But I'm not trying to cause trouble for Major.'

'Why should I believe you?'

'Dr Major hired me,' he said, despite himself, despite his principle of never explain, never give anything away.

'That doesn't stop you from looking for dirt on him.'

'True,' Plant agreed. How true.

'What are you up to?'

'It's confidential,' he said.

'Go on,' she said.

'He's had a couple of threatening messages,' said Plant. 'He's asked me to look into it.'

'What sort of threats?'

Plant shrugged. 'I haven't actually seen them.'

'"All is discovered, flee while you can"?' she suggested.

'How did you know?'

'How did you?' she said, 'if you haven't seen them.'

'Dr Major told me.'

'Ah,' she said.

'How did you know?' he asked again.

She looked at him with those blank blue eyes, impassive now.

'Isn't that what they always say?'

'Sometimes they're more specific,' said Plant.

'And that's what you're trying to find? The specifics?'

'Yes.'

'Got anywhere?'

'Not really.'

'Not really?'

'Not at all.'

She nodded.

'I wondered it if might be an old girlfriend.'

'Why not a young girlfriend?'

'I meant one from the past.'

'What's wrong with the present?'

'Sure,' he said. 'Could be. Something in that area. I'm just working through the possibilities.'

'So why did you want to know about the séances?'

'I don't know,' said Plant.

'Something led you there.'

'No idea,' said Plant.

'You don't believe in the higher realms, do you?'

'I don't disbelieve in them.'

'That's not good enough.'

'I'm not sure I believe in anything,' he said.

'That's very sad,' she said.

'I don't know.'

'I do,' she said.

Plant shrugged some more. Uncomfortably.

'Think about it,' she said. 'Think about where you're being led and what's leading you.'

The daughter drove up in the car and gave a couple of blasts on the horn.

'You might think it's sex,' said Freya, getting up and hobbling towards the car while the daughter turned it round, 'but it isn't, you know. That's just the earthly image of the divine love.'

Plant opened the door for her.

'She put you straight?' the daughter asked.

'You can take a horse to water but you can't make him drink,' Freya said. 'It will take a lot more than that to put this fellow straight.'

And they drove off.

She hadn't told him anything about magic.

# Eight

Plant lurked down in the depths of the library stacks, back amidst the 130s, Dewey system, hoping that his vision of youth and beauty might reappear. So all right, it wasn't sex, it was the image of the divine love. He would settle for that. He didn't know what else to do. He hadn't even found out her name. He should have taken down the car registration number, a matter of basic tradecraft, and he hadn't even done that.

The array of studies in witchcraft and Satanism did not allure him. He had wandered down there not so much aimlessly as with some hidden aim, one not disclosed to his conscious mind, hoping that something would come to him. He knew that it would probably not be the vision of youth and beauty, though he kept hoping that it might be. If all else failed he could look up the old university calendars for the years Major had been on staff and see who was on staff with him then and go to the department and try to talk to whoever might still be there. But he was not sure that would be any more productive than lurking in the stacks. Conscious thought was not going to help him at this moment. He merely had to do something and think about it and hope that that conscious focus would allow something unsought to swim up from the subconscious and show itself. Sometimes the answer was to get into the car and drive somewhere, anywhere, and then with the conscious preoccupied with traffic and cyclists and speed cameras and pedestrian crossings, the subconscious would feel safe enough to begin its movements. And a thought would form. He could have done that now, but something had impelled him back into the library. Perhaps it was not just futile desire and the habit of primitive masculine predatoriness, perhaps all that was merely the conscious that was impelling him, driven by unconscious forces to position him in the right place at the right time. Like Major's career choice of magic. Who knew? Certainly not Plant. He never knew.

He stood there within the concrete walls, the steel shelves, the drone and buzz of the air-conditioning and the fluorescent lights, a prison compound rather than a seat of learning.

It was Revill who showed up.

'Welcome to the mind prison,' he said, reading Plant's thoughts.

'The mind prison?'

'Concrete walls do not a prison make nor steel shelves a cage. The mind is its own place. Wherein we make a hell of heaven, or heaven of hell.'

Plant gave his appreciative smile.

'And what brings you down to the occult arts?' Revill asked. 'Old Arch cast a spell on you, did he?'

'I thought I might find some of his books down here, but there don't seem to be any.'

'No,' said Revill. 'Thank heavens for small mercies.'

'I didn't know you were into this sort of thing,' said Plant.

'Can't say I am, really,' said Revill.

'Just browsing?'

'Just browsing.'

The conversation lapsed. And yet there was so much that might be said. If the conversation could be suitably steered.

'Feel like a drink?' Plant asked.

'Seems like a good idea,' Revill agreed.

*

Revill was in a white shirt and a crested tie and what looked like the same off the peg dark grey suit he had worn when Plant had met him over lunch. There was nothing well cut or elegant about it. He did not gleam like Major. Hair cut short back and sides, but some time ago. Black Oxford shoes, scuffed and unpolished. It was all so conformist Plant knew he couldn't possibly be straight. It was the flat, undemonstrative, conventional look, except conventions had changed and no one looked like that any more. His teeth had a yellowish tinge, which could have been the stain of tannin from tea, or the stain from smoking. Being English he was probably a heavy tea-drinker. Plant picked out the yellow-brown tinge on the second and third fingers. A smoker. Again, it might just be tobacco. He spotted the tell-tale hash burn on the tie, a neat little hole in one of the quarters of a university crest. When it had got to that stage it was hard to be sure whether the signs were deliberately there, or whether Revill had gone way beyond caring. He could have been pretending conventionality. Or he could have been parodying it, the deliberate proclamation of the straight that let the cognoscenti know he was totally bent, the cognoscenti being the dope smokers and substance abusers and doubters of the socio-political consensus. The non-believers. The ones who had no faith in the system, and who spent their energies avoiding its demands and no longer had any aspiration to its rewards. They might not any longer be active addicts. They might be ex-alcoholics. They might simply have thought their way through to the periphery of things and preferred it out there. It was the William Burroughs dress code. And there was no way of telling where they were at, indeed there was often nothing to be told, they had departed and were simply marking time. Ambiguity had become a way of life, which made things easier if you were so out of it that you no longer cared. Not even necessarily out of it stoned. Just out of it in terms of any social norms. Off at a tangent years ago and now lost in space. Ground Control to Major Tom. As for the manner, academia was a good cover, or used to be, every serious academic absent-minded or eccentric or off with the fairies, oblique, introverted, ironic, monomaniacal, catatonic, pretty well impossible to tell which, all you knew was communicating was a problem. Were they talking to you or holding some other conversation in their mind? Those years of lecturing had left them habituated to droning on in some private world, gazing into space above the students' heads, avoiding eye contact, disregarding the boredom and inattention and people eating and groping and sleeping and reading newspapers. How would you ever know if they were stoned or drunk or not? And with the spread of prescription drugs, Valium and Serapax and Prozac and anti-inflammatories and antihistamines, even the ones who imagined they were straight were spaced out beyond recovery. They were like burned out satellites, systems on the blink, still up there in orbit but communicating erratically and randomly or not communicating at all, and the cost of retrieving them too great to be worth it, left to just sit up there till an asteroid collided with them.

They walked across the lawns and through the quadrangle and the vice-chancellor's quadrangle and across to the footbridge and off campus, though the buildings immediately off campus were still university buildings, creeping into the adjacent suburb. Revill led the way down a street of old terraced houses and into a pub. It was pretty well empty. A couple of people played pool in the back.

'It used to be called the British Lion, but in presumable deference to Republican sentiment, they changed its name,' said Revill.

'Does that worry you?' Plant asked.

'Why should it?'

'Being English and all that.'

'I can't say it does,' said Revill.

'But you still remark on it.'

'Ah well,' said Revill, 'then perhaps it does.'

He ordered a schooner of Kilkenny.

'Irish,' he said. 'I'll leave you to puzzle out the implications of that.'

Plant ordered a middy of light and puzzled.

'Time was,' said Revill, 'the pubs round here would be full of students. Now they're all working to pay the fees for their degrees. They call it part-time but they're working full-time and fitting their classes in to suit the job. We spent the seventies fighting for options to give them a chance to choose their courses. And now they choose the options that fit in with the time that the hospitality industry lets them off work. Still, it means the pubs are quiet. In the end you've seen enough students to last a lifetime and more. Nice just to have a quiet drink. And you can't have one on campus because they closed the staff club down. Can't have staff getting together sitting around getting pissed. Or even not getting pissed. They might plot things. Of course they could always walk off campus and get pissed and plot things, but they're all too demoralised and institutionalised to think of it, so they just sit in their rooms drinking spring water out of plastic bottles until it's time to go home and nod off in front of the television.'

He took a long swig of ale and stretched out and smiled with satisfaction.

'It isn't the life you thought it would be,' said Plant.

'It was for a while. We had the good years. The best years ever, probably. The only time universities were universities. It may all be finished now, but it was good while it lasted. You look back to the 1920s, 1930s, you read any of the memoirs of those times, the universities were terrible, anybody with any talent couldn't wait to leave. Lots of them didn't bother to finish their degrees. They were getting nothing out of it. Go back to the nineteenth century, things were even worse. Barbaric. Before that they barely existed. Just centres of reaction. Good wine cellars, sinecures for younger sons, like the church. Any real thinking was going on outside the universities. So if it's like that again now, that's just getting back to how it always was. But the sixties and seventies were different. Just that brief while. Bright kids. Kids from backgrounds that could never have conceived of university before. And a sense of excitement. That there were things to be learned.'

'And Vietnam,' said Plant.

'Vietnam, sure. But it wasn't only the war. The war was part of it, it got people thinking. But there are always wars. It's been a continuous war for the last century, two centuries, some of them get media notice, some don't. But sure, Vietnam got people thinking about the nature of the society that wanted the war. They started thinking about issues. The implications of what they were taught. The nature of power. The possibilities of change. People got involved. They talked to each other, for heaven's sake. Look at this.'

He gestured at the empty pub.

'A place like this would've been full. People talking, arguing. There'd be staff and students here.

They learned more sitting around places like this than they ever learned in a classroom. They'd talk to people from different subjects. Now no one knows anyone. Historians only know historians, physicists only know physicists. But all that war protest meant people got together from different disciplines. It was a university for the first time ever. Biologists talked to classicists, literary critics talked to economists. That was the revolution. It was like the English revolution, the civil war. The troops never did that much fighting. Most of the time they sat around guarding bridges and fords and crossroads. And this was when people had never been outside their own villages before. For the first time ever, ordinary people met other ordinary people from other districts, not just the handful they'd grown up with. They started talking to each other, sharing life experiences, comparing notes. That was the revolution. That's what started the political ferment. The Levellers and the Diggers. Of course,' he reflected, 'it all came to nothing. Repression set in. Just like now. But that moment existed. As it did for us. I feel privileged to have known it. Certainly can't complain.'

He stood up. 'Same again?'

'Yes,' said Plant.

Revill picked up the glasses and took them back to the bar.

'When did you leave England?' Plant asked when he returned.

'Thirty-something years ago,' said Revill.

'And you still take the glasses back to the bar,' said Plant.

'Go on.'

'It's not an Australian habit. Unless you're trying to ingratiate yourself with the barmaid.'

'I do confess I tried, but she wasn't interested. My days as a barmaid masher are over.'

'But you had them?'

'Gave it a go. Back in the old country.'

'They always give you new glasses in Australia,' said Plant.

'Ah, so they do,' said Revill. 'They certainly don't in England. At least not when I was there. You took your glass back and they filled it up and the slops that spilled over they poured back into the barrels when they cleaned up each night. Waste not, want not.'

'You knew Major in England?' Plant asked, settling into interrogative mode.

'No, spare me.'

'Isn't that an Oxford tie?'

Revill looked down at it. 'Yah, as we used to say there.'

'You were both at Oxford?'

'Apparently. So he says.'

'You doubt him?'

'Have to doubt everything he says,' said Revill. 'But he was probably there. Maybe,' he couldn't resist adding with a grin.

'You both came out here about the same time?'

'Pretty much.'

'Was he caught up in all the radical ferment?'

'He was caught up in everything. Whatever it was, he would be there. A young man on the make, our Arch.'

'And you weren't?'

'On the make? I don't think I was ever that focused, to be honest. I was more concerned with having a good time. I'd found England more than a trifle constricting. Can you imagine carrying your beer glass back every time you wanted a drink? As you so perceptively point out, I still do it. All unconsciously. How's that for social conditioning? It seemed a lot more open here. It wasn't, of course. But I didn't know that at the time, did I? I just plunged in. Still, it was fun while it lasted. Fun times.'

He sighed, contentedly.

'And how long did it last?'

'Until the end of the seventies. Then there was the big shift. Reagan. Thatcher. They began to roll everything back. Worldwide. Our client state rolled over ecstatically and said, me too, screw me too. Worldwide they began to roll back all the gains of the seventies, and the sixties. Now they've rolled back the gains of the fifties and are in process of dismantling the welfare state of the forties. Soon we'll be back to the rise of fascism. Except it's already risen and in place, of course. But it's more efficient this time. Without all the theatrics, so we never noticed it happening. Such is the great degradation of the times.'

'Is that how you see it?' Plant asked. 'Degradation?'

'How else can you see it?' said Revill.

'And the good old days weren't degraded?'

'I wouldn't say that,' said Revill. 'I don't think there was any doubt they were bad. Difference is, we had fun. Of course, while we were off our faces having fun, big business was getting itself organised to go global. And the forces of reaction were looking at us all having fun and starting their schemes to stop all that. Without doubt there was no lack of degradation. We were just so caught up protesting against the war and trying to radicalise the universities, we never saw the big picture. If you wanted to take a conspiracy view of it, you could say all the radical fun was just a smokescreen behind which the real dirty work was going on. You could even go on to say the smoke was the smoke of burning off, a controlled little fire to pre-empt a real conflagration from ever happening. Let the kids have their protest, make sure it's all monitored and infiltrated, and pick off the ringleaders and potential future radical activists before they're old enough to get out there in the real world and do any real harm and change anything.'

'You think it was like that?'

'Sometimes I do. Sometimes I sit and think about it and think about the way we are now and I think it must have been very like that. But at the time, how were we to know? At the time it was all very exciting and it seemed all very radical. And we fell for it.'

'Fell for what exactly?'

'What exactly? I think it would be very hard to

establish what exactly. But in broad general outline, I suppose it was ego. Vanity. Couldn't resist protesting how radical we were and drawing attention to ourselves.'

'In what ways?'

'Oh, standing up and being counted. Always a silly thing to do.'

'And how was that done?'

'Your friend Major,' said Revill. 'You were asking about his radical involvement.'

Plant nodded. Affirmatively. Encouragingly.

'Well, I doubt now how radical he was, but he was always involved. There were these so-called radical study groups on campus, sucked us all in. He was always there. I went along with them. No choice really. How could I not? If I didn't it would look like I didn't care, like I wasn't for the revolution. Couldn't have people thinking that, could I? So I used to go along. Hated it. I'd rather have been down the pub than staying back in some smelly seminar room after classes finished, listening to some boring graduate student mouthing some string of clichés about Lollards or radical pirates. I mean, really. But it was a matter of if you're not with us you're against us. Classic provocateur stuff. And the place was getting polarised. There were all the dead-heads sticking their dead heads in the ground. The last thing you'd want to do was get identified with them. Of course the next last thing I wanted to do was sit around in study groups. People want to study, go study. You don't sit around in groups. It was like those reading parties they had in nineteenth-century universities, go off in the vacation for a hike round the Lakes or the Massif Central, get to swim naked with some seedy old tutor. I've got nothing against sex. I'd got nothing against gays. But if you wanted sex, all you had to do was go down to the pub and take your pick. Or be picked. You didn't have to sit around the bloody department till half past seven at night discussing George bloody Orwell with half a dozen half-baked teachers' pets. George bloody Orwell, the man was an Etonian policeman, for heaven's sake, he was a bloody spook. Hung around the left and named names to the security services.'

'Is that how many there were, half a dozen?'

'Maybe a dozen, not any more. Anyway, I did it. For a while. At the time it was just a bore. As far as I was concerned. If Major wanted to score some private school squatter's daughter, I couldn't see why he didn't just ask her back to his room. Shut the door. But he liked all this carry-on. The business of having protégés. A tribe of camp followers. Planning for the future. Fix him up with a job or a grace and favour cottage when he got old and senile.'

'You don't approve of followers?'

'Never had them, somehow. Some people have them, some don't. It's not a matter of approval or disapproval. I never felt easy about disciples. There's always one going to betray you. And the rest just parroting everything you say.'

'But Major did.'

'He's not alone in that. Sad, really. One of the traps of the job, getting dependent on always having someone around listening to you, nodding in wise agreement.'

'But you're not tempted.'

'I could have been tempted. It just never happened. I start to hold forth and people shuffle around and get nervous and sort of creep away. I make them uneasy. Put them off their golf. The ones that stay, you get suspicious of. You wonder why they're still sitting there. How come they haven't left? Who are they reporting back to?'

He gave Plant an appraising look and then turned away as if he couldn't bear to see what he thought he saw.

'My old mother,' he said, 'was a lot wiser than I ever gave her credit for. Her favourite phrase, the one she used most, was "Not for the likes of us." You come from the working class, you learn to know your place. Don't draw attention to yourself. Don't get too clever. "Act daft," that was her other phrase. Whatever you do, don't let on. Not a matter of being stupid, just a matter of not making them think you're too clever. I should have followed her advice. I did for a while. I never even joined the Labour Club at Oxford. They were all too upper class for me. I felt out of place. And why draw attention to your politics? You come from nowhere, no point in getting pushed back down there. If you've got subversive thoughts, keep them to yourself. Get a good job. Wear a tie. Don't answer back. When you get a chance, do what you believe in. Shaft the system. Just don't let on. As long as you look straight and reliable, no one's going to question you. So I started out all right. You order a few radical books for the library that should have been there. Quite a few. But you mix them in with orders for the usual boring old stuff. You give your lectures on the world of the epic and show how the old epic values of war and militarism get questioned. No need to talk about US foreign policy, just stick to the ancient texts. It still makes the point. There are ways of doing things.

'But then people started coming along with this "if you're not with us you're against us" line. Make a stand for peace. Declare yourself. Sign here. And the radical intelligentsia, as they called them, which you couldn't not belong to, could you, they started on the necessity of analysing causes of the war. There are always wars, what you have to do is look at the structures of our society, why the system needs wars, give a radical analysis of the internal forces. Which was all very true and interesting and important, and we did it. What we didn't have to do was draw attention to ourselves. But we did. We got vain. We wanted to be leaders of the revolution. To be honest, I never did. I was quite happy being in the background. Lurking in the shadows. But somehow people kept winkling you out. And they used your own vanity to help push you into the forefront. So that you could get picked off. And you did. You got noticed. You got on a list. And once you're on a list, you're on a list for life.

And the people who stuck their heads in the sand are running things now. Together with a handful of high-profile lefties, who had to have been provocateurs, otherwise they would've been picked off and silenced instead of given the show to run. So yes, in answer to your question, those days were pretty degraded too. But they were fun.' He looked round the empty pub. 'And I don't see much fun round here anymore. That's the difference.'

'No more sexy young students sidling up to you,' said Plant.

'Oh, they're probably still around. If you're trying to do anything political, remotely political, you've got to imagine they're setting you up. Poor kids, they've been busted for dope and offered the choice, screw your tutor and find out what he's up to, what subversive thoughts he's thinking, or face a charge of possession. That sort of thing. Of course, the first few times you think they're after you for your body, or at least for your mind, which they were, of course. Pillow talk. Find out what you think and what you're planning and report it all back.

'And then you begin to become frightened of your students, are they setting you up? What lies behind their questions? And some conservative little prick suddenly starts spouting radical ideas and comes and wants to talk to you and get help on how it is, and you don't trust him, or her, you don't believe people can change. And once you stop believing that, where are you? What sort of radical thinker have you become?'

'So you don't trust students?'

'Not especially, no. Not that they're any different from your colleagues, of course. Why would you trust them either? No cooperative spirit. All out for themselves, desperate careerism, always ready to cut a private deal whether it's with the head of department or the government, do anything for a grant or a promotion. So they come along too, or they write to you from some other university, saying they're running this radical study group or this radical journal or this radical conference, give us a paper, why would you, why would you stick your neck in the noose? They might be legitimate, of course. You never know. But if they are, especially if they are, they'll be monitored and their journals or their conferences infiltrated. And if they're not genuine, then they were a trap from the beginning.'

'You belonged to some radical cell?'

'Of course not. People belonging to radical groups are easily controlled and monitored. All those groups are infiltrated. But if you're independent then they don't know what you might be thinking or doing. So they take especial interest. That, I suspect, was my downfall.'

'So the good old days weren't so good after all?'

'No reason to think they've changed,' said Revill. 'Still the same but with less fun.'

It always amazed Plant the way people with a dark and suspicious view of the world, people with a sharpened sense of surveillance and informers and the secret state, were always so ready to talk. Perhaps not all of them. Perhaps there were some who were so paranoid that they never talked at all, never went out, were never seen. So there was no knowing about them, assuming they existed. But the others, those who were open about their conspiracy views, never ceased to puzzle him. They sounded paranoid yet talked so openly. Here was Revill raving on about never trusting a student or a colleague, and yet telling him, telling someone he had met only once before and in no way could be said to know, how he suspected everyone because of his, Revill's, radical or subversive or aberrant or however he saw them views. Unless of course he thought he did know, his suspicions alerting him. And letting him, Plant, know that he suspected that he, Plant, could not be trusted. It was all of a piece with the transparent disguise, the interviews and funerals suit, and the Oxford tie. It might have looked conformist and respectable in 1959, but that was a long time ago. Now he just looked like a freak. Perhaps that was the intention. Perhaps he needed to demonstrate that he was indeed a freak, and did it this way rather than put a safety pin through his lip and dye his hair green, which had after all become sadly conformist.

# *Nine*

Major phoned.

'Do you have anything for me?'

'Not really,' said Plant.

'Not really?'

'Not at all.'

'Ah,' said Major. 'Well, laddie, I have something for you.'

'Oh, yes?'

'Another one.'

'Another what?'

'Another anonymous communication.'

'That's good,' said Plant.

'I didn't think so,' said Major.

'Perhaps not,' Plant conceded. 'But it will give me something to work on.'

Major grunted.

'You still have it? You haven't destroyed it?'

'I still have it.'

'I should see it.'

'You want me to read it out?'

'I'll come and see it.'

'As you like,' said Major.

'Where should I come? And when?'

'Oh, God,' said Major. 'Where? When?' There was a delay as if he might have been leafing through his appointments book. Plant knew the trick. He used it himself. Especially when there were no appointments.

'What about tomorrow?' Major asked.

'Where?'

'The art gallery.'

'Which art gallery?'

'The Art Gallery of New South Wales,' said Major, irritably. 'You know where that is, I suppose?'

'I do,' said Plant.

'Eleven o'clock suit you?'

'Eleven o'clock is fine.'

'Right.'

'Just a moment,' said Plant. 'Where in the gallery?'

'Nineteenth-century Australian,' Major said, irritably again, a note of impatience that he might have been thought to be found anywhere else. 'Only stuff they've got worth looking at.'

'If you say so,' said Plant.

'I do,' said Major. 'Eleven o'clock,' he reminded him. Busy man.

'Do my best,' said Plant. Unnecessarily.

*

Major was gazing at a boating scene in the manner of the enraptured. Ladies in frills and flounces and furbelows, chaps in striped blazers. It could have been the brush strokes and composition or it could have been the sexual narrative that entranced him. Or the unity of form and content, text and subtext, perhaps. Major himself was resplendent in brass buttoned blazer and pressed summer-weight grey trousers and cravat. He matched the painting on the wall rather well. Maybe that was why he stood there. Plant broke in on his reverie.

'Morning,' he said. He resisted the nineteenth-century ambience and its pressure to add a 'Sir'.

'You got here,' said Major, still gazing at the painting.

'Can't deny it,' said Plant.

Major turned and gave him what Revill's old mother would probably have called an old-fashioned look.

'You have the missive?' Plant asked. It seemed the right word in the right place.

Major handed it across without a word, as if he were a senior Foreign Office chap slipping secret documents to his KGB controller in the good old Cold War days.

'All right to look at it here?' Plant asked.

'Why the hell not?' Major asked.

Plant looked at it. A4 paper. Computer printing. Effectively untraceable.

YOUR CHARMS HAVE FADED. DOOMSDAY DRAWS NIGH.

'Succinct,' said Plant.

He looked at the prepaid envelope addressed to Major at the college. Handwritten capitals, no doubt disguised, possibly traceable.

'So it didn't come through the university internal mail.'

'I'm not sure there is any to the colleges any more. Or if there ever was.'

'Right,' said Plant. 'Anyway, it doesn't necessarily rule out colleagues.'

'Colleagues?' Major snapped.

'Or former colleagues. Because they would no doubt realise internal mail could narrow down the field of suspects. So they would decide to spend big and use Australia Post anyway. Postmark doesn't help. Nothing distinctive about the paper or envelope.'

'How do you know?'

'Guessing, to be honest,' said Plant. 'But it looks like standard A4 paper. You can get it anywhere. Prepaid self-sealing envelope, get it at any post office. No need to lick the stamp or flap, so no DNA. No doubt whoever sent it used gloves, so no fingerprints. Totally anonymous. Unless there's a coded significance in the two black handprints on the printed stamp.'

'No,' said Major.

'North African magic?' Plant tried.

'Maybe. Except it's presumably Australian indigenous.'

'If it had been one of those stamps with native fauna it might have conveyed a message.

'What sort of fauna?'

'Maybe a wombat.'

'A wombat?'

'Eats roots and leaves.'

'Who would send that?'

'Some dissatisfied girlfriend. You got any dissatisfied girlfriends?'

'Not that I am aware of.'

'All satisfied, good. Anyway, it's not a wombat.'

'No, it isn't,' said Major.

'Can I keep it?' Plant asked.

'Do you need to?'

'It's something to go on.'

'I prefer to burn the damn things.'

'I think I'd like to hang on to it.'

'Can't see why,' said Major. 'But suit yourself,' he added reluctantly.

*

'We can go to the café upstairs,' said Major. 'Talk about it there.'

'Let's do that,' said Plant.

The café had a splendid view over Woolloomooloo and the harbour, offering relief to those who had had enough art.

'Do you always meet people here?' Plant asked.

'I haven't been here for twenty years,' Major said. 'So the answer is no.'

'You don't arrange assignations in the university gallery when you're back in Oxford?'

'It's called the Ashmolean.'

'And you meet there?'

'No.'

'I wondered why you chose this,' Plant persisted. 'Whether it was a sort of habit. Or a policy.'

'My policy is not to waste time,' said Major. 'And since no one in this never-never land seems able to keep an appointment punctually, I chose somewhere to meet where I wouldn't be sitting around twiddling my thumbs while I waited.'

'But getting a bit of uplifting cultural input.'

'Yes,' said Major.

'It's the great Australian dreamtime,' said Plant.

'What is?'

'Being late for appointments.'

Major snorted and looked round irritably for service.

'You can always do crossword puzzles while you wait,' Plant suggested.

'Do one crossword, you've done the lot.'

'I'd never thought of it like that,' said Plant.

'Nothing to them. Waste of bloody time. Poor old Philby used to do *The Times* crossword every morning in Moscow. He said it was to crank up the cerebrations. Poor old sod. That would be enough to put you off them if nothing else did. People go on about them like they're part of some great tradition. Truth is they were invented in America in the 1920s.'

'Really?' said Plant.

'So what's the progress?'

'I can't say there is any. Not a lot to go on.'

'There's the note,' said Major.

'True,' Plant agreed. 'But I didn't have it till now. And even now I have it I'm not sure it tells us a lot.'

Major grunted.

'Do you find it particularly menacing?' Plant asked. 'Or just rather silly?'

'Silly?' said Major.

Plant waited.

'It depends what they have in mind,' said Major.

'You think it's building up to something?'

'I've no idea.'

'It could just be a joke.'

'I don't find it amusing,' said Major.

'A bad joke,' Plant suggested.

'It still has hostile intent.'

'Your charms have faded. Doomsday draws nigh,' Plant intoned. 'It could have. What about charms? Doomsday? Aren't they Anglo-Saxon words?'

'They're of Old English origin. Half our vocabulary is. Means nothing.'

'But it might suggest another Anglo-Saxonist?'

'It might. But not necessarily. Anyway, Old English used to be part of all English courses. It could just as well be a literature person.'

'What about "nigh"?'

'What about it?'

'A bit literary? A bit out of date? Literary archaism?'

'Might be in your part of the world,' said Major.

'Meaning?'

'Nox Americana and all that,' Major said. 'It's still in use where I come from.'

'So we can't narrow it down?'

'I wouldn't have thought so.'

'What about the charms? Do we take them as referring to your social manner? However loosely. Or does it suggest something more specific? Like magic charms.'

'No doubt it could.'

'So which charms is it that are intended?'

'How would I know?'

'The sender must think you do.'

'The sender's probably a bloody lunatic.'

'Maybe,' said Plant. 'But that doesn't preclude intention. Or even information.'

'I have no idea,' said Major.

'Well,' said Plant, 'I can't say I have either.'

Major ordered some sticky cake and tea. All those years in England. Plant ordered a coffee he didn't want and which his acupuncturist assured him was bad for him. Along with everything else he had ever enjoyed.

'The possibilities would seem to be the following,' he said. 'Tell me if I've missed any or if any don't apply.' He enumerated them. 'One, it could be some resentful girlfriend, or ex-girlfriend, or the boyfriend or husband of some girlfriend or ex-girlfriend; or two, some potential sexual harassment complaint from the depths of the past, doing it with students who now in late middle-age allege it has deformed their whole life; or three, a professional rival or a political feud; or four, someone you've been doing magic on or who thinks you've been doing magic on them; or five, a nut; or six, a combination of all or some of them.'

'Well,' said Major, steepling his hands and smiling over them, 'that certainly narrows it down.'

'Unless you can tell me who might have cause, it's the best I can do.'

'Haven't a clue,' said Major.

'And you've never offended anybody over the years sufficiently to provoke something like this?'

'I've probably offended a lot of people,' said Major, 'and shall continue to do so. Touchy lot, academics. Sensitive flowers. Same with students. How would you know? But nothing stands out.'

'Can we narrow it down at all?'

'You can rule out the magic.'

'You haven't been casting spells?'

'I am an historian of consciousness,' Major said, 'not a bloody wizard.'

'Or brewing up love philtres?'

'Never needed them. As Sir Henry Parkes said when recommended oysters, "I don't need these adventitious aids. Lady Parkes and I until quite recently have been in the habit of having connection seventeen or eighteen times every night, and we now have connection ten or eleven times."'

'The father of Federation,' said Plant. 'And your wife? Is she here with you?'

'Good lord,' said Major.

'We have to consider everything,' said Plant.

'She's visiting her family at the moment.'

'Where exactly?'

'Oh, out beyond the black stump. You can rule her out.'

'You're confident?'

'Yes, I'm confident,' said Major.

'You were caught up in the sixties protest movement.'

'Was I?'

'So Revill said.'

'Been checking up on me?'

'I had lunch with him and Dennis and Tony.'

'My commiserations. Sad old bunch of losers, aren't they? Pretending they're Evelyn Waugh or Kingsley Amis or Dorothy Parker or whatever. The twilight of the ungodly.'

'The sixties,' Plant said.

'They really are a long time ago,' said Major, 'despite what poor old Revill might imagine. It was more the seventies down here, anyway. Took a decade for the ideas to filter through. The laws of unequal development as poor old Revill used to say. Colonial bloody time-lag, if you ask me.'

'Could there be resentments from those years?'

Major sniffed. A long, reflective sniff.

'Never trust a chap who wasn't a radical in his twenties. Not that you'd want to trust many who were. It was just a phase. A fashion. A fad. The world moved on. Except for poor old Revill and his ilk.'

'And you moved on with it.'

Major grinned, all shining teeth and glistening spectacles.

'You bet I did,' he said.

'And there's no murky secret left behind in your past you'd want to tell me about.'

The smile remained, but fixed, frozen.

'To explain these notes,' Plant explained.

'Not a thing.'

'Well,' said Plant, 'that's about it.'

Major stood up, promptly.

'Right then.'

Plant got himself together and rose too. Major clapped him on the shoulder, avuncularly.

'Do your best,' he said.

Plant bore the blow and stood there, waiting for Major to make the move.

'Don't let me keep you,' said Major.

'You're not leaving?'

'Have to see a chap.'

'I'll leave you then.'

'You do that,' said Major. 'I'll hear from you.'

Plant left.

## Ten

Revill walked down the High Street of his native town. He would have liked to have strode, or stridden, or whatever it was. Alone. I strode with none for none was worth my stride. But it was more like shuffled. The faithful citizenry lurched from side to side in their hose and anoraks, swinging plastic bags full of plastic bottles and plastic packets, their walking sticks swinging out in the hope of tripping up someone eagerly and vigorously attempting to get past. The eager and vigorous were by definition alien and to be tripped up. This was no country for striding. Where was there to stride to? This was for hobbling and lurching, sudden stops that might engender a collision, maybe even a fall, at least a split plastic bag and a spillage of shopping into the gutter, or sudden directional signals from a swiftly raised walking stick that might prod someone in the ear or raise the hem of a skirt. He might as well have been in the Shambles. He ducked into an alley and sidled down to the Shambles. For old time's sake. The alley was worse, smelling of urine and fish and chips and vomit and something for the moment indefinable.

The Shambles was devoid of the butchers' shops that had given it its name. Gone to supermarkets and shopping malls everywhere. He remembered a past of raw bones in the gutters and maleficent dogs fighting over them, toothless crones in the malodorous alleys leading to Court Number One and Court Number Two, an ambience of medieval menace, men in striped aprons with bloody cleavers, windows festooned with rabbits and hares and pheasants and partridges shot by the local squirearchy or poached by the local rural proletariat. Now it was all travel agents, seven days in St Lazarus, fourteen days in the Mal Dives, Disneyland weekend break.

But modernisation had its limits. Another alley, another street down, and he was in the dark ages. Half-timbered buildings leaned over the broken pavements, each storey built out further over the street, each roofline buckled and sway-backed and irregular. The ground floors had been shop-fitted into Chinese takeaways and Indian restaurants, best Balti out of Birmingham. Bicycle repair shops hung on from before the green revival of non-fossil fuel transportation. Second-hand bookshops pre-dating internet searches lurked behind grimy windows. Pigeons cooed on the roof of the old Friary. He came to the pub.

\*

He stood at the bar and waited for service. A thin ray of sunlight caught the corner of the old wooden table. The smell of stale beer was wafted slightly by a breeze coming in through the open doors. He didn't recall that there had been a back door. Perhaps it was only opened in the morning to air the place. Perhaps the doors were only open to air the place and it wasn't opening time yet. No one was there. No one came.

It was not how he'd envisaged it. He had expected a triumphal return, when he first left. A prosperous spell in the colonies, and then the barmaids all over him. 'Ooh isn't he brown.' 'Ooh isn't he firm.' 'Ooh isn't he rich.' 'Ooh isn't he nice.'

That last evening before he'd left.

'We'll all be waiting for you. All of us. Remember us.'

Then Nell's mother had poured a bottle of soda water over his head and barred him for life.

Well, life with parole was only nine or ten years, fifteen at most, and he'd certainly done that. Done a lot longer than he'd expected. But he was back now. No regrets. Brown and firm and rich enough. And nice. He fingered his moustache but he'd shaved it off at the end of the seventies when it ceased to signify Zapata and Guevara. When Zapata and Guevara ceased to be signified at all. Except on the mud-flaps of trucks in Thailand. After the seventies it gave the wrong signal. As far as he was concerned. He picked his nose instead. That was the moment Nell walked in.

'Still got your filthy habits.'

'Hello, Nell.'

'The usual?' she said.

'You remember me?'

'How can I forget someone who's always picking his nose?'

'I was just scratching.'

'You usually were. Lois's bottom usually.'

'How is she?' he asked. Not too eagerly, he hoped. The assignation promised. 'Next time you're back, lovey. Promise you. You see if I don't.'

'Pretty good for a grandmother with varicose veins,' said Nell.

'I can't believe it.'

'That's what she said the first time,' said Nell. 'Then it was twins. Then they started dropping their own.'

'Good lord,' he said.

'He wasn't that good in the end,' said Nell. 'He went off to an ashram and abandoned her.'

'Who?'

'Lord whatever his name was.'

'Good lord.'

'So you said. What will it be?'

'The usual, I suppose.'

'You can't get it any more,' Nell said.

'I thought you just offered it me.'

'That's right,' she said. 'So you wouldn't be able to have it. Like Lois. Or did you?'

'Did I what?'

'Have her.'

'Woof,' said Revill. Or maybe it was 'oof.'

'Or was it her "Next time you're back lovey. Promise you. You see if I don't"?'

He blenched. Blanched. Went white, anyway. Lost his colonial tan and firmness.

'Not another,' she cackled. 'I should have guessed. You men. Poor suckers. All of you.'

She cackled contentedly.

'So what will it be?'

He looked at the array of beer taps. He didn't recognise any of the brands.

'I don't know,' he admitted.

'The cheapest?'

'What are you having?'

'I'll have a lime and bitters, thank you kindly.'

'Bit early in the day for that, isn't it?'

'Always so witty,' she smiled at him. 'A joking word for every-one. That's how they remembered him. Dying for him to come back.'

'Were they?'

'They?'

'You?'

'Dying on my feet waiting for your order.'

'I'll have that one,' he said, pointing.

'The cheapest.'

*

'So how come you're back? I thought you'd been safely transported.'

'I escaped.'

'So it seems. You tunnelled your way out?'

'Metaphorically speaking.'

'With your bare metaphors.'

'How else?'

'Still got the earth beneath your fingernails,' she said. 'Or haven't you cleaned them since you left?

They should do a DNA test on them. See if they can find traces of Lois. Maybe they could clone a younger version of her from the fragments.'

'I never touched her.'

'Not for want of trying.'

He sighed. 'True enough.'

'Oh, we're dealing in truth now, are we?'

'I never lied to you,' he said.

She cackled.

'So how come you're back?' she asked again. 'To see where it all went wrong? You're not trying to tell me you're a success. Expensive taste in cheap beers. The stretch limo parked outside. This isn't meant to be a triumphal return, is it?' She looked at him sharply. 'No, I didn't think it would be,' she said.

*

'It was hard to get out. Impossible. I tried, but …'

'Incarcerated, were you?'

'It felt like it.'

'Like you were doing time.'

'In a way.'

'Time and a half, even.'

He nodded. 'Time …'

'Stood still, did it? Turned back upon itself. Didn't they give you a bent nail to scratch the days and weeks on the wall?'

'They gave me a computer in the end.'

'Some would say you were onto a very good thing,'

Nell said. 'Those of us who've had to work for a living.'

'I was working.'

'Oh, yes.'

'I was.'

'We're open eleven till eleven seven days a week. Do you know how many hours a week that is? Eighty-four.'

'You don't open at eleven on Sundays.'

'I'll round it off at eighty. Now you tell me how many hours a week you were teaching.'

'Four.'

'All year?'

'Two semesters.'

'How many weeks?'

'Thirty altogether. Well, twenty-eight.'

'Four hours a week,' she said. 'And I just knocked off four to make a round figure.'

'They wouldn't let me do any more.'

'Didn't they trust you with the minds of the young?'

'No.'

'Or bodies.'

'Some semesters I was down to one.'

'Body?'

'Hour.'

'And you wept all the way to the bank.'

'It was demoralising,' he said.

'We should have a welcome back party,' she said. 'And we could all stand around and weep for you. If we weep enough tears you'll be able to scrub your nails. Or sponge the stains off your shiny suit.'

'There aren't any stains. It's new.'
'It certainly stands out.'

## Eleven

In the evening the pub was alive, throbbing, horribly alive, pullulating with young faithful citizens in jeans and singlets, spilling out onto the pavement, milling in the street. Revill would have gone past, on the other side, if he hadn't agreed to be there.

'Come by this evening,' Nell had said. 'We can go out for a meal.'

Go out for a meal. Things had changed. Britain was liveable in after all. Oh, why had he ever left?

The jukebox pounded out its bass from the public bar. The hours of lugubrious silence he had spent there, all gone, all gone.

A scrawny, shaven-headed youth came out of the door, backwards, a step to each thump of the beat, as if impelled by the force of the sound waves. He stood on the pavement's edge gesticulating, as a large, no less shaven-headed figure emerged from the door. The large figure was throwing out his arms in vigorous, dismissive thrusts.

'Go on. Shoo. Git.'

'Who you calling git?' the scrawny youth asked.

'Vamoose. Out, out, out.'

'I'm fucking out,' said the youth.

'Out of sight,' said the big man. 'Skedaddle.'

'Skedaddle yourself,' said the scrawny one. 'Git,' he added for good measure.

The big man stopped shooing and reached a hand

to his hip. It hung there momentarily where a holster might once have been worn and moved on down into his trouser pocket. He took out a handful of small change, palmed it across to his left hand, and began throwing one and two pence pieces at the scrawny youth.

'Ouch,' said the youth.

He bent down to pick up the coin. Another one hit him on the head as he scavenged in the gutter. He backed away, ducking as the coins were hurled at him. They were aimed with precision. Too precisely for the youth to bend down and collect them. He tried but he only succeeded in making himself a target. He backed off down the street, calling out imprecations.

The big man threw the last of his coins and stood there on the pavement, waiting till the scrawny youth was out of sight. Then he turned back into the public bar.

*

Revill went into the lounge bar. It was a class betrayal, he knew. Or thought he knew. It would have been, years ago. But it was less menacing. Indeed, it was comparatively empty. The jukebox penetrated there too, though fractionally less loudly, and there was room to get through the door, get to the bar, even get served.

'You again,' said Nell.

'You said this evening.'

'I didn't expect you to turn up, though,' she said.

'I always turn up.'

'Do you, now?'

He couldn't remember. He thought he'd been reliable. Reliable to a fault. Always at fault. It came back to him. That familiar note. That note of belonging.

'This man giving you trouble?' said a voice behind him.

'As ever,' said Nell.

A hand gripped his shoulder and half turned him round. He turned the other half voluntarily. The hand reached towards his stomach but it waited halfway there, open, flat, rather large, attached to the arm of the shaven-headed coin dispenser, waiting to be shaken. He shook it.

'You remember Will,' Nell said.

'How are you, Will?' said Revill.

'Not good,' said Will.

'No?'

'No,' said Will. 'This place is getting me down.'

'Looks like a thriving trade,' said Revill.

Shaven-headed singleted figures writhed and jostled at the public bar, packed solidly, a wall of living meat.

'Maggots,' said Will. 'A rabble. I'd gas the lot of them. Exterminate the brutes.'

'Not tonight, dear,' said Nell.

'And as for that jungle music ...'

The beat beat on.

110

'Whenever he hears it he wants to reach for his gun,' said Nell.

'Except you hid it.'

'You bet I did,' said Nell.

Will raised the hatch and let himself in behind the bar.

'What's your poison?' he asked.

Revill pointed to whatever he'd drunk that morning.

'You can't drink that,' said Will. 'Not that piss.'

'I'm in your hands,' said Revill.

Will looked at them, turned them over, palms up, palms down. They seemed very big. He poured a glass of something lethal.

'Cheers,' said Revill.

'No cheer in this place,' said Will.

*

Will backed the Range Rover down the street, maintaining a steady pace despite the knots of drinkers spilling and staggering over the pavement and onto the road. They dispersed only as he drove amidst them. They snarled in at the windows, raising their glasses as if to slop beer over the roof and windscreen.

'They're too cheap,' said Will. 'They won't even spare two p's worth of piss for the pleasure of throwing it at us.'

He distorted his face into a simulacrum of the faces outside, pressed it to the windscreen like a death rictus. The drinkers attempted to respond in kind but the four-wheel drive was moving too fast for them to adhere to the windows without risking crushed feet. They contented themselves with thumb and finger gestures. Will gestured back. Mine host.

'Spare us,' said Nell.

The bells of the cathedral rang out tidings of joy and invitations to contribute to the cathedral fabric restoration fund. They swept past its shadow and Will pressed a disc of Elgar's 'Pomp and Circumstance' marches into the CD player. He sang along to 'Land of Hope and Glory' as they sped through the Midland villages, North Piddle, Wyre Piddle, Piddle in the Hole.

*

They drove to an Indian restaurant in another town.

'At least you can go to another town,' said Revill.

'We're running out of them,' said Nell.

'Peasants,' said Will.

'He gets aggressive and they bar him.'

'The towns?'

'The restaurants.'

'Not the whole city?'

'The pubs.'

'Ah.'

'The shops.'

'Oh.'

'Soon we're going to have to sell up and go.'

'Never too soon,' said Will.

'What will you do?'

'We thought of the Falkland islands,' said Nell.

'Kill a few Argies,' said Will.

'So business isn't good?' said Revill. The end of empire, the death of old England, the impoverishment of post-industrialism, the flight of capital. His analysis was confirmed. There was nothing to come back to, after all.

'Business is very good,' said Will. 'Business is too bloody good to give it up.'

'It's just the public that he hates,' said Nell.

'The customers,' said Will. 'And the excise. And the health inspectors. And the council. And the Inland Revenue.'

'Otherwise everything's fine. Home sweet home. As you saw.'

'I see,' said Revill.

'No you don't,' said Will.

He glowered across his vindaloo. Beads of sweat ran down his forehead. Fire darted from his throat and eyes.

'We became the victims of our success,' said Will. 'We got in the good food guides. Suddenly we were devoured by locusts. The phone never stopped ringing. They asked for reservations. In a pub, I ask you. We don't take reservations. They asked for the menu. We don't have menus. We printed menus. But the food was always running out. They expect to have everything on the menu. They expect you to have cellars full of deep freezers so you can serve up everything. We serve fresh food and when it runs out it runs out. So they got nasty. Very aggressive, if I may say so myself.'

'And you would know,' said Nell.

'I would indeed.'

'That's when he started throwing customers out,' said Nell.

'Requesting them to leave,' said Will.

'Brandishing a bar stool over their heads.'

'That only happened once,' said Will.

'Till the next time,' said Nell.

'So they stopped coming.'

'I see,' said Revill.

'No you don't,' said Will.

'Maybe not,' agreed Revill.

'It took us two years to get out of the good food guides.'

'But Will and the health inspector achieved it,' said Nell.

'And your dog,' said Will.

'Blame the dog.'

'I wasn't blaming it,' said Will. 'I was giving it credit. Showing it affection.'

'He was stroking it,' said Nell. 'I can't imagine why. Then he picked up a plate from a table and this toffee-nosed old biddy said "You've just touched an animal".'

'Too right, I had,' said Will. 'I told her I'd rather touch an animal than any of the customers. Her included. At least you can't get AIDS off a dog.'

'She made a complaint to the health inspector,' said

Nell. 'He paid us a visit and Will got into a fight with him.'

'I offered to put the dog on him so he could see for himself. Six rounds with the dog or six with a customer of his choice. Whichever he preferred. Aggressive bastard thought I meant fisticuffs. I said of course not, I meant sit at the bar with the dog for six rounds of best bitter. He said it was an unhygienic suggestion and closed us down.'

'Really,' said Revill.

'Close enough,' said Nell. 'We'll gloss over the details.'

'Then we got invaded by the nappy-rashers and the baby snatchers. The breweries have been closing down all the old pubs in the town centre. We were the only one left. The only one that would serve British Youth. So we serve them.'

'You've seen our friendly service,' said Nell. 'You can imagine what the rest were like.'

'The rest all went broke. You either cater to the rabble or you go out of business.'

'So we have the trade,' said Nell.

'I hate it.'

'But you like the money.'

'No, I don't,' said Will. He emptied his pockets of small change and heaped it on the table. 'Here, take it, I hate the stuff.'

Nell scooped it up and put it in her handbag.

'So what are you going to do?'

'Sell up,' said Will. 'Go and buy a disused coal mine and live in it.'

'And how are things with you?' Nell asked.

'Hell,' said Revill.

'That's good,' said Will. 'That's what I like to hear.'

'I was trapped. I couldn't move.'

'I have dreams like that,' said Will. 'I wake up in the middle of the night and I'm totally paralysed. Can't move my arms or legs or head. Can't breathe. Can't speak. Can't call out.'

'This wasn't a dream,' said Revill. 'This was reality.'

'Ah,' Will laughed, 'if only it was so easy to tell the difference. Take this vindaloo.'

'I have. It's rather good.'

'But is it real? Or are you dreaming it? Are you going to wake up and find it was only pie and peas?'

'Pie and peas?' said Revill.

'That's what you eat down there, isn't it?'

'I didn't.'

'I read it somewhere,' said Will. 'Ozzie tucker. I knew a chap called that. They called him that because he was so unappealing. Raw and coarse.'

'Sure it wasn't another dream?' said Nell.

'It could have been,' Will conceded. 'I thought I went to school with him but you're right, how can you ever be sure?'

'I was sure,' said Revill.

'So you knew him?'

'I was sure I was stuck.'

'In the end you wake up,' said Will.

'I woke up and I was still stuck.'

'That's serious,' said Will.

'I couldn't get out.'

'But here you are,' said Nell.

'Escape from Devil's Island,' said Will. 'I do like a good yarn.'

'You twisted your sheets into a rope and climbed out the window?' said Nell.

'I woke up one morning …'

'Just as the sun was rising,' sang Will. The heritage of English song.

'And decided, I don't have to do this any more. I am taking early retirement.'

'I like that,' said Will. 'Determination. Decision. A good pension fund.'

'Exactly,' said Revill.

'And how long had you been there when you showed this sudden determination?' Nell asked.

'Thirty-three years,' said Revill.

'A mystical number,' said Nell.

'Quite a long time, though,' said Will. 'Pretty well two life sentences.'

'It was,' said Revill.

'What took you so long?' asked Nell.

*

'It was all right to begin with,' said Revill. 'Then when it wasn't, it was too late. I'd apply for these jobs and nothing would happen. I was blacklisted.'

'Is that how they do it?'

'I should hope so,' said Will. 'Stamp out subversives.'

'He has a deep commitment to tradition and authority,' said Nell.

'Tradition and authority,' said Will. He raised his glass. 'Queen and Country,' he said.

'Here we go,' Nell groaned. She raised her glass. Will glared at Revill.

'Come on, sir.'

Revill looked round. The Indian waiter smiled and raised an orange juice in the air. Revill brandished his half of bitter.

'Sometimes they just write anonymous letters,' said Revill.

'Saying what?'

'Like saying, do you realise the candidate has genital herpes?'

'Thought that would be par for the course for you chaps,' said Will. 'Occupational disease. Surprised it's nothing worse.'

'And did you?' Nell asked.

'That wasn't me. Someone told me that's what happened to someone who applied for a job.'

'I thought these things were confidential.'

'They wanted to know if it was true.'

'And they asked you?'

'They must have known you'd had body contact,' said Will.

'And did you?'

'Did I what?'

'Have genital herpes.'

'It wasn't me they were asking about.'

'It is now,' said Nell.

'Fifth Amendment,' said Will. 'Your only hope. Or ask her why she's so interested. Come to that, why are you so interested, my dear?'

'So what you're saying,' said Nell, 'is you went to Australia and spent thirty-three years lying paralysed in bed with genital herpes.'

'I'm saying I couldn't get another job because I was blacklisted.'

'What's the definition of a blacklist?' Will asked. He spluttered fragments of pappadam across the table at them. 'The menu in an Indian restaurant.'

Nell gave him a withering look.

'It was a clue in the *Telegraph* crossword,' said Will.

'No it wasn't,' said Nell.

'Got to keep up the old values,' Will insisted. 'Especially when you're sitting around with blacklisted subversives. The walls may be covered with red carpet, but we wouldn't want your old boyfriend to feel he was amongst intimate friends. Not with his genital herpes.'

'I don't have genital herpes,' said Revill.

'I bet you say that to all the girls,' said Nell.

'Well, we're not about to ask for visual verification here,' said Will.

'So what did you do wrong?'

'Oh, you know, speaking out against the spread of American imperialism, globalization ...'

'Nothing wrong with that,' said Will. 'Mind you, the colonies have been going a bit bolshie lately, all that American republican stuff.'

'They don't think of themselves as a colony any more,' said Revill.

'There you are then. Serves you right. You should never have left your own country.'

'I should have stayed put and become a Little Englander?'

'Put the Great back into Great Britain and throw the Welsh and Scots and Irish out,' said Will. He raised his glass. 'Rivers of blood,' he intoned.

'So you made your escape and now you've come back to find out who wrote anonymous letters about you,' said Nell.

Revill shrugged.

'To see where it all went wrong. In your shiny suit.'

He looked down at the lapels.

'It's not shiny.'

'It's been pressed too many times by unskilful hands,' said Will. 'Like Nell.'

'It's new,' he protested.

'It probably was once,' said Nell.

'In the days when the world was wide,' said Will. 'Takes a while for fashions to catch up in the colonies, I imagine.'

'I suppose they hand them out when you leave,' Nell said. 'Isn't that what they do in penal settlements?'

'No,' said Revill.

'You didn't buy it, did you?' Nell said. 'The man in

black. Or the Count of Monte Cristo. Is that it?'

'Is that what?'

'You spent all those years in the convict settlement and now you've tunnelled your way to liberty and you've come back to get your revenge on us like the Count of Monte Cristo?'

'Why would I want to be revenged on you?'

'That's what you've come back to discover,' said Nell. 'I don't mean us specifically. I just mean people in England.'

'Everybody wants to be revenged on somebody,' said Will. 'It's only natural. An eye for an eye and all that sort of thing. Darwin.'

'I've always thought of you as my friends,' said Revill.

'Nobody thinks like that any more,' said Will. 'In the words of the late, great Mrs Thatcher, there's no such thing as friendship.'

'Society,' said Revill.

'Come again.'

'She said there's no such thing as society, not friendship.'

'Slip of the tongue,' said Will. 'It's what she meant to say. Amounts to the same thing. Can't go on giving handouts to old friends. User pays, these days.'

'We had one of your friends in the pub,' said Nell. 'Asking after you in a friendly manner.'

'Who was that?' Revill asked.

'The magician,' said Nell.

'Go on.'

'Some Oxford fellow,' said Will. 'Name of Sapper. Miner. Something like that.'

'Major?' said Revill.

'Could be,' said Will. 'Looked like a corporal to me, but you can't tell these days. Services have gone to the dogs. He said he used to work with you. On one of those chain gangs, I imagine.'

'He said he wrote books on magic,' said Nell.

'Asked if Nell had kept any old nail clippings or locks of hair of yours he could take away and work on,' said Will.

'What did he want?' Revill asked.

'Cast a spell, I imagine,' said Will. 'What else would he want? I told him we'd done our damnedest to cast you out years ago. Wiped the slate clean. Had no recollection of you. He wouldn't take no for an answer. The wife filled him in.'

'I did not,' she said. 'I didn't take to him.'

'She has to say that. Otherwise I'd have taken to him.'

'How did he track me down here?'

'He said you used to talk about the place all the time when you got pissed. Which was all the time. Which sounded convincing, the getting pissed all the time bit,' said Nell. 'He said you'd told him to call in here and we'd give him a good time.'

'I think he said it was you who'd give him a good time, Nell, my dear,' said Will.

'When was this?' said Revill.

'Hard to say. He's been in a few times, over the years.'

'He's no friend of mine,' said Revill.

'Didn't think he could be,' said Will. 'You were never the sort of chap to have friends. I told him that. He walked alone, I said. That's why he went to the colonies, I told him.'

*

They drove back to the pub. Will pulled up before they reached it and they looked along the street. Crowds of drunken youth milled around spilling lager on the pavement and into the gutter. The jukebox beat out its beat.

'I can't go in there,' said Will.

'Thriving trade,' said Revill.

'It's too disgusting,' said Will.

He backed out of the street.

'England, my England,' said Will. 'Can't even go into your own pub. See what you've come back to. A rabble. What we need is a good war. Conscription. That would straighten them out. Thin them out, anyway. Either that or transportation.'

The half-timbered houses loured over the street. Rats rustled in the drains. The Black Death hovered all around them, waiting to resume its territory. Is this where I want to be, Revill asked himself, is this the promised end?

# Twelve

Revill had never intended to settle back into his native town. Not really. Perhaps he had wondered, lingering before the windows of the real estate offices around the cathedral. A lost vision of a sort of Trollopean or Hugh Walpolean retirement. Mrs Henry Wood, maybe. Walking through the cathedral cloisters of a summer's evening, as Henry James had once done. Still an institutionalised vision, inevitably. Just across the road from where Dr Johnson's father used to hold his book sales. He headed for the station, took a short last drink in the Jeeves bar of the Star hotel, and caught the train to Oxford to look up his old tutor.

'How nice of you to call,' said Harbinger, 'all the way from where did you say it was, the utter antipodes?'

'Yes,' said Revill.

'The penal settlement.'

'Well, that was some time ago.'

'But you still wear prison clothing? Your sumptuary laws require it?'

And he had given all that thought to what to wear. He had felt uneasy about the Monte Cristo suit after Nell's comments. Anyway, it might seem too servile to those demands of Oxford that he refused to acknowledge, back in subfusc. He chose denim. I am not looking for a job, this is not an interview suit, I am not a suppliant, I am free. But he wasn't. He was back in England. He had got the codes wrong yet once more.

'Reasonable enough for the climate, no doubt. You could always pass for an American. They had our first prison settlement, after all. Perhaps you should wear a baseball cap. They tell me you can buy them with the university crest in one of those shops in Broad Street. The way they live now.' He whinnied in a malign sort of way. 'I had a man once went to Australia. Name of Revill. Never knew what became of him.'

'That's me,' said Revill.

'What a coincidence.'

'I am he,' Revill added for good measure.

'What sort of man was he, do you remember?'

'They say he was one of your brightest students. Then you sent him to Australia and forgot about him.'

'Forgot about him?'

'Forgot to bring him back.'

'Left him there did I? For the term of his natural life?'

'Yes.'

'What a terrible story! How remiss of me.'

'Yes,' agreed Revill. 'Why did you do it?'

'Do?'

'Why did you send me there?'

'Where?'

'Australia.'

'Oh, I think you'd have to ask him that.'

'Was it for something I did?'

'Did?'

Revill let it hang there.

'Did you do anything?'

'I don't know.'

'Well, if you don't know, who would?'

'Was it some sort of penalty?' Revill persisted.

'Like an own goal?'

'Yes.'

'But you never were a sporting man, were you?'

'No,' said Revill.

'Didn't row with the college boat.'

'No.'

Spotted as an outsider from the outset. Against the government.

'Was it political?'

'Ah, political.'

Ah, political.

'Of course being bright isn't everything. As you must know.'

'I'm not sure,' Revill began.

'It's all a matter of degree.'

'I suppose it is.'

'Though not degrees.' He beamed at Revill. 'People used to ask me every year when the results were announced, are you happy with them? And I would say, yes, of course, a couple of firsts, a couple of seconds, a third, a fourth and an aegrotat. A bit of everything. A good range. Very happy. I mean, you can have a first class degree but that doesn't make you a first class man.'

He looked at Revill piercingly.

'Do I know you from somewhere?'

'You taught me.'

126

'Really? Where?'

'Here.'

'Here?'

'Oxford.'

'Oxford? Funny sort of place. Down the rabbit hole. I always think of Matthew Arnold's lines, don't you? "He came as most men thought to little good, But came to Oxford and his friends no more". Beautiful lines, don't you agree? That dying fall. Beautiful sentiments. Such plangency.'

'I suppose so,' said Revill.

'Well, very nice of you to call. Have you seen your old tutor since you've been back? You should drop by and visit him. It would be a nice thought. Always assuming he can remember you.' He chuckled. 'Or himself.'

Revill walked out into the endless twilight. The all but indescribable emptiness of North Oxford. Untrodden gravelled driveways. Fallen leaves, forever falling. Leadengrove unleaving. The eternal hours before dinner. The bells ringing out for chapel, for hall, for the hell of it. As if he'd never been away. But he had. Without a doubt.

# Thirteen

'Shame you didn't let me know earlier,' said Major. 'Could've fixed something up for you.'

A poisoned chalice. A diseased honey-pot. Some toxic icon from the reams of popular fiction Major had rifled over the years.

'Too late now, of course. Programme filled up for the rest of the year. You wouldn't draw an audience. Love to fit you in, but you know how it is.'

Revill knew how it was. It was however you wanted it to be.

'That's all right,' he said. 'I don't especially want to do anything.'

'You never did, did you?' said Major. 'It must be you, then.'

'What must be me?'

'You must be you.'

He didn't answer that one.

'When Lucy told me she'd seen you slouching towards the Bodleian and asked you to dinner, I had to wonder, was it really you? Heading for a library? Can never be sure with you characters from the colonies. Could be an imposter.'

'Why would I be an imposter?'

'It's hard to imagine, I agree. If you were claiming to be someone else it might be different. But I agree. It's hard to see what's in it for anyone claiming to be you. No hard feelings, of course, old chap.'

'Why wouldn't I be me?'

'Ah, that would be telling.' He tapped the side of his nose. 'I could give you a thousand reasons.'

Revill frowned. Major laughed and slapped him on the back. 'You're quite sure you're not an impostor?'

'Not at all.'

'Not at all sure?'

'Not at all an impostor.'

'The colonies used to be full of them. That E. Phillips Oppenheim novel, perhaps you know it.'

'No I don't.'

'Not much read these days. But it has its point. And the Tichborne claimant, of course. Nearer to home. You don't have any distinguishing birthmark? A recessive penis? Something unique?'

'No.'

'Irredeemably ordinary, ah well.'

Revill smiled thinly.

'You could be one of our secret service brethren, not really you at all, got yourself murdered and now you're just pretending to be you. Amazing what can happen.'

'In the world of E. Phillips Oppenheim.'

'Well, he was one of them. Or claimed he was. Could have been an impostor, of course. It was always denied. Very rich field.'

Revill understood.

'You're cultivating it.'

Plowing, tilling, reaping. Especially reaping.

'Inauthenticity,' said Major. 'A theme for our times.

Or The Theme of our Times, really.'

'Really.'

'Really. It got me Erasmus funding. Socrates funding. *Inauthenticité sans frontières.* A burning issue now they've abolished internal passport controls. Some suspect chap like you flies in. Not necessarily you, but like you. Gets through passport control once. Never checked again. Could be anybody.'

'So it's not a literary study.'

'Heavens no. Absolutely not. Literature's a liability, strictly between you and me. The social implications are the things to go for.'

'What, not your old Marxist readings?'

'No, no, no, absolutely not. Don't even mention the word.'

He took a look over his shoulder, the automatic academic reflex of years of caution in the common room spread to his own living-room.

'No, border security and all that. The war on terror. Immigration. That's the big theme. How to stop it, in effect.'

'Keep people in their places.'

'If only we could.'

'And they give you money for this?'

'Serious money,' said Major, beaming. 'Travel. Top hotels. Top level research grant. Topping research assistants.'

He leered lasciviously. Revill shook his head.

'So you've abandoned magic?'

'Abandoned it, no. Put it on the back burner for

a while, yes. Let it simmer away. Bubble, bubble. Nothing wrong with having two strings to your bow. Don't want to be stuck playing a Jew's harp all my life.'

'Inauthenticity.'

'It was either that or food labels. No, I tell a lie. Diaper labelling was a goer, too. European community standards. The future is in your hands. Don't want shit leaking all over them. But that was more the strictly linguistic chaps.'

'And this was literature?'

'No, literature's out. Cultural studies. A solid background in the popular. Ghosts, magic, crime.'

'Crime?'

'Crime and spy fiction. But the spies aren't the problem, really. Nor the criminals for that matter, not the professionals. It's the amateurs we're worried about. Civilians. Crawling all over the place. Never know who they are or where they are. Can't have chaps like you cropping up without warning all the time.'

\*

'Your problem, of course,' said Major, 'was pulling back from the brink. Recoiling from the fatal shore.'

Revill swallowed some more of the rough Bulgarian red.

'Interesting drop, eh?' said Major, topping up Revill's glass. 'Better than that antipodean plonk they try and sell us here.'

'Different,' said Revill. Gasped.

'Holding off, that was your problem,' said Major. 'Drink up. Lots more where that came from. All that anti-elitist stuff. You were in the vanguard in those days. Then you were outpaced. Not even outmanoeuvred. You just hovered on the brink while the smart money strode ahead. It's one thing to introduce Jack London and Dashiell Hammett into the syllabus, but they were still literary. Apart from being commos.'

'Yes,' said Revill. 'That was the point.'

Major cut him off.

'You failed to go the whole hog. Lord Archer. Tom Clancy. *The X-Files*. You could have made a breakthrough. But you lost your nerve. A two-minute delay. Fatal. The future rushed in and you weren't part of it. In the end you were no different from the old mutton-heads who'd hired you. Now where are you?'

'It's all such rubbish,' said Revill.

'Immaterial,' said Major. 'Or totally material, to be precise. But you never were a very convincing Marxist, were you? Never understood the material base. Too much of the old humanist all the time. Too many idealistic notions. You could never make the leap.'

'The leap?'

'Never effect the break.'

'Couldn't I?'

'Clearly not.'

'I believed ...'

'There you are. You believed. That was your problem. Belief. The old grand narratives died decades ago. There is nothing to believe in now.'

'Except success.'

'Oh, you don't have to believe in success,' said Major. 'It comes to those unrestrained by belief. You just grab it when it shows itself.'

He brandished the bottle of Bulgarian red menacingly. Revill declined.

'Don't be ridiculous. I got this in especially for you as soon as Lucy told me she'd seen you. I knew you'd be uneasy with anything too expensive. Let alone too good. What's Revill's level? I asked myself. If it is Revill. What rough drop should I get for the rough beast? What about a few bottles of Bulgarian red for the old bugger? Good old bad old ex-commie red. That'll test him. See if it's really him or an impostor.'

Revill held his hand over his glass. Major poured the wine anyway. It flowed over Revill's fingers and onto the table.

'Silicone finish,' said Major. 'It won't hurt it. I said to Lucy, No tablecloths tonight. Not for Revill. He always spills his wine. Can't hold it. Always leaves a patch of red for his host to remember him by. After all, what else has he got to offer?'

Then Lucy came in and served dinner.

## Fourteen

Revill awoke to a postmodern hell. Ahistoria. Transgenderania. Stealth bombers circled beneath the ceiling. Tyrannosauri snarled up at them from shelves around the walls. Pink, plastic pre-pubescent girls sat with their legs wide apart inveigling cowboys and unknown figures in Nuclear Biological Chemical protective clothing. He tried to sit up and cracked his head on the slats of the bunk above him. An odour of urine and vapour rub pervaded the narrow cavity in which he was lodged. How had he got in there? Surely not voluntarily. They must have got him drunk and rolled him in. Maybe they had some kind of egg-slice stretcher for depositing guests. Should he call out and say he was done and could they slip it back underneath him and serve him up? Morning sounds were everywhere. Chirpy music interspersed with chirpy voices. Once you could have been sure the posh voices were on the radio and the regional accents the new day's badinage with the milkman and the baker. Now he could no longer tell. Nor did he know if milkman and baker still provided their daily service in these regions. The vowels sounded Australian, anyway. Some awful soap sold cheap to cable or daytime television. Oh where were the blackbirds and robins of yesteryear? Even sparrows. He looked round the room again. Not a wooden car, not a threadbare dog. All uncompromisingly denatured. Not a spider's web nor a whining mosquito, not a rustling cockroach or a scurrying lizard. He listened in vain for the melodious cry of the currawong. No kookaburras rent the morning air. What was he doing here?

He struggled to be free. Was it the cry of the wild, the antipodes calling? Or some primal instinct of escape. But vertical bars held him in. It was like being in a cot. It was being in a cot. Shades of the prison house. He put his fingers round the rails and rattled them. He waited, shivering in the chill, a chill deeper than the chill of the morning.

*

'I saw you on the baby-minder,' said Lucy. 'CCTV. We put you in the old nursery so we could keep an eye on you.'

She pointed to the miniature camera gazing balefully down at him, and her robe swung open.

He averted his eyes. Oh Lord. Who was watching the baby-minder monitor right now? Or was it all being recorded on videotape?

She wrapped her robe back round her, like a Victorian piano demurely swathed, its little legs on castor wheels sticking out beneath the tasselled hem, its keyboard pressing boldly against the clinging folds. Play me.

'Archer put the bars up so you wouldn't fall out,' she said. 'He thought you might be a wee bit, disoriented. You know.'

She smiled sweetly, ever so sweetly.

'So much flying. And drinking.'

He gripped onto the bars, his knuckles whitening, his eyes clenched shut. Do you clench eyes? He opened them again, anyway.

She came closer.

'I'll set you free,' she said.

She smiled.

'If you like, that is.'

'Oh I like, I like.'

'It's not exactly bondage, but some people do get off on closed spaces. I believe.'

She pressed down on the rail. Her robe fell open again. Breasts. Pubes.

'I think you should move your hands,' she said.

He looked at them anxiously, no, he hadn't touched her, they were still clenched to the rails.

'Otherwise I won't be able to lower the defences.'

'Aargh,' he said. 'Ah, yes.'

He let go. His hands.

The cot rail sank down. If only he could.

'Grab onto me and I'll have you out of there,' she said.

He waved his arms ineffectually, helplessly. She took him in hand, grasped his wine-dark shirt cuffs, tugged his shoulders, torso, stomach free of the duvet.

'I suppose you're decent,' she said. 'Or should I close my eyes? And think of England?'

Later he wondered if he should just have taken her then and there. Surrendered himself then and there.

Whichever was least gender specifically offensive. But he stood, knees shaking, tumescent, in his unconcealing cheap shirt without shirt-tails. While she languorously shook out her robe and wrapped it around her again and again till she got it right. But where could they have done it? Not back in the cot. And the floor was strewn with naked, amputated dolls and moribund erector sets. There was nowhere to put a foot without circumspection. Let alone anything else. Maybe they could have done it standing up. Thrown her robe over the seeing eye. But the walls were lined with protuberant shelves on nasty looking brackets. It was impossible. She must have known that, surely. She lived there, didn't she? Safety in the nursery. If it was safety she wanted.

*

He sat at the kitchen table, all egg shell fragments and burnt toast crumbs, like the debris of a NATO human rights mission.

'Archie not up?' he tried, without much conviction.

'Oh, he left before dawn to pick up his plane.'

'His plane?'

Visions of an executive Lear jet.

'Well, not his. His flight.'

That was some relief. Though why couldn't he catch a bus like other people? Or a train. Or drive.

'He says first-class rail is so expensive now he might as well fly. I think he enjoys it.'

'I'm sure he does.'

'He said to say sorry he had to go but make yourself at home.' She smiled winningly. Winsomely. 'What can I offer you?'

He cleared his throat cautiously.

'Tea or coffee?'

'Oh, either,' he said, eagerly, an excess of eagerness.

'You sound thirsty.'

'Oh yes, I am,' he said.

He felt dreadful. Was it just the awful Bulgarian red, or had Major slipped him some evil magician's potion?

She filled the kettle and plugged it in, took down a couple of canisters from the splendid array on the kitchen shelves. She put tea in the teapot from one, and a plastic packet and rolling papers on the table from the other. By the time the kettle had whistled she had rolled a joint. She lit it while the tea brewed, took a few serious puffs and then passed it across. He didn't refuse.

'Does it take you back?' she asked.

He wasn't sure.

'I remember being quite shocked,' she said.

The good thing about sharing a joint was you could be inhaling when it was your turn in the conversation and you could hold your breath till your turn had passed without giving offence.

'You sat there reading the paper and smoking,' she said. 'I suppose I was young and romantic. But it quite shocked me.'

138

He was lost. He had no idea what she was talking about.

'Anyway, I took a puff and it must have calmed me down.' She sighed. 'I suppose I'd expected you to be looking into my eyes.'

He tried looking into them now. There seemed to be tears in them.

'Whispering undying love,' she said.

She coughed on the smoke and produced more tears.

'But you had eyes only for the papers.'

She passed him across the morning's *Telegraph* that lay on the table.

'Sorry,' she said, 'I should have given it you before.'

He shook his head.

'I don't read the papers any more.'

'Only if you've been making wild, passionate love all night,' she said.

'Wild, passionate love?'

'Don't you remember?'

'Remember what?' he asked

'That night we spent together.'

This was one time sucking on a joint wasn't going to work. He burned his lips, burned his fingers trying to detach the roach from where it had bonded to the burned skin. It still didn't help.

'You don't remember?'

How could he confess that he didn't? He had no recollection at all. How could he have forgotten? Was it some insane fantasy she had imagined?

'How could you have forgotten?' she asked. 'Oh, Lucy, what a humiliation.'

'Are you sure?' he said.

It wasn't the thing to say.

'I can see it must have been a memorable occasion for you,' she said.

'I don't ...'

'Have I been so terrible all for nothing?'

'Terrible?'

'Madame Merle.'

'Madame Merle?'

'Now you'll say you don't remember lecturing me on *Portrait of a Lady*.'

How could he in a lecture class of four hundred a quarter of a century ago?

'I suppose you slept with us all and forgot every one of us.'

He tried to speak.

'Or is it only me you forgot?'

He bit on his burned lip to deflect the pain.

'You probably forgot as soon as you began reading the paper. Oh dear, somebody seems to be sitting at my breakfast table. Better offer her a joint so she doesn't disturb my reading. Can't imagine what she's doing here. No idea who she is. Have a puff on this, dear, and shut up, will you.'

She rolled another joint expertly. Her voice may have been tremulous but her fingers were steady.

'Oh God how I hate the seventies,' she said. 'Everybody so stoned all the time they don't remember any of it. It's as if none of it ever happened, and then nothing ever happened again.'

# Fifteen

Plant answered the phone in the middle of the night before he had thought through the logic of it. It was the middle of the night so why should he answer it? He was awake now, of course, but just because it had woken him did not mean he had to answer it. He could have just ignored it. Unplugged it. Gone back to sleep. And if a call in the middle of the night had to be an emergency, how did that affect him? In his self-contained life, what emergency could there be calling in from outside? It wouldn't be anything good. Hollywood calling. The Order of Australia. Jury service. It could only mean disruption and trouble. It was. The sensible thing would have been to have considered a little longer, let it ring on for the answering machine to take over, let it go away. But he hadn't. He had been fast asleep and unthinking and had picked it up. And now he had it hooked round his hand.

'That you, Plant? I've had another. I'm going to need you here. Get this little lot sorted out.'

'Who's that?' Plant asked.

'Major. Who did you think it was?'

'No idea,' Plant said. Gracelessly. 'Where are you?'

'Oxford, of course.'

'It's the middle of the night,' said Plant.

'Well it isn't here. It's the middle of the day. All systems go.'

Plant groaned.

'What's your problem? You got some sun-bronzed Aussie sheila there? Succouring some seductive succubus? Nurturing an incubus?'

'No,' said Plant.

'Right then,' said Major. 'Nothing else tying you down?'

'Well,' said Plant.

'Didn't think there would be. So get your arse into gear and I'll see you.'

'Where?'

'Oxford, of course.'

'I don't know,' said Plant.

'Usual fee.'

'I'll have to think about it,' said Plant.

Exchange rates, that was what he needed to think about. How much more did everything cost there?

'I'll need a fare.'

'No problem.'

'I'll need to arrange accommodation.'

'All arranged,' said Major.

'Already?'

'Put you up in college. Show you how the other half live,' said Major. 'You finished your degree, didn't you?'

'Yes,' said Plant.

'Put you on the books then,' said Major. 'Make it all official.'

'What books?'

'Inauthenticity,' said Major.

'Inauthenticity?'

'Name of the game,' said Major. 'Thought I'd put you on the team. Makes it more kosher. Nothing as persuasive as inauthenticity. And you're the ideal chap. Colonial, background in investigation, what could be more appropriate? I'll fill you in when you get here.'

'No,' said Plant, 'fill me in now.'

'Can't talk on the phone.'

'You're going to have to,' said Plant. 'What am I wanted for?'

'I told you, more of the same,' said Major. 'I had another one.'

'In Oxford?'

'Yes.'

'Posted where?'

'Oxford.'

'I see,' said Plant. 'So why not just hire somebody local?'

'I don't think so,' said Major.

'It's a local matter.'

'I don't think so.'

'Why not? Are you worried this might escalate and impact on your chances for that chair?'

'How vividly you put it,' said Archer.

'Is that a "Yes"?'

'Tell you when I see you.'

'Hold on,' said Plant.

'No rush,' said Major. 'Get your affairs in order. Give yourself a couple of days.'

'You're sure?'

'Maybe three. Not any more though. We need to act quickly on this one. Let me know when you're arriving. Get the shuttle from Heathrow. You can walk from the coach station to college. Just ask at the lodge and the porter will tell you how to get to your room.'

*

Plant sat in his room and looked at the panelling. That was how he was sure he was in Oxford. The panelled walls. There was all that timber in Australia, or used to be, why couldn't there be panelling? Because it was all turned into woodchips and sold to Japan, was that it? He thought back to his time at university. He thought back to more recent times, visiting Major in that college room in Sydney. Panelling was the touch of distinction that had been omitted. Would it have made him happier to have grown up amidst panelled walls? And leadlighting? Mullioned windows, little diamond panes of glass. Would his life have been richer, more rewarding? Was Major's life richer now, now he was back in the old world? Did the panelling and the leadlighting and the old stone walls take the sting away from poison-pen letters?

He looked out of the window. It was a classic view, inner quadrangle, close clipped lawn, tranquillity. Nothing to spoil it except the sight of Archer Major striding purposefully along the stone flags, avoiding stepping on the cracks, the sun glinting balefully on his spectacles.

*

'Rooms suit you?' Major asked. Not without a touch of smugness. See what I have been able to fix up for you.

'Very nice,' said Plant.

Well, they were nice.

'How come you could fit me in at short notice? Do you keep them vacant for visitors or something?'

'Absolutely not,' said Major. 'Rooms are at a premium here. No, you were lucky. They're the visiting fellow's rooms. But this blighter fell through at the last moment, pulled out, they offered him a visiting chair in the States with a salary attached. What a hide! Telling us he had to go where the money was, couldn't afford to grace our ancient halls without a fee. I can see his point but he might have put it more tactfully. Don't appreciate being blackmailed. Won't be inviting him again. So since he dropped out on us, I was able to fix you up.'

'With the rooms or the visiting fellowship?' Plant asked.

Major laughed.

'Good point.'

'So what am I?' Plant asked.

'I've never been quite clear what you call yourself,' said Major. 'Private investigator, is that it?'

'Here,' said Plant. 'What am I here? A visiting fellow?'

'Ah, I see,' said Major. 'Not exactly, not quite. Needs an election for that.'

'You can't fix it?'

Major bristled.

'Well, it would need a college meeting, no need to put us through all that.'

'Us?' said Plant. 'You? Me? Which us?'

'The college, in this instance. Which means all of us. That's the meaning of collegiality. Might take a spot of time. You might be gone before the meeting got called.'

'You think?' said Plant.

'Formalities, formalities,' said Major. 'Still, see what I can do. I can't see why there need be a problem. Should be able to arrange something. Visiting scholar, maybe. Could mean eating at High Table, of course.'

'I might enjoy that.'

Major looked at him dubiously.

'You think? Twice a week. At least it's not every night.'

'You think my antipodean table manners might not be up to it?'

'Oh, someone will put you right on that. But you'll have to get yourself a gown. Ask one of the scouts. They'll probably be able to sell you one.'

'I'll put it on expenses,' said Plant.

Major looked at him hard. He laughed.

'Yes, well,' he said. 'Have you had breakfast?'

'About four o'clock this morning over the Alps.'

'Not that airlines stuff,' said Major. 'What's the time?' he asked.

'I don't know,' said Plant.

'Don't you have a watch?'

'No.'

Major snorted.

Sometimes Plant ascribed it to his Puritan ancestry. A refusal of ornament. Other times he thought it might have been a bad memory of handcuffs from a past life. And it gave him the excuse to ask the time from other people, check on their wealth or pretensions.

Major thrust out his wrist and exposed a Patek Philippe.

It told Plant something. Wealth or a high level of debt. Taste or pretension. And as for time, get your servants to tell that for you. Never use your own watch, you might wear it out.

'Just make it,' he said. 'Let's go.'

He opened the door and strode out.

'Do I need anything?' Plant asked.

'Just your wallet,' said Major.

Plant had been thinking more in terms of the missing gown. Or a tie, maybe. Whatever was expected. And then the polished oak table, silver service, toast, Frank Cooper's Original Oxford marmalade, of course, what else, elderly college servants in white jackets, a view of the fellows' garden, copies of *The Times*, still a broadsheet, with the classified advertisements on the front page.

But Major led him out through the porter's lodge and into the streets, cutting between delivery trucks and girls on bicycles and groups of camera-carrying tourists, along pokey lanes and into the Covered Market. Dead pigs and dead rabbits and dead pheasants hung in front of the stalls. There were cheeses and vegetables and polyester T-shirts and denim jeans, but the smell of dead flesh was the dominant impression. Major opened the glass door of what seemed to be, amidst the steam and condensation on the windows and the smell of cooking fat and frying flesh and living flesh and old clothes, a workingman's café, circa 1938.

'Get you a real breakfast,' said Major.

He ordered sausage and bacon and black pudding and egg and tomato and fried bread and tea. Plant stood in line aghast.

'I'll just have tea.'

'Need to keep your strength up in this climate,' said Major. 'Never know where the next meal's coming from. Best black pudding south of Ilkley moor.'

'I don't eat meat,' said Plant.

'No meat in black pudding,' said Major. 'One hundred per cent blood.'

'I'll pass.'

'Fried egg?' said Major.

Plant shook his head.

'Worried about cholesterol?' said Major. 'Battery hens? Animal rights? Is that it?'

Plant nodded. 'That sort of thing.'

'Toast,' Major suggested. 'I'll order it anyway. Toast and marmalade. Can't go far wrong with that.' He seemed to say it regretfully. 'You're not allergic to wheat, are you? An anti-glutenist?'

'No,' said Plant.

'Well, that's something,' said Major.

He led them to a cramped table in the corner. The place was partitioned off from the market hall by two walls of glass windows. The condensation on the glass obscured any view outside. By the same token no one could look in. The tables seemed to be predominately occupied by derelicts and bag ladies. Plant found himself shrinking into the corner.

'Been coming here since I was a freshman,' said Major, 'when I used to miss college breakfast by five minutes every day. Whatever I did. Then I discovered this place. Saved my life. Saved my bacon, at least. Hasn't changed a jot. Keeps the riff-raff out. But the connoisseurs know it. See that old codger over there.'

Plant looked at a distraught, wild-haired figure against the wall. Staring eyes. Missing teeth. Ragged shirt collar. Patched, stained jacket.

'One of the top Middle-Eastern archaeologists of his time.'

'Really?'

'Well, his time was a long time ago,' Major laughed. 'But his stuff stands up. Even if he hardly does. You'd never think he was one of our best sources of political intelligence for half a century. Knew Philby's father. And see that old biddy.'

He indicated another dishevelled, tragic ruin.

'Wrote the last word on Céline. Or was it Colette? One of those Frog art writers, anyway. Said to have been his lover. Or hers. Whichever it was. Maybe it was both of them.'

He chewed his pink pig and black pudding vigorously.

'Of course, you get a few people slumming it. But you can pick them.'

'Really?' said Plant. 'How?'

'They don't eat anything,' said Major. 'They leave food on their plates. Whereas the cognoscenti don't leave a scrap.'

Plant looked at the archaeologist's plate. Wiped clean. The same with the lover of Céline or Colette. Not a trace left. He spread some marmalade on his toast.

'A change from airline food,' said Major.

'That's true,' Plant agreed.

*

'So,' said Plant, 'you've had another note.'

Major tapped the side of his nose with his forefinger.

Plant looked round. It was of course possible that someone was disguised as a derelict or a don and had a directional microphone pointed at their table and wasn't there for the sausage and bacon and black pudding and egg and fried bread and pot of tea at all. The Middle-Eastern archaeologist could have been still garnering political intelligence, or the lover of Céline or Colette meticulously recording pillow talk.

'No hurry,' said Major.

He had had Plant scurrying across time zones and through war zones and beneath depleted layers of ozone and now he said, No hurry.

'We'll take a walk,' he added.

And now, after a thirty-hour journey, he proposed a walk.

'Be good for your circulation,' said Major. 'After sitting cramped up all that time. Don't want you getting DVT.'

'What are the symptoms?' Plant asked.

'Often there aren't any. You just keel over and snuff it. Apart from that, pain in the calf. Like some voodoo doctor jabbing a pin in your simulacrum. Very hard to diagnose.'

Plant felt it. He felt pain everywhere. He felt his arteries contracting and clogging from the sight of Major's breakfast. He felt his heart in spasm from the icy grip of Major's hand on his upper arm, as Major steered him out for their walk.

## Sixteen

They went out of the Covered Market, scurried across the High Street between the buses and the bicycles, and down a dark alley. Major seemed to have a penchant for narrow lanes and constricted alleyways, shooting down them like an interventionist cardiologist. He took another couple of twists and turns and then led Plant through an iron kissinggate beside a discoloured stone wall.

'The Meadows,' Major said.

'You always come here to talk?' Plant asked.

Major gestured expansively. Trees, grass, gravelled paths, squirrels.

'The lungs of the city,' he said. 'One of them, anyway. The other's the Parks. Always take the opportunity to walk through them. Keep the circulation going.'

A couple of more determined circulation conscious types jogged by, their garish running gear disrupting the antique quiet of it all.

'Yes, I had another note,' said Major.

'You have it?'

'Yes, I kept it for you. Not carrying it around next to my heart though.'

'What did it say?'

'Same old guff. Prepare to meet your doom. The day of reckoning approaches.'

'I'd like to see it.'

'You shall.'

'Where was it posted?'

'I told you on the phone. Here.'

'England?'

'Oxford.'

'So it could be somebody from here after all.'

'Somebody here though not necessarily from here,' said Major. 'Though of course once a member of the University you're a member for life. Get to vote for the Professor of Poetry if you've got an MA.'

'A former student?'

'Undergraduates, we call them,' said Major. 'Enough of this student nonsense.'

'Someone you taught,' said Major.

'No, not someone I taught.'

'But you think it is someone here.'

'Yes, I not only think it is someone here, I know who it is who is here.'

'How did you find out that?'

Major tapped the side of his nose again and gave a self-congratulatory grin. The gesture seemed to mean low cunning rather than silence this time.

'My beloved wife, actually,' he said. 'Bless her fluttering little heart. Spotted him by the Bodleian on one of her shop-to-die missions. Must have seen him going in or coming out. Can't imagine she'd have been in there herself. Anyway, she tracked him down and dragged him in for dinner.'

'And he confessed?'

'Oh Lord no, it hasn't got to that stage yet. That's what I need you for. The toes in the fire and the light flex round the testicles.'

Elderly dons sat on park benches feeding nuts to grey squirrels. They might have done some interrogations for their country in past imperialist wars. Perhaps they had served their time in Northern Ireland. Places like Oxford and Yale had the effect of distancing the petty details of dominion from the comfortable rewards of the specialist advisers. Napalm and depleted uranium shells were worlds away.

'So who was it? Anyone I'd know?'

'I would say so. I believe you assured me that you had met him.'

'Met him where?'

'In Sydney.'

'Someone from there, uh-huh. So who?'

Major smiled some more. Something flickered behind his eyes, like a lizard's tongue, but he held onto his revelation for a little longer, squeezing it out as long as he could manage. He pointed out the college rowing club barges moored along the banks of the river. He explained that it was called the Isis here but became the Thames once out of Oxford. An early paradigm of the inauthenticity project he was working on. And on whose books Plant was now duly enrolled.

'You want me to guess?'

'No,' said Major. 'That might spoil it. You might guess correctly. Or you might guess wrongly, which would be even more worrying. No, no, I'll tell you. Revill, of course. Who else?'

'Revill? Is he in Oxford now?'

'He is.'

'Have you seen him?'

'Yes. Positive identification,' said Major.

A rowing eight went by, the coach bicycling along the footpath, shouting through a megaphone. It didn't seem like Revill's world. Plant wondered why he had returned. Could it be simply to torment Major? He could see there might be a satisfaction in that.

'What do you think?'

'Do you actually know it is Revill?'

'Well, he was in Sydney when the notes began. And then he comes over here and the notes continue. Posted from here. Who else?'

'It could be more than one person.'

'It could,' Major conceded. 'A whole team out to destabilise me. I'm not sure I warrant that sort of attention. Perhaps I do. Keep me out of the chair. But if that's the case, why wasn't I getting the notes before I went away? If it was someone in place here, why hadn't they been sending them before?'

'You know Revill. You think he's likely?'

'Oh yes,' said Major, 'I know him. And yes, I think he's likely. He'd stoop to anything. And get it wrong, of course. Get himself spotted. Never had what it took, poor Revill. Started out with every advantage, and dropped the ball. Look at him now. You've seen him.'

'Yes, I've seen him.'

'Pathetic,' said Major. 'Pathetic.'

'So what makes you think it's him?'

'Motive, means and opportunity, as you chaps say.'

'What motive?'

'He's a loser,' said Major.

'Anything else?' Plant asked. 'Or is that sufficient cause?'

'Anyone who has stuck at associate-professor for thirty years has to be a loser. Never made full professor. Just couldn't cut the mustard.'

'But you're not a professor.'

'Nor am I in the colonies,' said Major. 'Any antipodean academic would give up his chair for the fellowship of an Oxford college.'

'Is that so?'

'There is a pecking order in these things.'

'What used to be called the great chain of being,' Plant suggested.

'If you like,' said Major.

'And in your estimation Revill is pretty low in this scale of things.'

'In his own estimation,' said Major. 'Never underestimate low self-esteem. It is a potent motivation.'

'For what?' Plant asked.

'For resentment. For envy. For desperate measures.'

'And you see these notes as desperate measures?'

'I see them as potentially heading that way,' said Major. 'That's why I called you in. To get it sorted out before anything too desperate occurs.'

They turned and walked along beside the Cherwell. Occasionally other pairs of stooped figures, immersed in conversation, would come towards them, falling silent as they passed. On the river itself another couple were in a punt, their communings even less accessible to monitoring. It seemed a favoured spot for private confidences and whispered conspiracies.

'How can you be sure it's Revill?' Plant asked.

'He's here, isn't he?'

'Yes, but …'

'Amazing bloody coincidence.'

'Perhaps.'

'One gets to know these things.'

'How?'

'One just does.'

'Magic?'

'Intuition,' said Major. 'Common sense. But what I don't have is hard evidence. That's where you come in, so keep an eye on the little weasel'

'I see,' said Plant.

'It shouldn't take long.'

*

They came to the edge of the Meadows and another gate. Major took them through it into the Botanical Gardens, and into a heated glasshouse. Condensation dripped onto tropical foliage.

'Thought it might freshen you up a bit,' said Major. 'Given your name and all that. When I first got back from Australia I used to come in here for a climate detox. Better than going cold turkey. Best to adjust gradually, I found.'

The air was heavy and humid.

'I'll remember,' said Plant.

'The point about Revill,' said Major, 'is that he is bonkers. Stark raving mad. He's an old Leftie, you know. Totally unreconstructed. Reads the poems of Uncle Ho every night before getting into bed. Poster of Che Guevara on his shithouse wall. You know the sort of thing.'

'That makes him mad?' said Plant.

'In this day and age, absolutely. The world has changed and he refuses to recognise it. He's stuck in a time-warp. That's why his work is no good. In so far as he does any. That's why no one publishes him. That's why he never made full professor even when they were giving away personal chairs with breakfast cereal. That's why he's still stuck in the colonies. He should have followed the example of Yannis Ritsos. Starved himself to death when the Berlin wall came down.'

'I see,' said Plant.

'Good,' said Major. 'The point is Revill doesn't see it. He's convinced there's a conspiracy against him. He's convinced he's on some blacklist that stops him from getting promoted or getting another job or getting into print or getting laid or getting any damn thing. As if anyone cared. He'd a florid case of acute paranoid schizophrenia. And as such capable of doing anything.'

'Except getting promoted or getting into print or getting laid,' said Plant.

'Precisely.'

'How do you know all this?'

'Know it?' Major exclaimed. 'Everyone knows it. You can't not know it. You've only got to be in his company for a couple of minutes. It pours out. An endless bloody litany of persecution and paranoia. The longest complaint in English since *Piers Plowman*.'

'You've been in his company?'

'The bloody wife invited him to dinner,' said Major. 'Yes, indeed, I have been in his company. Again. And let me tell you nothing has changed from when I used to be in his company every bloody day.'

'When was that?'

'When I had to work with the maniac.'

'And how does he feel about you?'

'About me?' said Major. 'The same as he feels about everyone else, presumably. Hostile. Envious. Resentful. That's how he normally feels.'

The brisk walk followed by the tropical glasshouse had made them both flushed. Plant could feel beads of moisture trickling down inside his shirt. Major seemed ablaze with rage or excitement or high blood pressure. He took off his glasses and wiped them on a handkerchief. Not a man for disposable tissues.

'What does your wife feel about him?'

'What's my wife got to do with it?'

'You said she invited him to dinner.'

'Oh Lucy's like that, collects strays all over the place.

She'd invite anyone to dinner. Saw him wandering through the streets and picked him up out of the gutter.'

'She likes him?'

'I wouldn't imagine so. Just a social reflex. Sees this poor old antipodean sod looking displaced and disoriented and feels she should do the right thing. You know how they teach them at those expensive private schools.'

'She knew him in Australia?'

'No idea, honestly.'

'She must have known him to recognise him.'

'There you are then. There's your answer.'

He flashed his watch and, muttering about time passing, led them out of the glasshouse, out onto Magdalen Bridge.

'By the way,' he said, turning back before striding away, 'you're invited for dinner tonight.'

'Tonight?' said Plant. He could feel exhaustion, if not sleep, spreading throughout his limbs. The brisk walk had done nothing to enliven him. The Botanical Gardens had not refreshed him.

'Yes, Lucy, bless her little heart, felt you would appreciate some decent home cooking after all that airline food. Can't think where you'll get it, though.'

'Well,' said Plant.

'Fine, settled,' said Major.

'I don't know your address.'

'Thought you were supposed to be a detective,' Major said. He took out his pigskin wallet and handed him an embossed card.

'Just a short walk up the Woodstock road,' he said. 'See you seven-thirty for eight.'

Plant ventured a weak smile.

But Major had already turned and gone.

## Seventeen

Plant trudged up the Woodstock road, buses and bicycles roaring past him. What he would have liked to have done was sleep. But sleep evaded him. He had lain on his bed through the afternoon and failed to sleep. He told himself it was night in Australia, it was natural to sleep, but his body clock refused the message. There were too many contradictory signals. Footsteps through the quadrangle. Footsteps up the staircase. Chiming clocks and bells. And now it was time to go out again he felt sleep might at last be creeping up on him. Even as he walked. He looked at the buses resentfully. There must have been one he could have taken, more than one, surely, if he had known where he was going and where they went.

North Oxford cast its pall of gloom over him. Haunted looking Victorian houses, every freeborn Englishman's home a bijoux baronial castle, in the mode of nineteenth-century Scotland or the ante-bellum South. Three storeys high and more. High trees, damp leaves on gravel driveways, derisory rooks and starlings in the trees, rabid bats, a paralysed stillness of hidden croquet lawns and dusty stairwells leading to dusty attics. He sneezed, once, twice, three times. Either he was allergic to it or he had caught something on the flight.

Plant crunched up the driveway and stood before the door. He noted the spy hole inserted at eye level and the security alarm box on the wall and the horseshoe mounted above the lintel. He rang the bell. Major answered the door, spectacles and teeth gleaming, admitting him to a hallway festooned with the all-weather outerwear of the British bourgeoisie, Wellington boots and umbrellas and Burberrys and plastic raincoats and anoraks and flak jackets, all colour-coordinated like military issue combat gear. Their superabundance seemed to underline the pervasive chill of the house.

'Take your coat?' Major asked.

'I don't have one.'

'Of course, you chaps never wear them, do you? Ah well, *chacun à son gout* as we say over here in United Europe.'

He led the way down the corridor, adorned with framed eighteenth-century prints of views of the Oxford colleges, and into the dining room. Plant knew it was the dining room because there was a dining table set for dinner. French windows opened out onto a lawn, or would have done if they had not been closed. Major saw him looking at it.

'Croquet? Fancy a game?'

'It's all right,' said Plant.

'You probably don't know the rules, anyway. A bit late to try and teach you now. Lucy will get restive if we don't eat on time. How about a drink instead?'

'Thank you,' said Plant.

'Wait till you've tasted it,' said Major. 'I got in a case of Bulgarian red especially for Revill and the bugger hardly touched it.'

'I'm not a big drinker,' said Plant.

'I wouldn't say I was a *big* drinker,' said Major. 'But I can at least put a civilised front on it.'

Whatever that meant. Plant pondered it. Did it mean he could drink a lot and not show it in an uncivil way, or that he didn't drink much at all but could give the civil impression of keeping you company?

'Unlike that piker Revill. Never had the staying power. Tragic sort of a life when you come to look at it. Which generally I must say I would prefer not to. And generally I've managed to avoid having to. Bad enough when I had to work with him.'

He poured a glass and handed it across to Plant.

Plant sipped it cautiously. It was particularly rough. Coarse. Harsh. The sort of drink that seized you by the throat and shook you till you choked. Major hovered over him, the bottle tilted to top up the glass.

'The first taste is always the worst. Best thing is to belt down a glassful and after that it doesn't seem so bad. Not too bad at all. Does the trick.'

'What trick's that?' Plant asked, his voice strangulated.

'Oh, warming the cockles of your heart, promoting geniality, unleashing confidences, followed by indiscretions of word and deed, spilling it over the tablecloth, and maudlin self-pity.'

'I see,' said Plant.

'I'm sure we will,' said Major.

He turned as a door opened.

'My wife, Lucy,' he said.

She emerged with a ruddy glow, a sort of effusion of morning dew, or the bloom on a plum, sweaty from the kitchen, from bending over the stove or the cooking sherry, which would have had to have been better than the Bulgarian red, or maybe just the glow of blonde, bulimic wellbeing and happiness. She gave Plant a bland, blonde smile.

'Have a drink, dear,' said Major, 'or have you already done that?'

She took a glass from the sideboard and held it up, brushing her hair back with the other hand, curly blonde hair, pink forehead beaded with sweat, mad blue eyes.

Plant braced himself for a North Oxford evening.

'We're having chilli rellenos,' Lucy said. 'I hope that's all right.'

'Sounds fine,' said Plant.

'Since you don't eat meat.'

'No,' said Plant.

'Nor do I,' she said. She smiled winningly. 'Archer will just have to go and chew on a bone in the kitchen if he feels unsatisfied.'

'Give a man meat,' said Major. 'Love the way all you Aussie's stick that on your rear bumper. Very provocative.'

'Yes,' said Plant. 'How did you know I don't eat meat?'

'Real Aussies drive utes, that's another gem,' said Major. 'How did I know? Had breakfast with you, if you recall. Made your feelings quite clear.'

'I hope I didn't put you to too much trouble,' Plant said to Lucy.

'Oh, I already knew.'

'Really?'

'Must have been on your file,' said Major. 'How about American food? You eat that, don't you? No ideological objection to it like poor old Revill? No, didn't think you would. That's something. Pompous little prick. All that holier than thou commitment. What a sad old word for a sad old world.'

'I don't find it sad,' said Lucy.

'Good for you, blossom.'

'I think things were much more fun when people had commitment,' she said.

'Don't worry, poppet, I'll get you committed,' said Major.

'I used to enjoy those days,' she said.

'Which days were those?' Plant asked.

'Oh, don't start her off,' said Major.

'When we were students,' she said.

'Speak for yourself, flower child,' said Major. 'While you were swanning around as a student princess, some of us were out there working for a living.'

'But you were still like students,' she said. 'You were all so young. Nowadays academics seem so ancient. Positively decrepit. But then they used to be young. Hardly any older than we were. And full of commitment.'

'That tired old word again,' said Major.

'It made it all so exciting. All those things we'd only read about. Suddenly there they all were. Demonstrations. Marches. Free-speech rallies. Love-ins.'

'Oh my America, my new found land,' said Major.

'You may mock,' she said.

'Indeed I do,' said Major.

'It had been so dull till then. Like England. And then suddenly all those things were happening. Poetry readings. All these writers would come along.'

'They'd go anywhere,' said Major. 'They're hardly in demand.'

'They are. Now they're big names. But then they were just starting out and they'd sit around the pub after readings.'

'Waiting for nice little middle-class girls to take them off for a fuck.'

'I wouldn't have thought you were in a position to talk,' she said.

'I'm always in a position to talk,' said Major. 'That is the nature of being a university lecturer and tutorial fellow.'

He stood up and brought the Bulgarian red over to Plant.

'Have another drink while dinner burns,' he said.

'Oh, shut up, Archer,' she said. 'This is what you kept doing to Revill.'

'What did I do?'

'You kept needling him.'

'Needling him? I injected him with controlled substances? Surely not.'

'You kept sticking pins in him.'

'That's more like. Prod the pretentious little prick. He'd have been found drowned in the college fountain in the good old days.'

'At least he still cares,' she said. 'He still believes in things.'

'In what?' Major asked.

'The good times,' said Lucy.

'Spare us,' said Major. 'He was just a pushy little prole who leapt on the leftist bandwagon and forgot to get off and ended up high and dry. No one wanted to publish him and no one wanted to hire him and no one was ever going to give him promotion.'

'They might have.'

'Not a hope. No worries on that score. Best time he can hope for is early retirement. As I seem to remember telling him. Grab it and go. Disappear into the distance, I seem to recall advising him. The remote distance. And the sooner the better.'

*

'So what are you doing here?' Lucy asked Plant.

'He's working on my inauthenticity project,' said Major.

'Is he so inauthentic he can't even answer for himself?'

'I sincerely hope so,' said Major. 'I hope he's the real thing. Native born laconic.'

'Well, we are going to have a jolly dinner conversation,' said Lucy.

171

'Same as usual, light of my life,' said Major. 'Plant will just sit there silent like so many dawns in Australia, as the poet put it, and you can rabbit on, no less Australian albeit an introduced species, and I shall nod wisely.'

'Why do you need someone from Australia?'

'Long history of inauthenticity,' Major said. 'Convict settlement and all that. Tichborne case. Merle Oberon.'

'You could just have asked Revill,' she said. 'He gave these brilliant lectures on *For the Term of His Natural Life* about the Tichborne case. He said the novel wasn't about the convict system at all. Or at least that wasn't its real point. Its point was the foundations of contemporary Australian society. Australia was set up on a prison model with guards and trusties and informers. It was Clarke's way of showing how contemporary society was controlled by a network of informers and by a military trained to keep the population down. And it's never changed.'

'He was always a paranoid bastard even back then,' said Major.

'Back when?'

'Back in the mists of time when you were a doting student, dearest. Back in the last century. Before they stopped him lecturing.'

'They stopped him lecturing?' Plant asked.

'Not before time,' said Major. 'Became too crazy. They had to take him off and confine him to small groups where he couldn't do too much damage.'

'It was political,' said Lucy. 'They were trying to discredit him.'

'They didn't have to try,' said Major. 'He'd discredited himself.'

'In what way?' Plant asked.

'Flipped right out. Saw everything as a plot. Every lecture a tour round the secret state. The student sitting next to you may be a special branch informer. The CIA is funding feminist criticism and deconstruction and literary theory. The MAN Booker prize is a capitalist conspiracy of mind control to degrade literary value. He'd have been questioning the Holocaust next.'

'How do you know?' Lucy asked.

'I have my sources.'

'What sources?'

Major pointed to his eyes and ears.

'How do you know he wasn't telling the truth?' she asked.

'Have you been smoking your funny cigarettes again?' Major asked.

She got up and cleared away the dishes from the first course, refusing any help, taking them out to the kitchen.

'Nothing to do,' Major assured Plant. 'All she has to do with them is stick them in the dishwasher without dropping too many.'

He filled up their glasses with more Bulgarian red.

'There will now be a short interruption until normal service is resumed and we get pudding or not as the case may be. Make yourself at home, as it is laughingly

173

called. I have to make a phone call, if you will excuse me.'

He went off to his study or wherever he phoned from. The cavernous house was silent. No muttered conversations on the phone. No sounds from the kitchen. After a while Plant picked up his glass and went out to join Lucy in the kitchen.

# Eighteen

She was standing outside the kitchen door looking into the garden. The door was open. The extractor fan was whirring above the oven. Strings of garlic hung each side of the kitchen window. Plant coughed politely.

She visibly jumped.

'Oh, it's you.'

'Sorry to surprise you. I just wondered if I could help.'

'I told you no,' she said.

She came back into the kitchen, keeping an arm behind her.

Plant sniffed. Dope.

'Smell's good,' he said, walking towards her.

'Archer doesn't approve,' she said.

'Why's that?'

'Oh, it would take too long to explain now,' she said, taking a deep drag. She handed the joint across. Plant inhaled. It nearly choked him. It shared a generic roughness with the Bulgarian red, but he held it in without coughing. Just a few splutters. She grabbed it back and took another couple of deep drags before returning it. Then she walked across to the sink and splashed water over her face and rubbed her teeth with her fingers. Plant stood there with the roach. She took a last deep drag and then stubbed it out in the sink and ran the tap some more and ripped the improvised cardboard filter into shreds and flushed

175

them away. Then she wiped away the trace of ash on the sink, washed her hands and face vigorously, dried them, took a swig of Bulgarian red, rinsed it round her mouth, gargled, and spat it accurately down the plughole. She smiled at him.

'All done,' she said.

Plant splashed water on his hands and face in deference to her precautions. He passed on the gargling. He figured just sipping at the Bulgarian red should be enough, its bouquet fierce enough to neutralise any other odour. He poured some down his throat to make sure. They were back at the dinner table when Major reappeared.

'Something's come up,' he said. 'Going to have to go into college.'

'Off you go then,' said Lucy.

Almost peremptorily, it seemed to Plant.

He turned to Plant.

'Do you want a lift back?' he offered. 'Nice of you to come. Lucy always appreciates a visitor. She feels she's in the gulag here.'

Plant looked at his glass, wondered about taking a last sip.

'Come on, time's up,' said Major. 'That's it, decent thing done, don't expect a repeat. Life's too short, as Dr Leavis said about reading *Tom Jones*.'

'He might not want to go yet,' said Lucy.

'He's had his dinner, time he went to bed.'

'Perhaps he'd like to stay and have a drink and talk.'

'Well, he can always say.'

'I know I would,' she said. She smiled at Plant sweetly. 'I spend all day cooking, I like to sit and talk when I've finished. I don't like it when everybody rushes off immediately they've eaten.'

'Can't be helped, poppet,' said Major.

'I know you can't,' she said. 'But Plant mightn't want to go yet.' She turned to him. 'Don't feel you have to go just because Archer's heard the call of the wild.'

'I'm in no hurry,' said Plant. 'It's early morning for me now, anyway.'

'Cock-a-doodle-do,' said Major. 'Don't get too vigorous. You plan on borrowing the family bicycle?'

'Family bicycle?'

'Oxford custom.'

'Oxford custom?'

'To get back to college on.'

'I think I'll be right,' said Plant.

'Leave you two to it, then,' said Major. He flashed his gleaming smile. 'Toodle-oo.'

'Toodle-oo,' said Lucy. She did not invest it with much feeling. It was not, after all, much of a feeling sort of utterance.

The front door closed with a resonating clatter.

'One of his floozies,' said Lucy. 'Charms them off the trees. God knows what they see in him.'

The charm is ended, Plant reflected. Could Lucy be sending the notes? He looked at those bright blue eyes. The face around them crinkled into a deep smile.

'Now we can have a smoke at leisure instead of

lurking behind the bicycle sheds like naughty school children.'

'Is that what you used to do behind the bicycle sheds?' said Plant.

'Amongst other things,' she said.

'I see,' said Plant.

'Still do,' she said. 'It's amazing how you grow older but nothing changes.'

'Isn't it?' Plant agreed.

She got up and turned on the CD player. Leonard Cohen called lugubriously from another century. Then she fetched her stash from the kitchen and began rolling.

*

'So the evening with Revill wasn't a success,' Plant suggested.

'Oh, I wouldn't say that,' she said. 'If I said that I'd have to consider all the other evenings.' She inhaled reflectively. 'And what a wasteland that would be. No, compared with all of them I'd have to say the evening with Revill could have been worse.'

'It got argumentative?'

'Not especially,' she said. 'Archer is always argumentative. Anyone who knows him just shuts up and lets him drone on.'

'And Revill knew him.'

'I think they just bored each other,' she said. 'They certainly bored me.'

178

'So why did you invite Revill to dinner in the first place?'

'Oh, I'm just stupid,' she said. 'You know me, I don't know anything. I used to think they were all friends. Colleagues, you know. I couldn't believe it, when I first started going out with Archer, how they all hated each other. As a student, you never imagine that. You think they're all, I don't know, scholars or something. Working together to advance knowledge. And then you find out they're all working against each other to bring each other down. It's no different here. Oxford,' she added, to pin it down, where they were, gesturing vaguely with the joint between her fingers. 'If anything it's probably worse. There's more at stake. Or more to grab. Or more to envy. I suppose that's why I invited Revill when I saw him. Reminded me of Sydney. A breath of fresh air. I'd forgotten all the competitive stuff, all the backbiting. All I remembered was the sun and the beaches and being young and everyone having a good time. Were you ever a student, Plant?' she asked.

'Yes.'

'When?'

'A while ago.'

'Then you know what I mean. What it was like then. When we believed in things. We thought things could be done. The world would keep on getting better. We wouldn't repeat the same old mistakes. And things mattered. We didn't just shrug our shoulders and say, what the fuck. We didn't sit around with the television off because we couldn't bear to watch the news. If the news was bad, we protested. We fought it. We weren't defeated then. Now it's as if all the stuffing has been knocked out of everyone. It's like they're all under a spell or something. Sleepwalking. Afraid to wake up. Like those 1950s science fiction movies they run on late night television.'

'That's what they were about,' said Plant.

'What?'

'Sleepwalking. Mass conditioning. Propaganda and fear. They were about McCarthyism and the Cold War.'

'Well, that's what everything seems like to me now. And the Cold War's supposed to be over. Years ago. But it wasn't always like this. That's why I remember what it was like being a student. They were the good times. And now they've gone. For everyone. It's not just a matter of getting older. Things have changed. I thought inviting Revill round would bring it all back. But it didn't. He and Archer just fenced around all evening getting drunker and drunker. As dreary as each other. Archer kept on about how well he was doing and Revill kept on about how his career had been ruined, and you couldn't tell them apart.'

'And has Revill's career been ruined?'

'I've no idea,' she said. 'He kept on about being blacklisted and targeted and immobilised and Archer kept saying that was all in his head, why would anyone bother to blacklist someone like him. And Revill went on about his radical past and Archer said, so what, he'd had a radical past and look at him, nothing but success. What a joke. But Revill believed him and got more depressed and Archer kept pouring him more wine and stirring him up and telling him he was full of self-pity, which he was, and Revill told Archer he was full of shit, which was also true, and they went on and on and altogether a delightful evening was had by all.'

'Does your husband have any enemies?' Plant asked.

'Apart from his wife, you mean? What a strange question.'

'What a strange answer.'

'Do you think so?' she said. 'I thought all husbands and wives were mortal enemies. Till death them depart. And even after.'

'I don't know,' said Plant.

'Well, aren't you the lucky one,' she said. 'Oh, no, we're not really enemies. We're just, you know' – she searched for the word – 'married,' she said. She gave a big smile. 'I think that's the word for it.'

'I wasn't thinking of that,' said Plant, not strictly honestly. He had thought of it. It had struck him as a possibility. He proceeded on a course of elimination.

'I was thinking of people outside the family.'

'Like colleagues?' she said. 'I imagine they're all enemies. From what he says.'

'Colleagues, former colleagues, students.'

'Girlfriends, you mean?' she said. 'I would imagine he's got up the noses of a few. Whether or not he got up any other parts of their anatomy remains open to question.'

'Have there been many?'

'Anatomical parts?'

'Girlfriends.'

'Now how would I know?'

'You brought it up,' said Plant.

'I don't think so,' she said. 'Or if I did, I was only vocalizing what was in your mind.'

'I don't know about that,' said Plant.

'I do,' said Lucy.

Her eyes were a searing blue.

'Yes,' she said, 'I imagine he would have a few enemies in the old girlfriend category. Even in the current girlfriend category.'

'How serious?'

'What is this?' she asked. 'Are you planning on blackmailing him or something? Kidnapping. You're thinking of kidnapping him and now you're wondering if anyone would want to buy him back. Probably they wouldn't. Though I shouldn't have said that, should I? I should be encouraging you to go ahead and kidnap him. Send his little finger through the mail. I can tell you, it would take more than his little finger to get me to fork out.' She took another drag. 'Or perhaps not. I'm basically a soft-hearted girl. I expect I would try and get him back. Though I don't think you should bank on making a lot of money out of it. I may be soft-hearted, but I wouldn't want to pay out a lot. I mean, in strictly cash terms, it would be better if you just bumped him off and I got to claim the insurance and we split it between us. He's always saying he's worth more dead than alive. Something with which I tend to agree.'

She looked at Plant doubtfully.

'I think I must be stoned,' she said. 'This is getting far too like those old movies they run late at night. Not the science fiction ones. More like *Double Indemnity*, that sort of thing. Gritty realism. What did you have in mind, Mr Plant, with this line of questioning?'

'Nothing like that,' he said.

'Oh,' she said.

He couldn't tell whether she sounded disappointed or was just working on her English accent, the sort of English accent that always sounded disappointed. The Oxford accent.

'Is he getting threats?' she asked.

'Threats?'

'Threats. You know, threats.'

'Why do you ask?' he asked.

'Why do you ask?'

'Oh,' said Plant, 'I don't know, just something that was said.'

'By whom?'

'I don't remember, really,' he said.

'I don't believe you, really,' she said.

They smiled at each other.

'Well, there we are,' said Plant.

'Yes, indeed,' said Lucy.

She got up and replaced Leonard Cohen with Lou

Reed. All her old records, Plant reflected. And then he reflected again, these were not her old LPs, salvaged from the past. These were reissues on CD. She had bought them again. She was not one to have allowed technological obsolescence thwart her return to the seventies. He wondered if she had downloaded them yet once more onto her iPod.

*

'Do you want to stay the night?' she asked, passing yet another joint across, Debbie Harry succeeding Patti Smith as mood music.

Plant took the opportunity to inhale and say nothing. It took all his willpower to do just that. Not cough. Not choke. Not show alarm.

'There's a spare bed,' she said. 'We put Revill in the children's old bunk because he was sort of incapable. Archer said he was afraid he might fall out of a single bed and injure himself. Personally I suspect it was some sadistic torture fantasy. Trying to plunge him into psychological regression. You can have the bunk if you want, of course.'

'I'll pass.'

'In fact you can take your choice of any of the beds,' she said. 'I don't imagine Archer will be back.'

'I think I should get back to college.'

'You too,' she said.

She stood up suddenly.

'Well, you'd best be on your way,' she said.

Plant struggled to his feet.

'Some other time, perhaps,' she said, sweetly.

*

He walked back to college and found he enjoyed it, warming up in the soft night air. And the evening had not been without its pleasure, whether from the Bulgarian red or the handful of joints or the heady scent of danger and desire as Lucy leaned towards him was immaterial. A crescent moon revealed itself amidst scuds of clouds, perched beside spires and towers, shining above crenellations and shadowing gargoyles. There was not a lot of traffic and he could feel the medievalism of it all wash around and over him. His footsteps echoed back from down the centuries. He could feel the vortex of it around him. He felt a pang for the experiences he had missed and then the pleasure he was experiencing now. He trailed his fingers along limestone walls to assure himself of their very palpability, smiled at the reduplicated chimes of quarters and hours from church and chapel clocks. Across the college lawns and gardens, owls and bats kept up their silent marauding. Yes, he reflected, not a bad life at all.

# Nineteen

It was not difficult to find Revill. He was sitting in the window of the King's Arms, gazing out blankly at the passers-by. Plant, who was one of them, waved and went in and joined him.

Revill was alone and, given that it was eleven-thirty in the morning, disconsolate or bored or desperate. He expressed no surprise at seeing Plant. He expressed nothing except a great weariness.

'Can I get you a drink?' Plant offered.

'Pint of Flowers,' said Revill.

'Flowers?'

'Flowers' bitter, the beer that Shakespeare drank.'

'Was it?'

'Well, it comes from Stratford-upon-Avon, and it has his portrait on the labels. What passes for his portrait, anyway. Though it's not generally thought to be authentic.'

Plant went through possible introductory phrases as he stood at the bar. Fancy seeing you here. Well, what a surprise. Last person I expected to bump into. They all sounded unpersuasive, indeed underlined the inherent falsity with which he would have had to deliver them.

'I heard you were over here,' Plant said.

'How did you hear that?'

'I had dinner with Dr Major.'

Revill shuddered. 'God help you,' he said.

Plant put the two pints on the wooden table and sat down.

'Following me around, are you?' Revill asked.

'Not at all.'

'Uh-huh,' said Revill.

'Do you want to be followed around?' Plant asked.

'It might provide a bit of company,' said Revill. 'You forget, you know. You forget how basically unfriendly the English can be. The Southern English, anyway.'

'Is this the South?' Plant asked.

'For the purposes of this discussion, yes,' said Revill. 'It's an extension of London, really. Like Cambridge. I know they used to say the North begins at Watford. But not any more. The South has expanded. It reaches up to Woodstock. If not to the furthest edge of the Cotswolds.'

'I'm not very familiar with the geography,' Plant said.

'Doesn't matter. It's sociology, really. The wealth is all in the South.'

'And that makes people unfriendly?'

'In my observation, yes. You might imagine they would feel comfortable and prosperous and outgoing. But they're not. They're terrified of losing what they've got. Property breeds fear.'

'You think?'

'The wages of sin. All property is theft. As we used to say when I was an undergraduate.'

'But not any more?'

'I don't know. I haven't been able to speak to anybody to find out what they say.'

'You sound miserable.'

'I am miserable. Despised and rejected of men.'

Plant looked startled.

'*Messiah*,' said Revill. 'I used to sing in it when I was a choirboy.'

'I hadn't quite picked you for a choirboy.'

'It was a long time ago,' said Revill. 'So was being an undergraduate. I'd forgotten how lonely it was. Being an undergraduate. I'd never been back. Well, I'd spent the odd couple of days in the Bodleian now and then. But then I was busy working on something. Now I'm not working on anything and the misery of it all floods back in. That perpetual loneliness. That sense of exclusion. A world going on and you know you're not part of it, and never will be. The English experience, I suppose.' He took a long draught of his pint. 'So what about you?' he asked. 'Are you working? Or is this a holiday?'

'Working holiday,' said Plant.

'Working at what?' Revill asked.

'A bit of research.'

'What on?'

'Actually, Dr Major hired me to work on his inauthenticity project.'

There was a silence. Then Revill laughed.

'It's a splendid concept, I must admit,' he said. 'If anyone ever questions anything, or says that's not true or that's not the way to do it, all old Archie has to say is, "But of course, it's all about inauthenticity. That's what we're into, how not to do it." I'll give him that, he's a shrewd operator. No institutional superego to retard his progress.'

Plant smiled but kept silent.

'Can't speak about your employer, is that it?' Revill asked.

'Not at all,' said Plant. 'I just don't know him very well.'

'Count your blessings,' said Revill.

'Would you say that he feels he's an outsider, too?'

Revill pondered.

'He probably does, actually. All that hearty manner has to be covering up some basic unease. And there's plenty to cover up.'

'Like what?'

'The emptiness within, I would have thought,' said Revill. 'The hollow man. Not exactly the archetypal hollowness, more the plagiarised spin off. But still as hollow as they come.'

'So you won't be going to his funeral?'

'His funeral?' said Revill. 'He hasn't died, has he?'

'No. A manner of speaking.'

'Oh.'

'You sound disappointed.'

'Disappointed?' said Revill. 'No, not really. I don't wish him dead.'

'Just suffering,' suggested Plant.

'I just don't want to have dinner with him again,' said Revill.

'What about his wife?' Plant asked.

'His wife,' said Revill reflectively.

'Yes, Lucy,' said Plant.

'Which Lucy of the thousand faces would that be?' asked Revill. 'Lucy Lockett or Lucy in the Sky with Diamonds, or our Nocturnal upon St Lucie's Day?'

'You've lost me,' said Plant.

'Donne,' said Revill. 'You can look him up in Blackwell's. Just across the road there. In the Eng. Lit. section under D. Lucy Lockett will be in the *Oxford Dictionary of Nursery Rhymes*. The Beatles should be in any good music shop.'

'Thank you,' said Plant. 'I might do that.'

'Short of things to do, are you?' said Revill.

'Is that your problem?' Plant asked, in as inoffensive a tone as he could muster.

'Part of it,' said Revill, 'I must confess, part of it. I thought I'd come back, use my last sabbatical, take a look round. But when you've decided to get out, there isn't a lot of incentive to do anything. It surprised me. I thought I'd potter around Bodley, work on something in the Upper Reading room, sit in Duke Humphrey and absorb the past. But suddenly the motivation's gone. I think it's knowing you're not going to teach any more. Thank heavens. No regrets. No more classes. No more preparation. But why sit up there researching a scholarly article which is just a hassle to try and get published when the work isn't even going to feed into your teaching? I used to resent the time teaching took, want to get on with

the research. But when there isn't any teaching, the research suddenly loses its point. Apart from the fact that the subject's been destroyed and no one cares any more. There's that too. Who'll ever read anything you write? You've spent your lifetime in a world that's suddenly dissolved. It must have been like that when the Soviet Union collapsed. All those Marxist academics suddenly without a context. Without a job, too. At least the job just about survived my lifetime. Working lifetime. Got me through to the pension.'

Plant nodded sympathetically. He tried for sympathy, anyway, hoped it seemed sympathetic. After a decent silence he took the conversation back to Lucy.

'Ah, Lucy Lockett,' said Revill.

'Yes,' said Plant.

Revill shook his head reflectively.

'How does she find it here?'

Revill shrugged.

'Is she lonely?'

'I imagine being the brash colonial in this town she gets the big freeze.'

'Dr Major too?'

'I think Major has always had his other life to keep him busy.'

'Really?'

'Uh-huh.'

'What other life was that?'

'He's always had his connections. From way back.

The university is just one of his fronts.'

'Fronts?'

'Covers.'

'Tell me.'

'He's your employer. Ask him.'

'I might.'

'You should.'

'And what would I find out?'

'Who knows?'

'Do you?' Plant asked.

Revill laughed.

'I don't want to speak ill of your boss.'

'Don't you?'

'Yes, of course, I do. What would give me more pleasure?'

'Go on then,' said Plant.

'I know nothing,' he said.

'But you have your suspicions.'

'Oh yes, I have my suspicions.'

Here he was again, checking up on his boss when he should have been checking up on his chief suspect, or his boss's chief suspect. Not for the first time, either. Funny how it always seemed to happen. Plant wondered whether he was in the right business. But then, he reflected, did anyone ever feel they were in the right business?

They sat and watched the undergraduates going in and out of the New Bodleian, going across to the Old Bodleian, coming out of Blackwell's with their books in Blackwell's bags, which was how you could tell they'd been into Blackwell's. Double-decker buses laden with tourists headed for the halls of learning and the sites of Oxford detective novels. Bicycles ignored the traffic lights.

'Another drink?' Plant suggested.

'I think I'll leave it at that for now,' said Revill. 'I just dropped in for a coffee but I decided coffee was probably more harmful than beer. But it's a bit early for serious drinking.'

'I thought serious drinkers started early,' said Plant.

'Could be. I just wanted somewhere to sit and think.'

'And now you've thought.'

'Not really. But I think I'll take a stroll in the Parks and call it exercise.'

'Dr Major took me round the Meadows,' said Plant. 'I haven't found the Parks.'

'Just along the road,' said Plant. 'That's why it's called Parks Road.'

'I see,' said Plant.

'I'll show you if you want,' said Revill. 'I used to walk in them all the time when I was an undergraduate. All those wretched Sundays. The Bodleian shut and nowhere to go. You'd get sick of sitting alone in your rooms. There's a limit to how many chocolate digestive biscuits and cups of instant coffee the body will take. So you'd go out for a dip in the drizzle. Files of disconsolate grammar school boys traipsing round the Parks hoping to bump into private school girls with loose morals.'

'And did you?'

'Can't say I did,' said Revill. 'But hope springs eternal. You never know, we might strike lucky today.'

# Twenty

They didn't. There were people walking dogs. And elderly dons or derelicts sitting on benches thinking thoughts too deep for words. The usual joggers, wired for sound. The Parks stretched out flat down to the River Cherwell. Revill led them towards it.

'Why do you say Dr Major has connections?'

'Well, he got a job here for a start,' said Revill.

'And you have to be connected for that?'

'I would have thought so. Unless you're brilliant, of course. They have been known to hire on merit.'

'Did you want a job here?'

'You always expect, deep down, always hope, anyway, that you're going to be called back. You never quite get to accept that no one cares, there are too many talented people, not enough jobs, not enough positions of power, influence, significance or fulfilment to go round. Once you've left, you've left.'

'Major came back.'

'Yes, interesting, isn't it?'

'Interesting? In what way?'

'There has to be a reason. He must have offered something they could use. And it wasn't expertise in Old English.'

'If he didn't have connections, he wouldn't have got back, is that what you're saying?'

'Pretty much, yes.'

'Couldn't he be brilliant?'

'If he could, he hasn't shown it,' said Revill. 'His work certainly isn't. Mind you, it's probably hard to shine in Anglo-Saxon. Not a lot to shine about.'

'What about his magic books?'

'Have you read any of them?'

'I've looked at a couple.'

'Blinded by their brilliance, were you?'

'Well,' said Plant.

'Dazzled by the intellectual grasp of the subject? Struck dumb by the secrets revealed?'

'I didn't find a lot of secrets,' said Plant.

'Well you wouldn't, would you?'

'Wouldn't you?'

'If you knew any secrets you wouldn't go proclaiming them to all and sundry, would you? You'd keep them to yourself. Or to whoever commissioned them in the first place.'

'I hadn't thought of it like that,' said Plant.

Revill gave a satisfied smile.

'You think he used his magic spells to get his fellowship here?'

Revill wrinkled his nose, one of those English gestures of thinking Plant was beginning to recognise.

'Indirectly.'

'Really?'

'Indirectly,' said Revill.

'In what way?'

'A government man.'

'A government man?'

'Does the state a bit of service,' said Revill. 'And

they would have fixed him up with a comfortable berth.'

'So what service does he do the state?'

'Oh, I don't know,' said Revill. Having introduced the topic, now he seemed to want to shrug it off.

'Are you sure?' Plant pressed.

'A bit of advice, I imagine. A bit of consulting. Spots some likely recruits. Reports back on the unsound.'

'But not magic?'

'Why not?'

'I don't know. Are you saying he's working on magic for the government?'

'Who knows?'

'But you're implying you know.'

Revill sighed. 'Do you know anything about the security services?'

'Only what I've read.'

'So what have you read?'

'Oh,' said Plant, 'the usual stuff. Infiltrating radical groups. Giving dissidents a hard time. Bugs, phone tapping. Safe houses. Is that what you mean?'

'Drugs?'

'That stuff about the CIA experimenting with LSD? Running the Far East heroin trade? Getting rid of the Taliban and restoring opium growing in Afghanistan? Yes, I've read that.'

'Magic?'

'I can't say I've read about that.'

'There you are then,' said Revill.

'Where am I?'

'Don't you find it interesting that nothing's been written on it?'

Plant reflected.

'Should it have been?'

'Everything else gets written about. Code breaking. Presidential assassinations. Death squads. Drug running. But there's almost nothing on magic.'

'Nothing or almost nothing?'

'Almost nothing. Just enough to indicate they have to have been playing with it. Bits like Aleister Crowley claiming he worked for intelligence. Dennis Wheatley in the war cabinet office. Using astrologers to shadow Hitler's astrologer. Psychic intelligence.'

'So you're saying they use magic but keep quiet about it.'

'Could be,' said Revill.

'And you're saying Dr Major is involved in this.'

'Why not?'

'And the fact that his books don't seem to show any belief in it and don't seem to say much doesn't mean he doesn't know much.'

'Sounds possible.'

'So you postulate a second set of books.'

'Always.'

'For government eyes only.'

'Now there's a thought.'

'Interesting,' said Plant.

'I think so,' said Revill. 'Much as I hate to concede that Major is a subject of any possible interest at all, I think that that is quite interesting.'

'And you know this for sure?'

'Who knows anything for sure?' Revill said. 'Especially in these areas.'

'Some people must,' said Plant.

'If they do, they're not going to be telling anyone,' Revill said.

'You really think it's likely?' Plant asked.

Babies in prams, dogs gambolling through the grass, old dons ambling by, young dons striding eagerly, loving couples punting down the river, the quiet and calm of it all.

Revill pointed to a row of buildings along the edge of the Parks.

'See those?'

'Yes.'

'Know what they are?'

'No.'

'The Science buildings. Know what goes on there?'

'No.'

'No,' said Revill. 'Who does? Where do you think they did the atom bomb research? Where do you think they did the chemical weapons research? Where do you think they evolved the satellite surveillance systems?'

'There?'

'There and countless places like them,' said Revill. 'That's what universities are for. To serve the state. They're not there to advance knowledge for itself. Who cares about that? Who's going to fund it? Follow the money trail. The money comes from government and the government wants something for its money.'

'What does it want?' Plant asked.

'Ways of keeping the people down,' said Revill.

'And you think they're using magic for that?'

'Why wouldn't they?' said Revill. 'Along with everything else.'

## Twenty-One

Major stuck his head round the door.

'Busy?' he asked.

Plant was resting after his exercise round the Parks. He had read novels in which investigators jogged regularly and worked out in gyms, but he was not that sort of person himself. If given the choice of role models he would probably have settled for the dressing gown and the meerschaum pipe and the seven per cent solution.

'Yes,' said Plant, 'working away.'

'Glad to hear it,' said Major. 'High Table tonight.'

'High Table?'

'Dinner in hall.'

'Fine,' said Plant.

'Do you have a tie?'

'A bow tie?'

'Just an ordinary one will do.'

'Yes, do you want to borrow it?'

'Wear it.'

'Now, do you mean?' Plant asked, innocently.

'For dinner. What about a gown?'

'Can't say I do.'

'You'll have to borrow one.'

'Do I need one?'

'Probably not, but I'll get you one all the same.'

'Thank you.'

'Pick you up just before seven.'

Plant sat at High Table. Major had steered him in and then sat elsewhere. It was not done to sit beside your guest, he explained. The undergraduates were clustered in a rabble at long tables running the length of the hall. High Table was on a raised dais at the end of the hall, set at right angles to them. Plant looked at the paintings of five centuries of past masters and former fellows hanging on the walls, beneath and between the slim perpendicular windows. The undergraduates kept up a dull rumble of sound like a railway station. Then the chaplain gabbled through a Latin grace, and the undergraduates briefly fell silent as they devoured their food.

'Harbinger,' said the genial faced old fellow next to him. 'And you don't have to ask, "Of what?"'

'Plant,' said Plant.

'What do you think this is?' Harbinger asked.

He prodded the crisp, dry solitary thing on his plate.

'Fish or fowl?' he asked.

It resisted his fork and skidded around.

'Or reptile? Frog maybe. Or what do you say to ersatz? Could it be soy?'

'I can't imagine,' said Plant.

'A cutlet, maybe.' He turned to the person on his other side. 'Could this be a cutlet?'

No one seemed to know. He stopped one of the white-jacketed college servants passing behind him.

'I'll inquire in the kitchen, sir,' said the college servant.

Harbinger made a determined jab at it and it slid off the plate and onto the floor. The servant came back and picked it up.

'I'll bring you another one, sir.'

'No need, no need,' said Harbinger.

'As you say, sir.'

'He'd just go out through the door and dust it off and bring it back again,' Harbinger explained to Plant.

Plant prodded his own offering cautiously. It was hard and resistant to knife or fork. He managed to slice off a fragment.

'Any idea what it is?' Harbinger asked.

'I can't say I have,' said Plant.

'You chaps still talk strine down there?' the fellow on his other side asked.

'I suppose so.'

'Well, you ought to know whether you do or not. Amazing concept. Love it. Rhyming slang, too?'

'There's still a bit.'

'Give an example.'

Was this what they called a viva? An oral examination to find out whether you knew anything after all, whether your written papers had been a fluke or sat for by a hired substitute. Or a fellowship dinner, to ascertain whether your table manners were good enough for acceptance.

'Keep out of the surf or the Noahs will get you,' said Plant.

'The Noahs?'

'Noah's ark,' said Plant. 'Shark.'

'You think it could be shark?' said Harbinger. 'Do you eat shark in Australia?'

'I don't,' said Plant, 'but people do.'

'What sort of people?' asked the second fellow.

'People who buy fish and chips,' said Plant. 'It's called flake.'

'Well, fancy that,' said Harbinger. 'And you think that's what this was? Fake. What an appropriate name.'

'Flake,' said Plant again.

'I think I prefer fake,' said Harbinger. 'Probably something Major cooked up. Sounds just his cup of tea.'

'He was in Australia, wasn't he?' said the second fellow.

'Yes,' said Plant.

'Yes,' said Harbinger. 'You can always tell.'

'How can you tell?' asked the second fellow.

'It does something to them. Accent or diet. And those native girls they bring back with them. So you know Major?' he said to Plant.

'Yes, I'm his guest.'

'Whose guest?' asked Harbinger.

'Major's guest.'

'How charming,' said Harbinger.

'Major's guest or the Major's guest or the major guest?' asked the second fellow.

'The first.'

'Primus inter majores.'

Plant smiled. 'Is there a major here, too?' he asked.

'Bound to be,' said Harbinger. 'Blighters are everywhere. Think they run the show. Have some more of that claret before they drink it all. The only thing worth dining in for. The only reason I still dine in.'

'Which is the major?' Plant asked.

'The secret service type beside Major,' said Harbinger. 'He used to be a major in military intelligence. Probably still is.'

'Major did?'

'Who knows?' said Harbinger. 'Wouldn't put anything past him. Perhaps they've come to take him away. Wouldn't that be something? Perhaps we should warn him. Major catastrophe looms. Prepare to meet thy dooms.'

'Can one have dooms in the plural?' the second fellow said.

'Oh, I'm sure Major can,' said Harbinger. 'He certainly deserves more than one. Not a doubt. I'm sure we all eagerly await that day of reckoning.'

'Aye,' the chaplain and the second fellow intoned together, like an assembly of peers in an unreformed upper house.

Plant looked at Harbinger, wondering. Harbinger smiled a satisfied, shifty smile.

'The ayes have it,' he said

'And is he the major guest?' Plant asked.

'The major? No. That's the chap next to the Master. Weapons inspector boffin. Used to be our fellow in bug research before he went off to the Foreign Office.

Bugs, bugging or buggery, take your pick.'

He peered at Plant's plate.

'A bug,' he said. 'Maybe that's what it is. Does it taste like a bug to you? I think I ate one once when I visited Australia. Indigenous cuisine. A witchetty grub.'

'No,' said Plant.

'You've eaten bug?'

'In the past.'

'And they are a part of Australian cuisine?'

'Yes,' said Plant. 'Balmain bugs, Moreton Bay bugs. They're crayfish.'

'Well, I'll be buggered,' said the second fellow.

'Not before dessert,' said the chaplain, all rosy red across the table.

Plant surveyed the array of gowned figures. They looked innocuous and unremarkable, genially swigging down the claret and toying with the food. A strange, closed medieval society that exercised its influence through the political and economic reaches of the nation. These were the people who advised on the end of empire and the end of history and the new world order. The people who genetically mutated crops and developed weapons of mass destruction and trained young politicians in the arts of deception. And practised magic. He found it hard to believe.

'The trick is,' said Harbinger, 'to have a quick snack beforehand. Line your stomach. Some of that fake and chips you eat. Or a bite of bug. And then just stick with the claret.'

'I'll remember,' said Plant.

'Wise man. However,' he continued, filling Plant's glass again, 'don't overdo the claret. You need to pace yourself for the port. That really is something worth waiting for.'

At a certain point all the undergraduates disappeared, but at High Table they kept on with course after course. Then at an arcane signal they all stood and filed out. Major hung back and intercepted Plant.

'I have to dash off, but you stay. I'll catch you tomorrow. Let me know what you think of the port. I think you'll find it's a damn sight better than that five dollar a bottle any port in a storm stuff they serve up in your native land.'

He disappeared with the secret service major.

The rest of them filed into a small room with armchairs and a table surmounted with bowls of fruit and nuts and a circular railway contraption bearing the port. Plant followed Harbinger in rejecting the fruit and sticking with the port. It carried him through into welcome oblivion.

## Twenty-Two

It would be wrong to say that Plant was woken by Lucy. He was already awake, his head heavy. It was impossible to sleep. The bells began their torture early. Indeed, they never ceased. The chiming clocks struck hours and half hours and quarter hours across the city throughout the night, churches, colleges, all out of phase with each other, so much for Greenwich Mean Time. The chapel bells summoning the faithful and unfaithful alike started around dawn, and built up steadily in number and volume. Followed by breakfast bells, if there were indeed breakfast bells. There was a dinner bell. But did they make sure you were summoned for breakfast? Hadn't Major said he'd always missed it? Plant was brooding on whether what he was hearing were breakfast bells when she burst into his room.

Burst was the only way he could think of it. The bedroom door was flung open, arms flung up wide, shopping bags flung up with them, and showering down, scattering their contents over the room. And she screamed. Hooted really, but it sounded like a scream. Someone outside in the quadrangle might not recognise the difference.

'I didn't think you'd still be in bed, I'm sorry, I was just looking to see if you were in here but I didn't expect to find you in bed. I mean, well' – she wrenched her watch round her arm so she could read the dial –

'it is ten thirty. Or eleven thirty. Or is it nine thirty? I never can work out these Roman numerals, why don't they use Arabic numerals? Is it another anti-Arab campaign? Anyway, it's quite late. Well, it's not early. Not that it matters. Sorry if I woke you up. Or were you already awake? Are you one of those people who does his best work in bed?'

Plant groaned.

'Do you have a hangover? Or did somebody sap you with a blackjack? You really are the classic private eye.'

He groaned some more.

'Just say if I'm talking too much.'

'Yes,' he said.

'I am?'

He nodded.

'Too much or too loud?'

'Both,' he said.

'Well, aren't you the gentleman?'

He shook his head.

'Another heritage classic,' she said.

He looked at her balefully.

'Do you mind if I open a window? It needs freshening up in here.'

She opened it anyway. Sounds of rumbling traffic and happy voices and more bells wafted in. She peered out of it.

Plant sunk deeper beneath the sheets as the cold air swept into the room.

She turned round and smiled at him pertly and began

gathering up *Vogue* and *Harper's* and *Cosmopolitan* and the *Spectator* and the *Literary Review* and the *London Review of Books* from the blankets and the floor and stacking them beside the door.

'I'm trying to control my addictive compulsive behaviour,' she said, 'by buying magazines. Instead of going out spending a fortune on clothes or books, I buy magazines about clothes and books. Then when I'm cured I'll be in a position to know what clothes and books to buy. My doctor said, "Well, we can't just replace one addiction by another, can we?" I don't see why not. Especially if it saves you some money.'

She smiled at him willingly. She was high as a kite, and happily so. No point feeling guilty and remorseful about it. She seemed to have the right attitude. Plant's attitude, anyway.

'Talking of addictive behaviour,' she said, sweeping Plant's clothes off the only chair in the bedroom and sitting down, 'how would you like a smoke?'

She opened her handbag and produced a slim, silver cigarette case.

'Isn't it delightfully retro?' she said. 'They'll be illegal next. A prohibited manufacture. Or licensed. Limited. If you know the right people you'll always be able to get yourself a cigarette case. But they'll be rare antiques. Or expensive counterfeits. Smuggled in from the former Soviet Union. Like guns.'

She produced a rolled joint and lit it with a silver lighter.

'One's little toys. Accessories for the wicked woman.

Yes, a smoker. Politically incorrect. Worse, a dope smoker. Dependent. Addicted. Anorexic. Bulimic. Suicidal.'

She handed the joint across.

'As a trained investigator you would be thinking all that anyway, so there's no harm in telling you.'

Plant reached an arm out of bed and took it.

'Don't you have any pyjamas?' she said. She laughed. 'Wowie. Don't they wear them in Australia these days? Is that because of global warming? My, you really are the original White Australian, aren't you? Don't you ever go to the beach? Or are you worried about skin cancers, is that it?'

Plant sucked on the joint and coughed and choked and sat up. He held onto it till he recovered, and took a second toke.

'You said your husband doesn't like you smoking,' he said.

'He doesn't like a lot of things I do.'

'Health reasons?'

'Sort of.'

'What, heart disease, lung disease?'

'Oh no, he doesn't worry about that. I don't think he'd worry about that at all. Get rid of me all the sooner.'

She took a deep drag.

'It's the influences it opens you up to. He says it opens you up to the lower astral. Black magic and demons and disincarnate entities.'

'Does he believe in all that?'

She shrugged.

'I thought he said he was just an historian of popular culture.'

'Is that what he told you?'

'Yes. But he believes it too? Even though he says he doesn't?'

'I've no idea whether he believes in it or not. In magic or in anything else, for that matter.'

'But he doesn't like you smoking.'

'No. And he always gathers up his nail clippings and burns them in the grate. Keeps his comb clean, burns the stray hairs.'

'Are you serious?'

'Oh, yes,' she said. 'I don't find Archer much of a joke. Not the sort that makes you laugh, anyway.'

'So he does believe in all that stuff?'

'Possibly,' she said. 'His attitude is why take a risk? It might be true. Enough people have thought it was true. So unless you've got clear evidence to the contrary, why take risks?'

'And he doesn't have clear evidence that magic doesn't work?'

'Do you?'

'I can't say I've ever really thought about it.'

'Well, Archer has. Thought about it. It's like Pascal said. You don't know if God exists or not, but you might as well assume he does. Nothing's lost if he doesn't.'

'Is it the same with the Devil?'

'I suppose it might be,' she said. 'Why, are you

feeling devilish?'

She got up from the chair and came and sat on the edge of the bed and looked into his eyes. Plant held out a hand towards the joint. She passed it across.

'Now it's my turn to ask the questions,' she said.

'Go ahead,' said Plant.

She crossed her legs and her skirt rode up her thighs some more.

'What exactly are you working on?' she asked.

'Inauthenticity,' he croaked, trying to hold in the smoke.

'I don't believe you,' she said.

She was very close and her eyes were sparkling.

'Why not?'

'Because I think you're lying.'

She took the roach from him and inhaled and blew smoke out in a narrow column towards his nostrils.

'You reckon?'

She held his cheek with her thumb and finger and shook it gently like you might shake a domestic animal. A horse, maybe. The squatter's daughter.

'Do it again, but slower,' Plant said.

'Fresh, too,' she said.

'It's the open window.'

'I don't think so,' she said.

She sighed.

'Where did you meet Archer?' she asked.

'In Australia.'

'And you began blackmailing him there?'

'I'm not blackmailing him.'

'Aren't you?'

'No.'

'Who is, then?'

'I don't know that anyone is.'

'So why does he grab the mail before I can see it?'

'Does he?'

'Yes.'

'Habit, maybe.'

'He never used to.'

'Can't help then,' said Plant.

'Has he hired you?'

'Yes.'

'What for?'

'To work on his inauthenticity project.'

She opened her handbag and took out a small business card. Plant recognised it. One of his own. Presumably one he'd given to Major.

'Research assistance. Investigative reporting,' she read. 'What about indexing?'

'I don't enjoy indexing.'

'But you enjoy poking around in other peoples' business.'

'Sometimes. It depends on what's involved.'

'And what does it usually involve?'

'What it says. Research assistance, invest...'

'I know what it says,' she cut him off. 'But when I was a student they taught us about the pleasures of the sub-text.'

'That must have been enjoyable.'

'I think you're a private investigator.'

'Do you, now?'

'Probably unlicensed.'

'Uh-huh.'

'But in effect, that's what you are. A snoop.'

'Uh-huh.'

'And I want to know what you're snooping after.'

She looked him in the eye, and then glanced over his bare arms and bare torso. 'Darling,' she added throatily, looking him in the eye again.

She did it well. Maybe when she was a student she had learned the pleasures of the drama, too. The essential note of self-parody, the over the top suggestiveness, the ambiguity of image and representation.

'If I were,' he said, 'it would be confidential.'

'Ah,' she said. 'All private parts and confidential dicks.'

'You're very good,' said Plant.

'Thank you,' she said. 'I can also be very bad. Quite extraordinarily wicked.'

'Is that so?'

'If you treat me right,' she said.

'Uh-huh,' said Plant

'I'll level with you,' she said, leaning towards him. 'Then you can level with me.'

'Maybe,' Plant said.

'I want to know why Archer hired you.'

'So you said.'

'If anyone should be hiring a private investigator, it's me,' she said. 'I know he has his little bits on the side. He always has done. I wouldn't object if he just told me. But he can't be honest. Never could. He has to have his secrets. He is the most secretive man I ever knew. And I can't stand it.'

She took out the silver cigarette case and lit up another number.

'And now,' she said, sucking in the smoke and letting it curl out of her nostrils, fetching little nostrils, twitching there in front of Plant, 'and now he hires a fucking private investigator. Why? What's he want an investigator for? I'm the one who wants an investigator. I'm the one who doesn't know what's going on. I'm the one he keeps the secrets from.'

'You think he has other women?' Plant asked.

'Too right I think he does. I know he does.'

She passed the joint across.

'Just like I have other men.'

She smiled at him. A sweet smile of satisfaction.

'So are you out to get even or to get even?' Plant asked.

'You'll have to run that past me again.'

'Are you trying for revenge or planning to equalise the score?'

'Make love not war, I say,' said Lucy.

'Do you happen to know who he's seeing?'

'Oh God, no,' she said. 'It's all too pathetic. He just makes a fool of himself. Prostrating himself before all these debutante types. Or whatever they are. Anyway, you know what they are, the *crème de la crème*, darling, enough to send his cholesterol level stratospheric, instant heart attack and all for nothing.'

'All for nothing?'

'They're not the sort of girls who sleep with the second eleven,' she said.

'I see.'

'I'm sure you do,' she said. 'But poor, pathetic Archer doesn't. He has these delusions.'

'You seem to know a lot about him without hiring an investigator.'

'Quite so,' she said. 'And no doubt he knows the same about me. So why's he hiring you?'

'I think you'd have to talk to him.'

'Don't be ridiculous,' she said. 'Have you ever tried to talk to Archer? You can't get a thing out of him.'

She manoeuvred herself further onto the bed. Plant moved over to give her more room.

'Why do you have to hold out on me?' she asked.

The eyes fluttering. Imploring.

The skirt riding up.

The hand at the neck of the blouse, fingering the button. Reflectively.

The slope of the ceiling pressed down. She leaned over him.

They sat there deadlocked. It was as if they had lost track whose was the next move.

The door opened and Major came in.

'Well, well,' he said.

'Hello, darling,' said Lucy.

'Morning poppet,' said Major. 'Still got your kit on, I see.'

'Would you like me to take it off?' she said, sweetly.

'Not right now, if you can bear it,' he said.

'Your nice Mr Plant was telling me what he was doing for you,' she said.

'No, I wasn't,' said Plant.

'He was about to,' she said, 'when you came in without knocking.'

'And what is Mr Plant doing for me right at this moment?'

'He has your interests at heart,' Lucy said.

'Is that so, Mr Plant?'

'Absolutely,' said Plant.

'I'm glad to hear it,' said Major.

'I knew you would be, darling,' said Lucy.

Major sniffed.

'You been up to your filthy habits again?' he asked.

'Which ones are those, darling?'

'Smoking.'

'Oh, no,' she said. 'Mr Plant offered me one but I declined.'

'Is that true, Plant?'

'Absolutely,' said Plant.

'Why don't we step into the other room and let Plant get dressed?' Major suggested.

'Mr Plant won't mind our staying here, will you, Mr Plant?'

'Well I have no wish to watch him rise.'

'If only he would,' said Lucy.

Major steered her out of the bedroom with a practised hand.

Plant dragged himself out of the sheets.

'Oops,' said Lucy, stepping back in. 'I seem to have dropped one of my magazines somewhere.'

She smiled at him sweetly.

'Lucy,' Major called.

She rolled her eyes, picked up *Marie Claire*, and went out again.

## Twenty-Three

When Plant had dressed and emerged from the bedroom she was gone.

'No Lucy?'

'I sent her packing,' said Major. 'You'd finished with her, I assume.'

'She called round to ask why you were employing me.'

'What did you tell her?'

'I didn't tell her anything.'

'Good man.'

'You haven't told your wife about receiving the letters.'

'No.'

'Why's that?'

'You've met her.'

'Yes.'

'Enough said.'

'Is there any reason not to tell her? I mean, if you're not telling her because you think she might have sent them, she's going to know you suspect her if you don't tell her you've received them.'

'Not necessarily. There are a lot of things I don't tell my wife.'

'She did indicate that.'

'And I certainly don't think she sent them.'

'Fair enough.'

'Do you?'

Plant hesitated.

'I don't know,' he said. 'It's not impossible.'

'Why would she?'

'Well, you'd be the one to tell me that.'

'What do you mean?'

'Well, without prejudice, as they say,' Plant suggested, cautiously, 'maybe she suspects you have some …'

'Bit on the side? She's been onto you about that, has she?'

'About what?'

'She's very insecure,' Major said. 'Comes from being a colonial. Feels she can't compete with all these Oxford ladies.'

'Ladies in the sense of being Lady this?' Plant asked. 'Like, titled?'

'Like titled, as you put it. Yes.'

'Your students?'

'Undergraduates. Colleagues. Colleagues' wives. It's the way it is here.'

'Could that provoke her to send anonymous letters?'

'Unfounded jealousy?' he said. 'I hadn't considered that.'

'I have.'

'So you say.'

'Is it possible? Or don't you think so, knowing her? Your wife, that is.'

'Can't imagine it for a moment. Not her style at all. She's more the direct action type. Throw the soup across the kitchen and follow it up with a barrage of onions.'

'So why not tell her about the letters?'

'I suppose I had thought it might be something in that area. Some guttering old flame. Which is what Lucy would have thought if I'd said anything. So I thought it best not to mention them. No need to stir her up.'

'So it could be some female friend feeling slighted or neglected or something.'

'I had thought that might be a remote possibility. Until Revill came into the picture.'

'Remote? How remote?'

'A possibility, then.'

'And is it?'

'How would I know?' said Major. 'You're the investigator. Investigate.'

'The only way I can investigate,' said Plant, 'is by asking questions.'

'Of course, sorry, old chap.'

'It might be better to tell your wife.'

'You think?'

'It would stop her asking me. And she might have some suggestions.'

'Like what?'

'I've no idea. But two heads are better than one.'

'You're quite a fount of wisdom, aren't you, Plant?'

Plant smiled. Benignly.

'So why haven't you come up with anything?'

'There's not been a lot to go on,' said Plant.

'What else do you need? You're wasting time going on about Lucy. You know it's Revill.'

'Do I?'

'Who else could it be? He's the obvious suspect.'

Plant gave his shrug.

'Have you talked to Revill?'

'Oh, yes.'

'And have you got anywhere?'

Plant thought about it. He should have thought about it before. But what with dining at High Table and the claret and the port and being woken, or at least greeted, by Lucy first thing, there had not been a lot of time to think. Not much thinking had been done, anyway. He put himself into delay mode. He was not sure why. Because he had not had time to think yet, perhaps. Or perhaps because at some deeper level he had been thinking, but had not let himself open up the answers.

'When did you see him?'

'Yesterday.'

'And what did he have to say for himself?'

'Not a lot.'

'That's not like him,' said Major.

'Not a lot of substance, anyway.'

'That's more like,' said Major. 'He always was a waffling little weevil.'

'Uh-huh.'

'So what did you talk about?'

'Oh, this and that.'

'You're not holding out on me, are you, Plant?' Major looked at him keenly.

'Why would I do that?'

'No idea. Don't care, especially. Just want to know if you are.'

'No, of course not.'

'So what did you talk about?'

'Oh, how he felt about being back in Oxford. Memories of lonely undergraduate days. The usual stuff.'

'I didn't hire you to write his biography.'

Plant smiled. 'Just background.'

'I don't need it. He's the obvious suspect.'

'Well, we haven't established that yet.'

'So when will you?'

Plant shrugged.

'It's not something that can be rushed.'

None of it was. Including reporting back to Major. Indeed, he was not sure he wanted to report any of it back to Major without some deep and serious consideration. And probably not even after that. If what Revill had been saying were true, he needed to go carefully. If only a fraction of it were true. Forget Revill's persecution delusions, if they were delusions, forget his paranoia, if it were paranoia, consider only the possibility that Major was working seriously on magic. A man who was careful about his nail-clippings and shed hair. Or even if he wasn't, that someone else was working on it. It was not the sort of thing you wanted to know. Certainly not the sort of thing you wanted anyone to know you knew. Certainly not something you wanted to mention without long and serious reflection. Official Secrets Act and all that. And

if you hadn't signed it and they didn't think you were
safe, then you were very unsafe. Very.

'So he didn't confess.'

'No, he didn't confess.'

'So what do you do now?'

'I talk to him some more.'

'Anything interesting turn up so far?'

'So far,' said Plant, 'it has been a matter of gaining
his confidence. Until I establish that, I won't get
anywhere. And if I try rushing it, he'll smell a rat.'

'You're not just dragging this job out because you've
fallen for the dreaming spires?'

'No,' said Plant.

'Or for any of the other local attractions?'

'No,' said Plant.

'Take care, then,' said Major. He grinned his grille of
a Japanese military staff car grin, circa 1938.

'I shall.'

'What's your next move?'

'Breakfast,' Plant said.

Major flashed his fancy watch.

'Too late now,' he said with another cheerful grin.

'I need something.'

'Don't you have a kettle?' Major asked.

'Probably there is one,' said Plant.

'Get yourself some instant coffee.'

'Hate the stuff.'

'Well, whatever.'

'Whatever,' Plant agreed.

'How did you enjoy High Table?'

231

'Interesting,' said Plant.

'Still want to be fixed up with compulsory dining rights?'

'Maybe just leave things as they are,' Plant said.

'Always the best thing,' said Major. 'Glad to see you're a natural conservative at heart, after all.'

He let himself out.

Plant went back into the bedroom. He tidied up the bed, plumped the pillows. A neatly rolled joint fell onto the floor. Lucy, bless her. He considered for a moment. What to do with incriminating evidence. Play it by the book and burn it.

He went out into the sitting room and sat in his chair and smoked it. The bells sang a gentle, joyful song. The sunbeams danced playfully on the leadlight windows. The day took on a new colour. One he could face.

## Twenty-Four

They met in a pub in town. The Crown. Revill had suggested it. 'If you feel like company for dinner some time,' he'd said. Plant had.

'It's where Shakespeare used to stay on his trips between London and Stratford. Bedded the publican's wife and begat the noseless poet Davenant.'

'Is that so?' said Plant.

'So he said.'

'Who said?'

'Davenant.'

'Why noseless?'

'Syphilis. But he didn't claim it was hereditary.'

'You like pubs with literary associations?' Plant asked.

Revill shrugged.

'It's centrally situated,' he said.

They had a couple of halves each, and then Revill suggested an Indian restaurant. Which wasn't. Not central, that is. A bit of a walk. But it was the best value, he assured Plant. 'Better than Chinese. Australia's better for Chinese. Or Vietnamese. But England's better for Indian. Though Australia's got better now they've let some Indians in. Trust the word of an Englishman when it comes to Indian restaurants. Apart from that there's not much left in England you can't get as good or better somewhere else. Beer, I suppose. I miss English beer. That's about it. Nothing much to come back for when you think about it.'

They walked down the High and over Magdalen Bridge and up the Cowley road.

'Oxford's always been terrible for food. Notorious. Unless you want to pay a fortune. And I don't. And I doubt it'd be any good anyway. There used to be these expensive places I could never afford when I was an undergraduate. You heard about them. Where the rich went. And took their rich girlfriends. Oh, the exquisite sense of privilege and exclusion.'

'Is that what you felt?'

'Exclusion? Of course.'

'And now?'

'Still too expensive. The price of tenure is low wages.'

'You regret it?'

'Not really. I was never that worried about making lots of money. It seemed good at the time, and tenure was worth having the way things panned out.'

'What way was that?'

'The political climate.'

'Which was?'

'Storm clouds over Europe. It became uglier. Or didn't you notice?'

'It seemed to get harder to get work,' Plant conceded.

'Blacklists,' said Revill.

'Really?'

'Of course. No one believes there are, of course.' He looked at Plant, waiting for the refusal to believe.

'I could believe anything,' said Plant.

'But do you believe this?'

'About blacklists?'

'Yes.'

'Convince me.'

'There you are, you see,' said Revill. 'Why do you need to be convinced? I would have thought it was blindingly obvious. Everyone knows it happened in the States. Back in the fifties. But that was somewhere else. And a long time ago. But they refuse to believe it's happening here. The UK or Australia. They refuse to recognise it when it's all around them. They say you're paranoid.'

'Is that what they say about you?'

'You haven't heard?'

'Why should I?'

'You haven't been checking up on me?'

'Checking up on you?'

Revill sighed.

'Isn't that what you do?'

'Once in a while,' said Plant. 'Tell me about the blacklists.'

'You want the definition?'

'Please.'

'A menu in an Indian restaurant.'

Plant looked up. It was not what he had expected. He had pigeonholed Revill as the politically correct radical. High minded. Probably tedious. Certainly not one for Paki jokes.

'Just something I was told in my home town.'

'Your home town here?'

'Uh-huh.'

'You go back to visit?'

'I have been known to. Once in a while,' Revill said. Plant noted the return of cautiousness.

'You still have friends there?'

'I was thinking of buying a cheap little terrace in the inner city for my retirement. My imminent retirement. But twenty minutes of walking through the streets changed my mind.'

'Why's that?'

'I think I've been away too long.'

'But you still see people there?'

'Have a pint at the local.'

'You still think of it as the local?'

'Which would that be?' said Revill. 'The Saracen's Head? The Green Man? The Mug Inn? The Old Talbot? The New Talbot? The Crown? The Barley Mow? The Cardinal's Hat? The Farrier's Arms? You name it, I've drunk in it.'

'Friends in all of them?'

'Just the odd joker,' said Revill.

'Drink in any of them regularly?' Plant asked.

'I'm not really your regular guy,' said Revill. 'As you'll find out if you go round checking up on me.'

'Why would I do that?' Plant asked.

'I'm still waiting for you to tell me,' said Revill. 'But I suppose there's no harm in telling you where I used to drink since I'm not likely ever to go back there. I think this is my last visit. I don't think I belong in England any more. If I ever did. Or anywhere else, for that matter.'

'Tell me about blacklists,' said Plant.

'What you notice is the chill,' said Revill. 'Suddenly you're out in the cold. I used to do a fair bit of freelance work. Book reviews, that sort of thing. First of all in the weeklies, then the dailies. Then I started getting radio work. Books to begin with. Then talk programmes, discussions, current affairs. You get known. They know you can get the work in on time. And you've got something to say. And you don't mind saying it.'

He laughed. Hollowly. A practiced, hollow laugh.

'But somebody minds. One day you don't get asked any more. And that's it. No one calls. Finish.'

'Maybe the producers changed,' said Plant.

'Oh, some did. Some got purged. I'm not saying I was the only one frozen out. There was a clean up of all the media after the seventies. And it wasn't just a matter of being dropped from one paper or one programme. It was everything. Papers, magazines, books, radio. Suddenly all the doors were closed.'

'A cultural shift,' said Plant.

'Yes.'

'But you take it personally.'

'Not especially,' said Revill. 'I was just saying people don't like to believe there are blacklists in our free society. It was a sociological observation. You want me to talk personally, I'll talk personally.'

'Talk personally,' said Plant.

'So you are checking up on me.'

'I find personal experience more persuasive than sociological analysis,' said Plant. 'More interesting, anyway.'

'Of course,' said Revill. 'That's why people read novels. Or used to. Now they read biographies.'

'What was your personal experience of being blacklisted?' said Plant, avoiding discussion of the death of the novel. 'Apart from getting no more work. A drop in freelance earnings.'

'The money was never that good,' said Revill. 'I didn't do it for the money. It was the chance to participate, you know. To be part of the chosen circle. The pundits.'

'And you miss that?'

'In some ways. Though it was a distraction. It gave instant ego gratification and kept you from doing any real work.'

'So why didn't you take the chance to get on with some real work when it all dried up?'

'Oh, I did,' said Revill.

He let it hang there.

'And?'

'I couldn't do it. It was like a paralysis. I'd never believed in writers' block. You just sit down and write. That's all there is to it. But now I found I couldn't any more. Now I'd got time, now I wasn't pumping out reviews and opinion pieces to deadlines, I no longer had any energy. I should have had more. But I didn't. I couldn't get things organised. I couldn't bring things to completion. Even filling up the car with petrol became too hard. The simplest things were like an ordeal.'

'You were sick.'

'I don't think so.'

'Depression.'

'The odd thing was, if I forced myself to do something, I could do it. If I could break through this sort of miasma, I could get things done. But it was like the willpower had been paralysed, and getting the willpower to break through was almost impossible. I'd manage for a while. And then the energy would go again. It was like it was jammed. Blocked, somehow. I'd have all these bits and pieces written. Opening paragraphs. False starts. Well, not so much false, they were fine. But they petered out.'

'Did you ever find out what was causing it?'

'Yes. Yes, I did.'

'What was it?'

Revill looked him in the eye.

Plant held his gaze. If he showed a flicker of doubt, he would lose him. One false note, one knowing smirk, one dismissive aside and it would be all over. The thing was to keep Revill talking.

'It's not just a matter of a list,' said Revill. 'Anyone can work out there are lists. The security agencies always have files on academics and intellectuals and writers and politicians and journalists and trade unionists. That's just intelligence gathering. The real point is what they do when they've got their lists. That certainly isn't ever talked about. Or written about.'

'What do they do?'

'What they don't do is make martyrs of people any more. All that McCarthyite stuff wasn't such a good idea. It purged the universities and the movies and government of leftists, but it had a lot of negative feedback. Now they do it quietly. No public hearings. Just feed information, true or false, to employers. Not even political information. It just needs a couple of people going round saying you're sexist or misogynist or homophobic or anti-Semitic and you're fucked. They know that. They have their people do it. So your politics are never an issue. Not explicitly. Can't even argue with them. It's done at another level. Simple character assassination.

'And that way you keep the media free of radicals. Contracts don't get renewed. People are let go. Or moved into dead end areas. But with the universities they had the problem of tenure. It's hard to get rid of people. Of course, they can block their careers. Make sure if they apply for a job somewhere else, they don't get it.'

'You applied for jobs?'

'Lots of times.'

'Without success?'

'Without success. Generally without even getting an interview.'

'You were disappointed.'

'Yes and no. But that's not the point.'

'What is the point?'

'The point is what controls can be applied. There

you are, in a secure job, paid to think. So they may cut off your freelance outlets, they may block your promotion, they may stop you from getting research grants, but it's very hard to sack you. Or it used to be. So you just sit there and think your thoughts. The ones the state doesn't like. The ones that question things. It's hard to get them published, but in the end you can usually find somewhere that will take them. Especially if your scholarship is sound. And once ideas get into print other people can read them. So how are they going to stop you?'

'You tell me.'

'Magic,' said Revill.

# Twenty-Five

Plant sat there in the shadowed Indian restaurant, drinking pints of draught Bass and eating pag saneer and malai kofta and dhal and nan. Scholarly voices held scholarly discussions at the other tables. Committed young researchers discussed genetic engineering and First World debt and information technology and the possibility that Milton was not the author of *De Doctrina Christiana*. While he sat there listening to Revill telling him how the secret services were using magic to immobilise aging left-wingers. What am I doing here? he asked himself.

What I am doing here is working for an Oxford don who writes books on magic and who has been getting anonymous notes about his fading charms and an imminent day of judgment, which he suspects are being sent by a former colleague, to whom I am currently listening. That is what I am doing here. And they may both be stark raving mad but I don't get that much work that I can pick and choose. And they may not be mad at all. Which is perhaps even more disturbing.

'How did you find out it was magic?' Plant asked.

'My girlfriend, initially,' said Revill.

'Go on.'

'She checked it out with some psychic who said it sounded like someone was doing magic on me.'

'And you believed her?'

'Yes and no. I thought about it.'

'What did she tell you to do?'

'Don't eat in other peoples' houses. Scrub yourself with salt in the shower.'

'Did it work?'

Revill shrugged.

'So what did you do?'

'I read up on it. Being the scholarly type.'

'Major's books?'

He snorted. 'I didn't get a lot out of them. Which was interesting in itself, I realised later. No, I looked up all the Frances Yates stuff and the Warburg Institute stuff and all the usual, you know, A. E. Waite, Montague Summers, Eliphas Levi, Cornelius Agrippa, Ficino. Visited a few psychic healers.'

'And?'

'The usual holocaust. I tossed out a lot of dodgy stuff from the house. Took down a lot of paintings. Threw out all the bric-à-brac people bring you from their travels. Phallic symbols, obscure gods, little dolls in native costumes and manikins and elephants and things that visiting academics from China and India and all those gift culture places foist on you.'

'Why did you do that?'

'On the principle that images are used to draw in occult energies. That's why the puritans tossed out images and icons, to stop these forces being attracted. Memory theatre. They memorise something in your house and send bad energy to it. Or someone gives you some object with a spell on it. Some artefact. A bowl. Or a book.'

'So you had a spring clean.'

'Yes, well, I needed to. I ended up living with beautiful bare walls, clear, empty surfaces.' He laughed. 'Not unlike a prison.'

'Did it work?'

'Yes and no. The place felt a lot clearer. In the end my girlfriend left too. She couldn't stand it any more.'

'Are you with anyone now?'

'No.'

A wilderness of loss and emptiness spread around him.

'And who was doing all this magic. Did you ever find out?'

'It took a while,' said Revill. 'I thought maybe, you know, it was some personal thing. Star-crossed lovers, jealousy. It may have been at some level. Jealousy and envy are horribly effective ways of motivating people. But ultimately I figured it had to be more than that. I had my suspicions. But it took a while to confirm them.'

'But you did?'

'Oh yes. I went to a few psychics. Psychic healers. That sort of thing. There's a lot around. But in the end, yes, my suspicions were confirmed. '

'And they pointed to Dr Major?'

'Why do you say that?' Revill asked.

'It seemed to be the direction we were heading.'

'You've been to his house,' said Revill.

'Yes.'

'Didn't you notice?'

'Notice what?'

'You couldn't have missed it.'

'Missed what?'

'The chill.'

'It was a bit nippy,' Plant agreed, 'but I thought that was just the weather.'

'It wasn't that sort of chill,' said Revill.

'What sort was it then?'

'The chill of black magic.'

'Really?' said Plant.

'It's a giveaway. Characteristic.'

Plant sat there silent. He thought back to Major's house. He supposed it had been chill, but he had probably assumed that was just the way it was in England. Miserable climate and economical with the heating. He hadn't been in enough English houses to make a comparison. He hadn't been in any, come to think of it. From an Australian perspective, the whole place was pretty chill.

'Look,' said Revill, 'I don't even like talking about this.'

'But you are doing.'

'Yes, well, that could be a mistake.'

'I find it interesting.'

'Why?'

Plant tried to think of an acceptable reply.

'Who are you working for?' Revill asked.

'Me?' said Plant.

'I don't see anyone else at the table,' said Revill.

Plant did some quick calculations. He could fence around some more, or he could play the honesty card.

His principle was generally, when in doubt, go for honesty. He found it easier than having to remember the lies he otherwise had to invent.

'Major has been receiving anonymous letters. He asked me to track down the sender.'

'I assume they weren't fan letters,' said Revill.

'Why do you say that?'

'Apart from the fact I can't imagine him attracting any fans, he wouldn't be hiring you to track them down if they were.'

'Maybe,' said Plant.

'Are you reporting all this back to him?'

'Would that be a problem?'

'A problem?' said Revill. 'What's one more problem?'

He called the waiter over and ordered two more pints of Bass.

'Look,' Revill said again, 'I don't even like talking about this.'

'Why's that?'

'Because it's too dangerous. How much have you read about it?'

'About magic?'

'About the security services using magic. Anything at all?'

'I think you asked me this before,' said Plant. 'I don't think I've read anything.'

'Exactly.'

'But you're saying this is a political strategy? Official policy?'

'I'm not saying anything.'

'You were earlier.'

'Yes,' said Revill. 'I wish I hadn't. I must have drunk too much.'

Plant waited. Revill took another deep swig of Bass.

'You read about the CIA and drugs. Mind control stuff for interrogation. And psychic spying. Using psychics to tune into affairs of state.'

'Somebody did talk to me about psychic spying.'

'Predictive Remote Viewing, they call it. The US military spent $26 million on research into it. But the important stuff is not about intelligence gathering. That's what they tell you they do, gather intelligence. Well they do. But that's only part of it. It's what they do with it, how they act on intelligence received that counts. It's all about control. If they can control you by black magic it's less public than assassination or show trials, isn't it?'

'I suppose it would be.'

'But they never mention using magic to control people.'

'Not that I've seen.'

'So that to talk about something so secret is to invite trouble.'

'If it's happening.'

'Oh, it's happening,' Revill said.

'And why are you targeted?'

'They don't actually tell you that,' said Revill.

'Why do you think?'

'A couple of possibilities. First of all they probably

automatically target anyone they think of as a dissident. Once you're on a list you're a target.'

'What was the second reason?'

'They have to practise, don't they? They have to see if it works. It's like the atom bomb, they had all the theory worked out, but they still had to see if it worked operationally. That's one of the reasons they dropped it on Hiroshima. And the other one on Nagasaki. Testing, you know.'

'And they were testing on you.'

'It could be.'

'Why?'

'Why me?'

'Yes.'

'I suppose I was in the wrong place at the wrong time. There was Major working on the theory. I just happened to be close at hand. And suspect. Wrong politics, wrong opinions. Or maybe he didn't like me.'

'I thought you and he used to share opinions.'

Revill laughed.

'Yes, I probably thought that too. But he was probably just hanging around the left looking for likely targets. Subjects, I think the psychologists call them.'

'And so he picked on you?'

'Not just me, I wouldn't think.' Revill said. 'I think you'll find it a lot more widespread than you might have suspected. The days you could just go and test things in Guatemalan gaols are long passed. Or so they say. You've got to look elsewhere for your experimental subjects.'

'Will I?'

'Assuming you're looking into it. Which I wouldn't recommend.'

'I'm looking into the threatening letters Dr Major's been receiving.'

'Sounds good to me,' said Revill. 'What did they say, these letters?'

'Your charms are fading.'

Revill chuckled.

'There you are then.'

'Where?'

'Someone must have figured what he's been up to. Magic charms. Unless you think it refers to his bedside manner. But I would have thought that had faded a long time ago, if it ever existed.'

*

'How does magic work?' Plant asked. 'Or is that too big a question?'

'Basically it's a matter of sending out negative energy.'

'And how do you do that? Bad thoughts?'

'Pretty much,' said Revill.

'You don't have to dress up in robes and sacrifice a goat and deflower naked maidens on an altar.'

'Only if it turns you on.'

'It's hard to imagine,' said Plant. 'Some basement of MI5 with a roomful of professional agents taking time off from satellite surveillance to stick pins in some voodoo doll. Or sitting round in a circle intoning "Get Revill".'

'It's hard to imagine a roomful of scientists sitting round in a circle developing the atom bomb. But they did. Or cultivating anthrax spores. But they do. At Porton Down. Just a short drive away.'

'Maybe,' said Plant.

'I think the principle is, if it works, do it.'

'And it works?'

'Oh, it works.'

'But you think a bunch of Oxbridge chaps, or Ivy Leaguers, are going to get into chanting spells and summoning up demons?'

'Why not?'

'It seems out of character.'

'You think magic is remote from MI5 chaps straight out of public school and Oxbridge.'

Plant nodded.

'A cultural disjunction?'

'Absolutely.'

'M. R. James, who's the generally acknowledged master of English stories of black magic, was a master at Eton and librarian at Kings. Where the spies come from. All the CIA directors used to be members of the Skull and Crossbones club at Yale. With its ritual initiations.'

'Maybe,' said Plant.

'No maybes,' said Revill. 'That's all documented.'

'Maybe they take it seriously, maybe they don't.'

'Anyway,' said Revill, 'the basis of western magic is

the Kabala.'

'Is it?'

'Read your Eliphas Levi and A. E. Waite.'

'So?' said Plant.

'The point about the Kabala is the magic power of names. The names of the lord, the names of the angels. Black magic basically inverts it and summons up demonic forces. But it's the same intellectual structure.'

'Go on,' said Plant.

'You probably won't like what I say.'

'I'm pretty broad minded.'

Revill gave a derisory grunt.

'So who takes the Kabala seriously? Whose cultural tradition is it an intrinsic part of?'

'Oh no,' said Plant. 'Not a Jewish conspiracy.'

'I said you wouldn't like it.'

'Do you like it?'

'The point about being a scholar used to be looking for the truth whether you liked what you found or not. That was the point of academic freedom and the point of giving people tenure. You could think the unthinkable without getting fired. Or fined.'

'And now?'

'Now there's a lot of mealy-mouthed political correctness that may have been well-intentioned originally but serves to stop you thinking the unthinkable.'

'And this is the unthinkable?'

'Take your own reaction,' said Revill.

Plant nodded.

'So where does it get us?' he asked.

'If you find it hard to imagine a bunch of spooks from MI5 or the CIA sitting around casting spells, how about Mossad? If you postulate a living rabbinical tradition, then it's no great leap. Recruit some Cabbalists, invert the values, there you are.'

It was a moment to take a long, reflective swig of Bass and say nothing.

'It's said to be the most efficient of all the agencies. Stands to reason they would make use of everything available.'

'So you're saying Dr Major was working for Mossad?'

'Not necessarily directly,' said Revill. 'But those organisations are all one global network. You work for one, you work for all of them. They'd all be developing the same programmes. Mossad's input to the CIA is public knowledge. So are the CIA's links with MI6 and ASIO.'

'You're not going to tell me Dr Major's name is really Mayer?' said Plant.

'I leave that up to you,' said Revill.

'Spare me,' said Plant.

'Anyway, at one level Major is irrelevant. He's just the hired hand. The point is who's behind it all.'

'And who is?'

'Who knows?' said Revill.

'That's helpful.'

'It's not a matter of individuals,' Revill said. 'Or

252

even nation states. It's not a conspiracy. It's simply what Chomsky says. It's just institutional practice.'

'Human nature,' said Plant.

'I don't think so,' said Revill firmly. 'I believe human nature is basically the same everywhere and basically good. But a small number of greedy, powerful people can manipulate it to their own advantage and to everyone else's detriment.'

'And they are who?'

'The ruling class,' said Revill. 'The rich.'

'So you really are an unreconstructed lefty. Just like Dr Major said.'

'Am I?'

'Sounds like it.'

'And is that a bad thing?' Revill asked.

Plant shrugged.

'But at another level, of course, Major is quite interesting. Here for once we have the human face of terror. Not the bland impermeability of the anonymous bureaucracies. The agencies that dare not speak their name. For once we see an actual practitioner.'

'Is that what interests you?'

Revill sighed. 'Not really,' he said. 'Not any more. Now I find it all very tedious and I'm sick of it. I just wish it would stop.'

'So what are you going to do about it?' Plant asked.

'Do about it?'

'Are you going to expose it?'

'And get myself killed?' said Revill. 'I'm obviously not the only one. If they're doing it on me, it's part of a pretty widespread programme. They might have been in trialling it in Australia, but almost certainly they'd have been working on it in Britain and the States too. It's huge. There would be hell to pay if it ever came out. So they'd make sure it never did.'

'Would anyone believe it?'

'Enough would.'

'And you're not going to confront Dr Major?'

'You think I'm crazy?'

Plant said nothing.

'You probably do, of course. But I'm not. It would be insanity. What would it achieve? Appeal to his better nature? You're joking. I'd just alert him that I knew and that would be the end of me.'

'You think he'd kill you?'

'I don't know whether Major would personally. More likely he'd pass the word along. I don't quite see him doing it himself. But he might. If he had enough involved in it. Why not?'

'But you've followed him over here.'

'Like hell I have. This is as much my university as Major's.'

'He works here.'

'So what? Once an Oxford man, always an Oxford man. The point is being a member of the university, not being one of the hired help.'

'You believe that?'

'Yes,' said Revill. 'I do actually.'

'So you didn't come over here to harass him?'

'I came over here on my last leave.'

'It sounds ominous.'

'Take the money and run,' said Revill. 'Make sure I use up all my travel allowances.'

'You're not bearding Dr Major in his den?'

'You're joking.'

'Or sending him threatening letters?'

'I am delighted to hear he's receiving threatening letters. I'd be delighted if he were exposed. But I never want to have to deal with him again.'

'And the magic?'

'My career's over,' said Revill. 'What does it matter? I'm out of it. No more corrupting the youth of the Athens of the south. I'm retiring. I hope to be free of it all. I just want a quiet life. For once. That's all I ask. I'm certainly not going to be talking to Major about it. Or anyone else. Far too dangerous.'

'But you're talking to me.'

'Yes, I am, aren't I?'

'Why?'

'I must have drunk too much.'

'Is that why you drink?'

'Is what why I drink?'

'To let it out.'

'Clever chap, aren't you?' said Revill. 'You could be right. Yes, it probably relieves the pressure. Partly right, anyway. I suppose since you're working for Major I thought this was a possible line through to him and his masters. Send along a message. I'm retired. I'm not teaching any more. I'm not writing any more. I'm finished. I'm no threat to anyone or anything. I just want to be left alone.'

'You didn't have in mind threatening Dr Major just to make sure.'

'Why would I do that? I'd only get myself in deeper trouble, wouldn't I?'

'Would you?'

'I'd reckon. Anyway, I don't propose to find out.'

'No,' said Plant. 'I don't think you should.'

'Is that an order?' said Revill.

'Friendly advice,' said Plant.

# Twenty-Six

Plant reflected. It was something he could do while he lay in bed. And he felt like lying in bed after the evening with Revill. It had involved too much to drink. Once again. Too much for Plant. He was not sure whether Revill normally consumed that amount. Perhaps he didn't. Perhaps drinking too much had been what had provoked his confidences. Or perhaps he normally did, and it was simply having someone to confide in that had provoked the confidences. Not so much drunk as the release of talking to someone, isolated in Oxford, and not so much Oxford even as all the previous years, the decades of desperation in Sydney. Plant was not sure whether it really mattered what had provoked them. As long as they were true. But could they be?

Out of two absences, Revill had erected an all-encompassing, omnipresent structure. On the basis that Major's books on magic revealed nothing about the practicalities and practice of magic, Revill postulated that Major had kept the real information secret and reported it to some government agency. On the basis of the lack of printed comment on the use of magic by the world's intelligence services, he postulated that magic was a top secret operational strategy. It was an extraordinary logical paradox. The negative made positive. Creation *ex nihilo*. But Plant could see that it might be true.

True! It sounded insane. But that did not prevent it from being true. The point, anyway, was whether Revill believed it was true or not. Maybe he had been persecuted, sidelined, blacklisted. But magic? It sounded crazy. Plant lay there listening to the bells. One of the functions of bells, he had read somewhere, somewhere in his recent researches, was to frighten off evil spirits. In that case Oxford should be a very clear environment. Or perhaps it was a very dark and evil environment, and needed endless bell ringing merely to make it tolerable to inhabit.

Given the choice of Major or Revill, Plant rather preferred Revill. There was no doubt Major appeared successful and Revill did not. That also made Revill more appealing. From what he had experienced of Major, Plant could readily believe he would cast spells on someone if he thought it would be to his advantage. He would probably do pretty well anything. But whether he was doing that, whether it was even possible to do that, Plant had no idea. Nor did he know whether ringing bells really did ward off evil spirits. Could all this be going on in the modern world? But there again, amidst the ringing bells and the grimacing gargoyles and the furled, gowned figures, was he in the modern world?

Do whatever you have to do, Major had instructed him. But he had no idea what that was. Could Major be a practising magician? It was possible. Priests still did exorcisms. Masons performed their rituals. Most newspapers ran an astrology column. But did government agencies use magic? It was something you would never know, of course. And if Major did do magic on Revill, was his use of magic political? He might have been a government man, he might have been researching magic for government agencies, but it didn't necessarily follow he was casting spells on Revill at Her Majesty's behest. It could have been from personal hostility or jealousy. Or it could have been, as Revill suggested, that he needed somebody to practise on. Would a government project practice on innocent bystanders? Yes, probably. But as far as most governments were concerned, a radical like Revill was no innocent, anyway. Maybe it was never official. Maybe governments never did use magic. Or never used it operationally. Plant tried to consider the various possibilities. How much of what Revill said should he accept, how much should he interpret?

He had tried to empty his mind of the magic business and see it as a case of professional jealousy. 'Did you and Major think of each other as rivals in those early years?' he had asked.

'Rivals?'

'Yes, were you competitive?'

'I can't say I was,' said Revill. 'I can't speak for him.'

'Which suggests you think he was.'

'Never thought of him in that way. Never thought that much of him, to be honest.'

'You didn't feel threatened by him?'

'Threatened?' said Revill. He looked at Plant keenly. 'Why would I? Should I have done?'

'That he had a doctorate and you didn't, for instance.'

'Lord, no. Not at all. A PhD is a stigma. The point about Oxford is the gentleman amateur. Effortless superiority. I might not be a gentleman but I'm certainly an amateur. And I used to be effortlessly superior in those days. Hubris, indeed. Have I paid for it? Have I, indeed. But that's the way it was.'

'So no rivalry?'

'Not at all. I suppose he might have felt a bit since he had to slog away for three years getting his BLitt and I never bothered. It could have made him resentful I suppose. But there again, at the age he was sitting around in Bodley casting Anglo-Saxon spells, I was out lecturing to classes of four hundred first-year students. So I didn't have it that easy. Just more fun. While poor old Archie carried on trudging away pot hunting.'

'Pot hunting?'

'Looking for trophies to put on his mantelpiece. Prizes, you know. To prove he wasn't as dim as he felt he was. He'd got his BLitt, for what it was worth, but you had to have something to say before they'd let you do a doctorate at Oxford in those days. Hard fact. Not critical waffle. So first thing he does when he gets to Sydney is enrol in a PhD. Not a shrewd move. Oxford thinks Oxford is the best. You get a BA from Oxford, you don't want to insult it by going and tacking on a PhD from the colonies.'

'Is that how it is?'

'That's how it seemed in those days.'

Plant gave his understanding nod.

'Look,' said Revill, 'A. J. P. Taylor the historian. He took a first at Oxford. Went off to Vienna and did some research and wrote it up as a book. Macmillan offered to publish it if he paid them fifty quid. He couldn't afford it. Namier said, come to Manchester, enrol for a PhD and submit your manuscript and then the local university press will publish it. He did, they did. The book came out, but he never took out the Manchester PhD. Felt it would take the gloss of the Oxford BA.'

'Amazing,' said Plant.

'Believe it or not,' said Revill.

'And now Major's got a job in Oxford. Despite his Sydney doctorate.'

'Yes, well,' said Revill. 'Things change. I guess he was more in tune with the way we live now.'

'And you don't resent it.'

'Why would I resent it?'

'Fame, success, esteem.'

'You think I would want to be part of that world?'

'I don't know.'

'Well,' said Revill, 'I know. And I wouldn't. Despite all its lures.'

'But they are lures?'

'For some.'

'And not for you?'

'A bit late now, wouldn't you think?' said Revill.

*

'I don't expect you to believe me,' Revill had said.

'I can believe anything,' said Plant, who could.

'I know it sounds insane. Some acid crazed fantasy.'

'You took a lot of acid?'

'Not really. I preferred mushrooms.'

'You took a lot of mushrooms?'

'You can't take too many.'

'Really?'

'After a few times you've had enough. You've seen what there is to see. You can't face it any more, really.'

'Is that how you felt?'

Revill laughed. 'I feel that way about a lot of things.'

Plant nodded sympathetically. He could identify with that.

Could it possibly be true? Or maybe partly true? Something to destabilize already paranoid dissidents. Feed them the idea that black magic is being practised on them. And watch them self-destruct.

He could envisage the discussions. He could hear the case being pitched. Appreciating the agency's scepticism. But it's a win-win situation. If magic works, it can be used to drive the targets mad. Incapacitate them. If it doesn't work, no problem. As long as the targets believe it works, that will drive them mad with fear and suspicion just as readily. So fund the project and let its existence be suspected, let the targets suspect it's happening. And whether magic works or not, that would work just as well.

All in the mind. Which was what magic was, of course. All in the mind. The power of negative thinking.

*

Plant took himself for a walk round the Meadows, hoping that something would come to him. Nothing did. Joggers, grey squirrels, other people similarly immersed in thought or reverie passed him by. But nothing came to him. In the afternoon he tried the Parks, and nothing came to him there. Swans, punts, more joggers.

In the early evening he dropped in on Major in his college rooms. Major handed him a sherry. It was the Oxford equivalent of the witching hour, when dons got stuck into their casks of amontillado prior to flitting off to dinner. Plant looked out of the window at the fine view of the graveyard alongside. Tiny bats swooped and soared above the tombs.

'How would you go about doing magic?' he asked.

'What sort of magic?'

'Like, oh, I don't know, casting a spell on someone.'

'Can't imagine that I would.'

'One.'

'One down, more to come?' said Major.

'How would one go about it?'

'Ah. Got some mortal enemies, have you?'

'No, no,' said Plant. 'It's a purely academic question.'

'That's what they all say,' said Major. '"Doctor, I have this friend who has these suppurating sores on his genitals and I said I'd ask on his behalf."' He gave his uningratiating car grille grin.

Plant grinned back.

'What sort of procedures would you use?'

'I wouldn't,' said Major.

'What do people usually do?'

'I imagine people do all sorts of things. Stick pins in little dolls. Write other peoples' names on scraps of paper and stick them on an altar beneath a sheep's head. Chant a few strange words backwards. There's no limit to what people will do.'

'So there's no set pattern?'

'Can't say there is.'

'No standard institutional practice?'

'Doubt it.'

'You don't draw a pentagram on the floor and sit round in robes.'

'I wish you'd stop this "you" business.'

'One,' said Plant.

'Why the sudden interest?'

'I was just wondering how people did it.'

'You sound like a sex-starved adolescent.'

'Does it involve sex rituals?' Plant asked.

'I'm sure it could if that's what you wanted.'

Maybe Lucy came in and participated in unspeakable rites. He tried to imagine what unspeakable rites might be. The drugged maiden on the altar. Drugged matron. Drugged, anyway. It didn't seem that unspeakable.

'Can you just do it on your own? Or do you need a coven of magicians?'

'I imagine you could advertise in the local rag under help wanted.'

'Seriously,' said Plant.

Major gave him a keen look.

'Is this part of the investigation?'

'What investigation?'

'The one I hired you for, squire,' said Major.

'Oh, that investigation.' Plant smiled. Winningly, he hoped. 'No, no, not really.'

'Not really?'

'Not at all.'

'What's that idiot Revill been filling your impressionable head with?'

'Revill?'

'Our suspect.'

'I can't say he's been filling my head with much at all.'

'Can't say or won't say?'

'Nothing to say,' said Plant. 'Why?'

'Aren't you supposed to be grilling him?'

'I'm not sure grilling is the best way to find things out.'

'You seem to be grilling me.'

'No, I was just interested, that's all. How people went about it. Magic.'

'Not the sort of thing they let on to outsiders, I would imagine.'

'But you write about it.'

'Those that do, do; those that don't, write about it.'

It sounded very self-deprecatory. Uncharacteristically so.

'So you don't really know how it's done.'

'One knows the principles,' said Major. 'But the

daily, squalid detail, no. There's an infinity of ways of attempting to manipulate mankind.'

'And they all work?'

'Who's to say?'

'Not you.'

'Not I.'

*

And that was as far as he got. If it was a secret government project, he was never going to find out, anyway. And if he did find out they would bump him off. He tried to reconcile himself to that and leave it alone. Leave it as a possibility and not worry about the details. No hanging off Major's roof and peering in on a gaggle of Foreign and Commonwealth Office types saying the Lord's prayer backwards. No breaking into his rooms and finding the secret staircase behind the bookcase leading down to the ancient Knights Templar's circular chapel beneath the college and hiding beneath the altar as the assembled company intoned 'Get Revill'. No hacking into Major's computer and intuitively deducing the password – abracadabra, what else? – and opening it up to a file of arcane invocations.

The details are unimportant, he told himself. They were not what he was looking for. Indeed, none of it was what he was looking for, was it? He was supposedly looking for the author of the anonymous notes. Investigating the ancient lore of the secret state was not part of his brief. Yet how else was he to find out if Revill was right in his suspicions? Did it matter, anyway, whether Revill was right or crazy? Either way he could have been prompted to send the notes.

His curiosity had been aroused, that was the problem. But curiosity, he told himself, was always a problem. And what would be gained by attempting to satisfy it? More to the point, what would be lost? There are some things that you are never going to know, he reminded himself. And the workings of the secret state are among the most unknowable. And best left that way.

## Twenty-Seven

Plant headed back to his room through the long, grey twilight. A scuttling movement in the corner of the quadrangle attracted his attention and he caught a glimpse of Harbinger emerging from the chapel like a vampire arisen from its tomb. He walked over and saluted him with a 'Good evening'. Harbinger looked up apprehensively, tugging his gown tightly around his chest and waist like a cerement.

'Have you got a moment?' Plant asked him.

'Very few,' said Harbinger. 'The sands of time, you know.'

'I wondered if I could have a word with you about a former student of yours called Revill.'

'Revill?' said Harbinger. 'The man they say I said was one of my best men and I sent him off to Australia and forgot about him?'

'Yes.'

'For the term of his natural life.'

'Yes.'

'You know the original title of the novel was just *His Natural Life*?'

'No,' said Plant, 'I didn't know that.'

'Rather more telling, don't you think? You don't have to see it as a formal sentence. Not a legal punishment. Just the human condition.'

'The Human Condition,' said Plant. 'Isn't that another title?'

'Oh, absolutely, we're good on titles here,' said Harbinger. 'The veritable home of lost allusions.'

'Do you remember him?'

'Whom?'

'Revill.'

'Not especially.'

'He came back here recently.'

'Ah, he escaped the prison island, did he?' said Harbinger.

'He came over on study leave.'

'Well, good for him. From the Chateau d'If to the Iffley road.'

'Was he in political trouble at Oxford?' Plant asked.

'Trouble?'

'Or after?'

'After?'

Harbinger waited, but Plant was an expert at the waiting game. They stood there silent in the gathering gloom. Small bats swooped around in the twilight, chasing late flies and early moths.

'Well, of course if you're political, you're likely to be in trouble, I always say. It's a tautology, really.'

'Was he political?'

'Well,' said Harbinger, 'to quote the young man in question, "Isn't everything political?"'

'I don't know,' said Plant. 'Is it?'

'Well, I don't know about that,' said Harbinger. 'My mind doesn't work in those regions.'

'Were you surprised he never tried to get back?'

'Get back?'

'To Oxford.'

'Oh. A lot of them try to get back. Many call but few are chosen.'

'Did Revill?'

'We already have one Marxist on the faculty,' said Harbinger.

'And you only ever have one?'

'We won't be appointing another in a hurry.'

'Was Revill a Marxist?'

'I'm not sure that's really any of your business,' Harbinger said. 'Unless trouble is your business.'

'That's a fair job description,' said Plant.

Harbinger grunted. He tugged his gown tighter, scowling like a cornered delinquent.

'Has anyone ever come along asking about him?'

'Now that would be telling, wouldn't it?'

'Would it?'

'It would be if I could remember.'

'And can you?'

'Can I what?'

'Remember whether anyone came asking after Revill.'

'Revill?' Harbinger beamed. 'Now who was he?'

'Your student.'

'Oh, there have been so many.'

'So many what?'

'Students, as you call them. Unless you mean chaps asking questions.'

'Have there been a lot of them?'

'A lot of what?'

'Chaps asking questions.'

'What sort of questions?'

'About Revill. Your student.'

'My student?'

'Yes.'

'There have been so many.' He rotated his neck, looking round the twilit quadrangle for ways of escape. 'So many,' he repeated elegiacally. 'How would I remember?'

It was not like interviewing taxi-drivers and bartenders and hotel receptionists and just slipping a tenner into an open palm or a top pocket. Maybe there was a way of getting Harbinger to talk. The magic word. The postcard ripped in two, ready to match the waiting other half. The special handshake. But Plant didn't know it.

'You know Dr Major?'

'Not one of mine.'

'Not one of your what?'

'Not one of my men.'

'But you do know him?'

'The Anglo-Saxon charmer?'

'Yes.'

'Hard to deny it.'

'Do you know him well?'

'I've worked with him. But I wouldn't say I know him well. I give those fellows a wide berth.'

'But you're from the same college.'

'Oh, the same college,' said Harbinger, 'yes, but not the same school.'

'When you say you've worked with him,' said Plant, 'what sort of work was that?'

'Oh, passed the odd charm across to him. Looked up a bit of marginalia here and there.'

'Was this magic?'

'No, not at all, just the results of wide reading. Serendipity, perhaps, but not magic.'

'But you worked on his magic research?'

'Can't say I have,' said Harbinger. 'Can't say I haven't. Can't say anything about it.'

'Because it's classified?'

'Classified?'

'Official Secrets Act.'

'Can't say,' said Harbinger.

And that was it. There didn't seem a lot more to say. Or, to put it the other way, there was a lot more to say but Harbinger was not going to be saying it. An academic lifetime of ambiguity and evasion had made him a grand master at avoiding saying anything. He glanced up at the night sky and flapped the enfolding sleeves of his gown. Somewhere a bell tolled. Everywhere, in fact, bells tolled.

'It's getting dark,' he said. 'I must fly.'

# Twenty-Eight

Plant phoned Major first thing the next morning. First thing after a lot of futile brooding. A civilised first thing.

Lucy answered.

'Oh hello,' she said, 'have you caught any villains yet?'

'Not yet.'

'Oh well,' she said, 'I'm sure you will.'

'Is Dr Major in?'

'Do you see him as a villain?' she asked.

'Do you?'

'Oh, wives can't testify against their husbands, you must know that.'

'They can if they choose to.'

'Is that so?'

'That's so. Are you able to tell me if he's in?'

'Able and willing,' she said.

'And?'

'"Willing for what?" you're supposed to respond.'

'Willing for what?' Plant responded.

'How about a spot of lunch?'

'And Archer?'

'Oh, no, not Archer, he's gone off to Brussels.'

'Brussels? What's he doing there?'

'Picking sprouts, I imagine. Did I hear you say yes to lunch?'

'You didn't, but I will.'

'I'll pick you up,' she said. 'Twelve sharp, college gates.'

*

A Peugeot convertible stood on double yellow lines outside the college. She lowered the roof and drove up the Woodstock road and out of Oxford.

'We'll go to the Trout,' she said. 'It's terribly touristy, of course, which makes it rather vulgar and déclassé in the eyes of the elite, but we Australians don't mind that, do we? Our natural element, as Archer puts it.'

They sat outside beside the river, amidst the tourists and the peacocks.

'I'll have a cider,' she said. 'If they say white wine isn't alcoholic, then cider must be positively alcohol negative, wouldn't you say?'

'No.'

'Well I would. And do,' she said. 'So a cider for me.'

'So why not?' said Plant.

He fetched cider for both of them. And smoked salmon sandwiches for Lucy and a ploughman's lunch for himself. It added a bucolic feel to things.

'Here's to country pleasures,' as Lucy put it.

They touched glasses.

'At least no one will see us here,' she said. 'That's the good thing about tourists. They frighten off the locals. Sort of place they'd never be seen dead in.'

'Who?'

'The people who won't see us here.'

'And you don't want to be seen with me?'

She put her hand on his.

'Oh, Plant,' she said.

'Yes?' said Plant.

She giggled.

'Nothing personal,' she said. 'In fact, I think you're perfectly presentable. For what you are and what's required. But it's a horrid, gossipy little town and I don't want tales getting back to Archer. I get enough tales getting back to me.'

'What sort of tales?'

'You're still pursuing your inquiries, are you?' she said.

'Uh-huh.'

'Any success?'

'Not really.'

'Are you going to tell me what these inquiries are about?'

'That's for your husband.'

'Ah, my husband,' she said.

She produced her silver cigarette case, sprung it open, held it out to Plant. He shook his head.

'Chicken,' she said.

She lit up a joint and inhaled deeply and then blew the smoke across at him. Plant took the opportunity of a bit of passive smoking.

'You're allowed to smoke outdoors,' she said. 'At the moment, anyway.'

'But not dope.'

'It's pretty well decriminalised now,' she said.

He could feel himself weakening and he could feel Lucy seeing it.

'Sure you won't have one? At least then we won't be passing numbers across to each other in a deeply suspicious way.'

'All right,' said Plant.

'That's better,' she said. 'I thought you'd come round. Do you always come round in the end, Plant?'

'It depends.'

'Well, it would, wouldn't it?'

The peacocks shrieked their alarming cry. Children hurled bits of sandwiches into the river to feed the fish. Plant tried to think of questions to ask to pursue his inquiries in the surreal, sunny ordinariness of the afternoon, but none came to him.

'Tell me about your husband,' he said.

'Archer?' she said.

'Yes, Archer.'

'Poor Archer, he married me because he thought I was landed property. But the banks own most of it. And an Australian squatter's daughter is not quite the county type he really wanted. Alas. Never presented at court. But there we are. Got the acres and I can do the curtseys. They love that, your lower class English. They love to think they can fuck landed property.'

'Is Archer like that?'

'Oh yes. All the English are. Paul Revill. All of them. Probably the only thing that gets them up.'

'Are we speaking from experience here?'

'About Archer? Well, I am married to him.'

'About Revill?'

'I'm just a country girl, Plant. And it was all a long time ago and in another country.'

'What about recently?'

'Recently?'

'Paul Revill.'

'Oh, recently.' She considered for a moment. 'What are you doing this afternoon, Plant?'

'Nothing.'

'You're sure?'

'Sure.'

She looked him in the eye.

'Feel like a roll in the hay?'

'Yes,' he said. 'But I make it a rule not to sleep with clients' wives.'

'How boring.'

'Just self-preservation.'

'Well, at least you don't claim it's ethical. How about ex-clients' wives?'

'Maybe.'

'Then you'll just have to pull your finger out and get the case solved, won't you?'

'I guess so.'

'Or I'll have to get rid of Archer.'

It was Plant who did the looking straight in the eye this time.

She put her hand on his wrist and smiled at him, enchantingly.

*

Plant was back sitting happily at his window, looking out at the medieval scene below. A watery sun shone on the geraniums, deep red against the soft golden glow of the college walls. All seemed pretty well with the world. And then Archer breezed in.

'How's the investigation?' he asked.

'So so,' said Plant.

'I'm not paying you to admire the view,' said Archer.

'I was cerebrating.'

'Celebrating what?'

'Deep in thought.'

'How about some action?' Archer suggested.

'What do you feel would be appropriate?'

'You're the investigator.'

'I am,' Plant agreed.

'How about putting a tail on Revill?'

'What, and watching to see if he goes to a mail box?'

'Or a female box,' said Archer, in his bright and chipper morning mode, all glistening teeth and gleaming gold spectacle frames.

'If you insist,' said Plant.

'I do indeed.'

'Have you got his address?'

'I'll ask the wife.'

*

Surveillance was not that easy. It would have been easier in a car, sitting comfortably behind tinted windows, listening to the radio and sucking on the varieties of confectionary the English so enjoyed. What the English called sweets and the Australians lollies and Americans candy. But Revill did not have a car in England. Nor did Plant. Anyway a car would have been a nightmare in the Oxford traffic snarls. But lounging around the streets was a problem. There were too many twitching lace curtains, too many concerned citizens eager to report pædophiles and terrorists and insurgents and drug dealers. He strolled down to where Revill had his flat and round the block and back onto the Iffley road. He considered renting a bicycle but rejected the idea as too grotesque. He was not sure he remembered how to ride a bicycle. And there was no way he was going to spend the morning in the grimy gutters, pretending to mend a puncture or fix a broken chain. He found a newsagent and bought a paper. The *Daily Telegraph*. Now the other broadsheets had gone tabloid it was the only one to hide behind. He felt ridiculously conspicuous. But at least it was Oxford and there was no shortage of the ridiculous or the conspicuous. Undergraduates with flowing hair and flowing gowns, horrid little buggers with carnations in their velvet jackets, anorexic young ladies in tights on ancient bicycles, joggers in jogging gear, rowers in white shorts and white sweaters, dons dressed up for a day of donning around, derelicts preying on the rich and privileged, cross-dressers, thespians, loud-voiced American tourists in check trousers and quieter Japanese tourists in blue suits.

Some time after ten thirty Revill emerged and made his weary way along the pavements. He crossed over Magdalen Bridge and sauntered up Longwall, hesitated outside the King's Arms but went on past, turned up South Parks road. Plant kept him in sight and followed. Revill was not one to look round. Think of it as exercise, Plant told himself. People pay good money to go to gyms to get this sort of circulation-improving activity. Or tourism, he tried, enjoy the feel of old Oxford, think of the centuries of study and discovery, or the æons of frivolity and futility that these old walls and poky windows have concealed.

Revill passed by the entrance to the Parks; he certainly was not out for health-giving exercise or a leisurely stroll with fond memories. He headed on up to Norham Gardens, across into the Banbury road, and northward, ever northward, like an Arctic goose or a homing pigeon. Plant knew where they were headed, not even a guess, a certainty. On they went. Eventually Revill turned into the driveway, crunched across the gravel, rang the bell. Lucy appeared in a morning halo of golden locks and a robe. She pecked him on the cheek and put an arm around him and drew him inside.

Plant took a bus back into town. Short of installing a listening device in the house there was little more he could do. He could see no point in hanging around the street, and he had done quite enough walking. He rewarded himself for all the exercise by calling in at the King's Arms for an early lunch: a pint or two of

Flowers and a slice of vegetable pie. He sat there alone and read his *Telegraph*, catching up on the latest doings of pædophiles and terrorists and insurgents and drug dealers. Funny old world, he reflected, Lucy's golden locks hovering in his consciousness there like a genie escaped from a bottle.

## Twenty-Nine

Lucy came round in a flurry, distraught, awry.

'It's terrible,' she said. 'You've heard?'

'Heard what?'

'About Paul.'

'Paul?'

'Paul Revill.'

'No,' said Plant.

But he knew. He knew it from the fear in her eyes and the aura of shock she carried.

'He's dead,' she said.

'Dead?'

'We just got phoned up. They said he was dead.'

'How?'

'They didn't say.'

'Why did they phone you?'

'They phoned Archer.'

'Why?'

'They asked him to go and identify the body.'

'Why Archer?'

'There was no one else who knew him. If Archer hadn't gone they would have had to fly somebody out from Australia.'

'He was English, though, wasn't he?'

'Yes. But he had no one left alive. No relatives.' She broke up. 'He was totally alone.'

He waited for a while while she wept, then pushed on.

'How did they know Archer knew him?'

'Through the college, I suppose.'

'I didn't know he had anything to do with the college.'

'Oh, yes. He'd dined at High Table. That was the last anyone saw him alive.'

'High Table?' Plant asked. 'Did Archer invite him?'

'I shouldn't think so. The bursar's secretary phoned up Archer for his address to invite him so I gave it them. But I imagine if Archer had invited him he would have known. Or asked me. Maybe it was his old tutor.'

'Harbinger? He couldn't even remember who Revill was.'

'That's just an act,' she said.

'So if Harbinger invited him, why wasn't he asked to identify the body?'

'Because he'd have put on his usual act about not remembering who they meant, I expect.'

Plant could believe it. It was all looking like one big act, Harbinger, Archer, High Table, maybe Lucy too.

'So who told you he was dead?' he asked

'The police.'

'The police? Why the police?'

She looked at him wide-eyed. Wet-eyed but wide-eyed.

'I don't know. I hadn't thought. You don't mean?'

She left if unexpressed, inexpressible.

'It mightn't mean anything,' Plant said.

'Oh God, you don't think he was murdered?'

'Why should I think that?'

'Why else would the police be involved?'

'Probably just routine,' said Plant, 'if they have to have a post-mortem.'

'Do you think?'

'I don't know,' said Plant. 'Why would he have been murdered?'

She looked at him in puzzlement.

'It could have been natural causes. Heart attack. Stroke. He smoked and drank a fair bit.'

'There was nothing wrong with him,' she said. 'He wasn't sick.'

'Things can just happen.

'No,' she said.

'Or it could be accidental. Or suicide.'

'Paul would never have killed himself.'

'So who would have wanted to kill him?' Plant asked.

'I don't know,' she said. 'I don't know that anyone did.'

'But you think he might have been?'

'I don't know.'

'Did he say anything?'

'Say anything? When?'

'When you talked to him.'

'I hadn't ...'

She tailed off.

'Hadn't what?'

'I didn't see him that often.'

'But you did see him.'

'Once or twice,' she said.

'What about?'

'Not about anything. I just happened to see him, that's all.'

'Happened.'

'Oh, the first time I bumped into him in the street, then he came to dinner, which was a disaster, and then I saw him one afternoon after that.'

'Just the one.'

'Maybe a couple of times, I don't remember.'

Plant looked at her.

'Why are you looking at me like that?'

'No reason. It's just the way I look.'

'No it isn't. It's a look you use.'

'Maybe.'

'There's no need to lie to me,' she said.

Plant smiled.

'The sentiments are mutual.'

'Are you saying I'm lying?'

He shook his head. 'You've hardly said anything,' he said, 'how could you be? A bit economical with the truth, perhaps.'

'That's outrageous.'

'Did he say he was worried someone might kill him,' Plant asked, 'the couple of times you met?'

'Why should he?'

'Only if he was worried about it.'

'I don't know what to do,' she said.

'In relation to what?'

'I don't know,' she said. 'It's all such a shock.'

287

'What did your husband say?'

'Archer? Why should he say anything?'

'Didn't he express shock? Surprise? Sorrow, even?'

'Archer?' she said.

'He doesn't express emotions?'

'He just said "Typical".'

'Typical?'

'Yes.'

'And what did that mean?'

'I've no idea. It's just one of his expressions.'

'He uses it regularly?'

'Yes.'

'But you don't know what it means.'

'It means, "What would you expect?" It's an expression of contempt, like most of his expressions. It's the sort of thing the English say all the time.'

'It's typical of them, you'd say.'

'Yes,' she said. 'I would.'

She looked round his room. There was not a lot to look at.

'I have to have a drink,' she said.

'I don't really have anything,' said Plant. 'We could go to the King's Arms.'

'Not there,' she said.

'Because Revill drank there?'

'Did he?'

'Didn't you know?'

'I think he drank at a lot of places,' she said. 'Like me.' She opened the door. 'Let's go,' she said. 'I'll show you somewhere different.'

'Did Revill drink there too? Where we're going?'

'You want to talk to me, you keep your insinuations to yourself.'

'Do I want to talk to you?'

'If you know what's best for you.'

'Oh, nothing but the best,' said Plant.

'I am not in the mood for facetiousness.'

'Sorry,' said Plant. 'It's just the way I am.'

'Always?'

'No, just sometimes.'

'I thought you might have been trying to cheer me up.'

'Cheer you up?' said Plant, the chivalrous, as befitted the traditions of his occupation. Had that been what he was doing? Surely not. 'Why would I be trying to cheer you up?' he asked, instead of taking credit for being a caring, if crass, sort of chap. Now he had no credit. And he had denied any suggestions of chivalry.

# Thirty

Once again the Peugeot convertible was parked on double yellow lines outside the college. Once again she lowered the roof and drove up the Woodstock road and out of Oxford. They passed pub after pub.

'I thought you wanted a drink,' Plant said.

'I needed to get out,' she said. 'I need some air.'

It was there all around them, far too much of it in Plant's opinion, but he sank deeper into the passenger seat and said nothing. They hurtled on past the airfield, where light aircraft came low over the road, practising take-offs and landings. He felt even more vulnerable to them without a roof.

'We can go to Blenheim. I bet you haven't done that.'

'No, I haven't.'

'You have to,' she said.

'Do I?'

'I'll take you round the park. We can have a drink after.'

'Whatever you say,' said Plant. He was becoming an expert on parks.

*

They walked through the archway into the grounds of Blenheim palace. Lucy explained how the trees represented the disposition of the British and French troops at the battle of Blenheim. There was no one in sight, just the trees rooted to the soil, the engagement endlessly deferred, commemorated in the park given to Marlborough for the victory of 1704.

'"But what good came of it, at last?"

'Said little Peterkin.

'"Ah, that I cannot tell," said he,

'"But 'twas a famous victory."

'It's a poem by Southey,' she said. 'Paul quoted it at me when I brought him here. Everything was an excuse for a political education with him.'

Her cheeks were pink, her eyes and lips glistened. It could have been the open car or the chill air, or it could have been rouge and lip-gloss. Or it could have been booze and dope and fear.

'I don't know if I should tell you this,' she said.

'Go on.'

'He told me these terrible things.'

They walked along the landscaped paths, the palace crouched on the rise behind them.

'I knew Archer didn't really like him. He'd joke about him. Dismiss him. But there was an always an edge about it. Too much of an edge if you've really dismissed someone.'

She ferreted through her bag and found her cigarette-case and lighter. She tapped a smoke out for herself. Plant refused. They stood there as she struggled to light it in the wind.

'I always thought it was because we'd had a scene. Just a brief one. Nothing much. Sneeze and you'd probably miss it.' She gave her hollow laugh. 'Paul seemed to have done.'

'How long?'

'Oh, I don't know,' she said. 'A couple of nights. A couple of weeks. A long weekend. It was ages ago. I have no bloody idea. Do you keep a record of everyone you've ever slept with and how many times you did it?'

Plant shrugged.

'Do you?' she insisted.

'I sort of remember.'

'Yes, you would,' she said scornfully. 'You probably keep a list too. All tabulated. Bloody men. They're either insanely jealous or they don't remember a thing.'

Plant tried the impassive look.

'I don't know how long it lasted. Nor how many times I slept with him. I just know I did. At some point.'

'And your husband was unhappy about that?'

'Probably not. But who knows, who knows?' she said. 'Anyway, it was before Archer and I were on together.'

'And since?'

'None of your bloody business.'

'So your husband didn't like Revill.'

'No,' she said. 'But that wasn't necessarily because of me.'

'What was it because of?'

'That's what I don't know,' she said. 'If I knew, I'd say. I just know there was something there.'

'And it wasn't friendship.'

'You're joking,' she said.

'But not downright hostility.'

'It was pretty hostile the night he came to dinner,' she said.

'So what were the terrible things Revill told you?'

'You won't believe me even if I tell you.'

'Try me.'

'No,' she said. 'It sounds too ridiculous.'

'And is it ridiculous?'

She looked at him. Biting her lip. There was anguish in her eyes. Or craziness. Desperation.

'I went round to see him one afternoon in that horrid room he was staying in. We had a couple of joints and he got really stoned and started raving on, the way people used to do. He said he hadn't smoked dope for ages. It affects you like that for a while, then you get used to it.'

'And?'

'He said Archer had been doing black magic on him.'

Plant nodded.

'Well?' she said.

Plant said nothing. There was a time for speaking and a time for keeping silent.

'I can't believe it,' she said. 'Here am I, plucking up the courage to tell you, and you don't even react. And you're not even fucking surprised.'

She burst into tears, sobbing there.

'Don't touch me,' she shrieked, as he moved towards her.

'I can't believe it,' she said.

'Believe what?'

'Any of it,' she said.

'I'm not sure I can,' said Plant.

'It's true,' she said. 'He went on for ages. He swore me to secrecy. He said no one must ever know, it was too dangerous. They'd kill him if they found out he knew.'

'What else did he say?'

'He said it was a secret government programme. So secret they'd kill to keep it that way. I don't know why he told me.'

'He must have needed someone to talk to about it.'

'Well, he got what he wanted,' she said.

'Maybe,' said Plant.

'What do you mean?'

'I'm not sure he wanted to be dead.'

She was crying again, her eyes full of terror.

'Did you tell your husband?' Plant asked.

'I asked him if it was true,' she said.

'Was that wise?'

She looked at him in contempt, her eyes brimming with tears, her throat strained, her voice strangulated.

'Fucking brilliant,' she said.

'You think it might have got him killed?' Plant asked.

Her face was frozen in the chill wind, her expression fixed in horror. Her lips were open but no words came through them. It was as if she had seen the Gorgon. They walked in silence. The wind cut across the artificial lake. Water birds paddled in silence beside the withered sedge.

'Say something, damn you,' she said.

'I don't know what to say,' he said.

'So who killed him?'

'We don't know that anyone did at the moment. It could have been natural causes. It could have been accidental.'

'How could it have been accidental?'

'Drugs, maybe.'

'He didn't do those sorts of drugs.'

'Didn't he?'

'No.'

'You sound very certain.'

'I am.'

'Maybe it was suicide.'

'He would never have killed himself.'

'You're sure of that?'

'He was too angry about Archer,' she said.

'Too angry to kill himself?'

'Yes. He was determined to get Archer somehow. He was sure Archer had ruined his career. He wanted to get even. Or something. Expose him. Flush him out. Make him run. I don't know what he wanted. He didn't say. He just went on and on about Archer and magic and Archer working for the secret services.'

'Did you believe him?'

She looked at him, her eyes red-rimmed, her nose and cheeks pink.

'Oh yes,' she said. 'I could believe him.'

'Why?'

'Why? Don't you believe it?'

'I don't know,' said Plant.

'Well, I do.'

'For certain?'

'For certain.'

'How?'

'Because Archer told me.'

'Archer told you he was practising black magic on Revill?'

'No, not that,' she said. 'He never gave me any details, obviously. He just said he was doing government work.'

'Government work.'

'Then he put his finger to the side of his nose in that sickening gesture he uses.'

'Meaning what?'

'Meaning it's a secret. "Nuff said," as he always says.'

'And that was it?'

'He shouldn't have told me even that,' he said. 'He made me swear not to repeat it.'

'But you have.'

She ignored that as self-evident.

'So why did he tell you?'

'Because he was always sneaking off to places without telling me where he was going. Because I never knew what he was doing. I thought he was screwing someone. We had a row about it. He said he had a secret life but it was not what I thought it was. He said

it was secret work for the government and swore me to silence.'

'Did you believe him?'

'Not especially. I certainly never thought it was magic. I've no idea whether he believed in magic or not. I sort of assumed it was just something he came up with to get research funding from whoever there was who might provide funds. Belief wasn't an issue.'

'But you believed him when he said he was doing secret work for the government.'

'Up to a point. I never knew exactly what it was he was supposed to be doing. I thought he was probably just spotting talent, you know, likely students, chatting to foreigners. I still think he was screwing his students. Or shop girls. Or something. So no, if you want to know, no, I didn't necessarily believe him. He might have been doing secret work, why should I care? It was a convenient story for doing what he always did, which was lie. It could have been another lie or it could have been the truth. It didn't really make any difference.'

'So what did you think when Revill told you?'

'I didn't think anything.'

'You believed him?'

She puckered her lips.

'You believed him enough to tell your husband.'

'Oh, Archer was being a pain. He was going on about things. So I just lobbed it into the conversation.'

'And what was his reaction?'

'What do you think his reaction was? You think he

got down on his knees and made a full and contrite confession?'

'Probably not.'

'He tapped the side of his nose with his finger,' she said. 'What else would he do?'

'And you left it at that?'

'Oh, I probably poured myself a drink. Or Archer made a phone call and said he had to go out. So I probably rolled a smoke and forgot all about it. That's what I usually do with Archer. Have a smoke and forget all about him. Which is what I propose to do now.'

She produced her silver cigarette case and lighter from her bag again. They sat on a fallen log and shared the joint. The wind lost its chill and the palace shone golden on the ridge and the lake reflected a cleared patch of blue sky, and everything was warm and vibrant and pulsating with the circumambient nature, the chlorophyll pulsing through the grass and the leaves, the earthworms writhing beneath the turf, the ducks and moorhens and coots clucking with more than contentment. And slowly the paranoia and the conspiracies opened out like daisies opening before the dawn sun, or mushrooms rising up as the thunder clouds gathered, and a helicopter throbbed along the horizon.

# Thirty-One

Plant hired a car and drove north-west. He would bill it to Major and hope for the best. It could hardly be more expensive than taking a train. Especially if you wanted to take a train that would get you anywhere in time to do anything with the day. He would have liked the BMW, or the Jaguar, why not, but there was always the possibility that Major would refuse to cover the bill. He went for the bottom of the line.

'Maybe a Siesta,' he said.

Or an Echo. Or a Plangent Cry.

The girl winked at him. 'Sweet dreams,' she said.

He was not sure how he was going to justify what he was doing. He could try the 'tying up loose ends' ploy, but he was not sure Major was going to care about loose ends. He focused his mind on getting out of Oxford before Major decided that with Revill dead there might not be any more anonymous notes and he could dispense with Plant's services. He turned off the road to look at the Rollright Stones on the way. A circle of eroded stumps on a high ridge. The old religion? Ancient magic? Ritual sacrifice? The stones told him nothing. He got back in the car and headed across the Cotswolds.

He still had no information on what had happened to Revill. Natural causes? Heart attack? Stroke? Revill had not struck him as the suicidal type. He seemed no more depressed than most academics Plant had encountered. If anything, he seemed to have come to terms with his depression and made it into a way of life, rationalised it into a social analysis and a political cause. Was that the way ritual sacrifice lay? Or removal with extreme prejudice? Is that what it was, if it wasn't natural causes or suicide? And if so, who would have done it? Who would have wanted it done? The possible answers were there but he left them to drift beneath the surface. They would emerge. In the meantime he took a quick detour through Blockley, because he remembered from his recent reading that Edward Kelly told Dr Dee that was where he had discovered the alchemical powders of transmutation, and then on through Chipping Norton where Kelly had found his wife. Edward Kelly, 'a perfect magician'. He switched on the car radio. Ella Fitzgerald singing 'That Old Black Magic'. He changed channels. Barry Manilow's 'Can it Be Magic?' He found a classical station. *The Magic Flute*. It was everywhere. Inescapable. It permeated the entire culture. And yet no one believed in it. Or did they?

At least he was out of Oxford. Major would not be able to find him and take him off the case for a couple of days. And there was nothing he could do in Oxford. No way would the local police welcome him and take him around with them on their inquiries. No way at all.

*

Plant trawled his way through the pubs, exhibiting his Australianness, trying to strike up conversations. It took a while but eventually he found what he wanted.

'Do we know someone called Revill who went to Australia?' Nell said. She laughed. 'If we kept a list of everyone who'd been transported to Australia we'd never get anything done.'

'Was he the fellow who went out to govern New South Wales?' Will asked. He loomed over the bar, wreathed in menacing smiles and beer fumes.

'He was back here recently,' said Plant.

'Here as in Great Britain or here as in this hostelry?' Will asked.

'I'm not sure,' said Plant.

'Makes it hard,' said Will.

'What's he done?' Nell asked.

'I'm afraid he's dead.'

'Dead?' said Nell. 'What happened?'

'We don't know.'

'Was it an accident?'

'It might have been.'

'I don't believe it,' said Nell.

'Somebody bump him off, did they?' said Will.

'Or suicide.'

'Not a chance,' said Will.

'So you did know him?'

'Well, I suppose if he's dead, it can't hurt him to admit it,' said Will.

'But you didn't see him as the suicidal type?' Plant said.

'Suicide? Not a hope. He was far too full of himself. Why would he kill himself? He'd got early retirement and a pension. All he ever wanted. Surprised he didn't go into the army and get out after twenty-two years.'

'He was a pacifist,' said Nell.

'That wouldn't have stopped him. He could have gone in as a chaplain.'

'Was he religious?'

Nell laughed. 'Not that I ever noticed.'

'Certainly not prone to guilt and self-laceration and remorse and suicide,' said Will. 'Which is not to say he shouldn't have been.'

'He wasn't depressed?'

'Of course he was,' said Nell, 'he was always depressed.'

'Part of his charm,' said Will. 'Switched it on for the ladies. Worked like a treat. "Let me tell you my sad story."'

'Is that so?' said Plant.

'Ask Nell, if you don't believe me.'

'He believes you,' said Nell.

'How's he supposed to have done it?' Will asked. 'An overdose?'

'I can believe that,' said Will. 'He'd take anything. Insatiable, I think is the word.' He tried it again. 'Insatiable. Yes. I think that about expresses it.'

'So it could have been accidental.'

'I don't know,' said Will. 'Why are you asking me?'

'Had he ever overdosed before?'

'Not so it had any effect,' said Will. 'Constitution of an ox.'

'I wouldn't have thought that,' said Plant.

'Looks are deceptive,' said Will. 'You look at me, you think, ah, the original iron and steel man. Whereas in fact I'm your original sensitive. Now Revill, he looked like a wet weekend, but he was as tough as depleted uranium inside. Take anything and bounce back for more.'

'Is that so?'

'Are you doubting my word?'

'No.'

'Because you shouldn't. I may be soft and gentle inside …'

'But on the surface he's all brute, aren't you dear?'

'If you say so, darling.'

'So what's your interest?' said Nell. 'Have you come to track down his killer?'

'I don't know that he was killed,' said Plant.

'He had enough enemies,' said Will.

'Did he?'

'The entire academic community and the secret services of the world, to hear him talk.'

'Before we get onto that,' said Nell, 'what's your interest?'

'Another pint of Directors, I should imagine,' said Will.

Plant said yes, he would have another pint and could he buy them a drink?

Yes, he could, said Will, with pleasure, any time and he'd have a pint of the same.

'Yes, when you've said what your interest is,' said Nell.

'Did he think someone was trying to kill him?' Plant asked.

Nell stood there impassively, the classic barmaid stance, how to outface a customer, waiting.

'That's my interest,' Plant said. 'Whether it was natural causes or whether it was accidental or whether it was suicide or whether someone might have killed him.'

'Who are you working for?' Nell asked.

'You're one of them Australians, too, aren't you?' said Will. 'Can tell it by your accent. I knew there was something funny.'

'Yes,' said Plant.

'You knew old Revill Down Under then, did you?' said Will.

'I was asking him a question dear,' said Nell.

'Sorry, dear,' said Will. 'Did you get that? She's asking you a question, Mr –, what did you say your name was?'

'He didn't,' said Nell.

'Plant,' said Plant.

'Well, he has now,' said Will.

'He still hasn't said who he's working for,' Nell said.

'No more he has,' said Will.

'It's confidential,' said Plant.

'Well, it would be, wouldn't it?' said Nell.

'How do we know you're not some sort of confidence man, then?' Will asked.

'You don't.'

'Makes it difficult,' said Will.

'One of Revill's former colleagues has been receiving anonymous letters.'

'And you met Revill in the course of your inquiries,' said Will.

'Yes.'

'Can't imagine him sending anything anonymous,' said Will. 'He always liked the sight and sound of his name too much for that. As for suicide, no, I can't see it. He'd got himself a good retirement package, got a new life to start. He was nosing around here looking for a new life, wasn't he, Nell?'

'If you say so.'

'Oh,' he said. 'Are you saying he was nosing around looking for his old life again? Treacherous little sod. Asking you to run off with him again, was he?'

'No such luck,' said Nell.

'Disappointed, darling?'

'It'll come,' she said. 'One day someone will ask and I'll be gone. You'll see. Quick as a flash.'

'If it's that quick I probably won't see,' said Will.

'He said he'd thought of buying a place here,' said Plant.

'And thought better of it ten minutes later,' said Nell. 'Who would want to buy here? What is there here?'

'Isn't it where he came from?'

'And where he couldn't wait to get out of,' said Nell. 'He'd have been mad to come back.'

'Of course, he could have been mad,' said Will. 'He always showed signs of incipient insanity to me.'

'There was nothing mad about Revill,' said Nell. 'He was shrewd and calculating.'

'Hard to see why he wasn't more successful in that case,' said Will. 'Though maybe he was. Landed himself an easy job. No heavy lifting. Relieved of most of his teaching because of his commie views. Not trusted to do any administration. Given early retirement to get rid of him. Pensioned off for the rest of his life. Seems like a pretty good deal, when you think about it. Maybe he was as shrewd and calculating as the dear wife says. Sort of thing she'd know about, too. Unlike simple souls like myself.'

'He seemed to think he was blacklisted.'

'Well, I imagine he was,' said Will. 'I mean, if you sit around reading what you like and writing what you like, you're bound to get into trouble in the end. It's just the way he was. I don't blame him. If anyone, I blame the people who gave him the job. They shouldn't let left-wing types like him into the universities. They're only going to cause trouble and upset people. Cause themselves trouble. He complained about being blacklisted and all that, but he complained about everything. Just a natural moaner. The original whingeing Pom, as you people call them. And you've got a point, I'll give you that. They're never satisfied. Always agin the government. We get them in here all the time. Bunch of wankers. Just like Revill. He moaned about how they took his teaching away from him, but it would have killed him having to do a full load.'

'Something killed him,' said Plant.

'Well, it wouldn't have been doing a full load,' said Will. He scratched his shaven head reflectively and had a reflective drink of his beer. 'Mind you, come to think of it, you never can tell. These types who seem so tough, seem to have all these inner resources, when they go they go. In no time. I've seen it before. Put them in a combat situation and they turn to water. Even in a non-combat situation. You'd think they don't have a care in the world, they've got such thick skins nothing can ever get through to them and then one day, pow, there they are, a few pills or a hose to the exhaust pipe and they're gone, never as much as a good-bye. When they decide to do it, they don't mess around, they just do it.'

'You think Revill was like that?'

'Could be,' said Will. 'Not impossible. Who's to tell?'

'Certainly not you,' Nell said.

'Which of us did she mean?' Will asked. 'Or does she mean both of us? Who can ever tell anything?' He drank some more of his Directors bitter and shook his head slowly.

'Did he ever talk about magic?' Plant asked.

'Magic?' said Will. 'Better ask the old witch about that. More in her line.'

'Magic?' said Nell. She gave a cackle. 'Cross my palm with silver and I'll read your fortune? That sort of stuff?'

'More like spells,' said Plant.

'Love philtres?' said Nell. 'We do a nice line in them. Want me to mix you one up?'

'They don't work on the wife,' said Will. 'She's become immune. Just in case you were getting ideas.'

'Was he into love philtres?'

'Him, or that horrible colleague of his?' Will asked.

'Which colleague was that?'

'Oh, the fellow who used to work with him Down Under. He came round here asking about him. The magician,' said Will.

'He was no magician,' said Nell. 'He was just another lecturer.'

'They're all lecherers,' said Will. 'But this one was interested in magic. The wizard of Oz.'

'He was interested in anything,' said Nell.

'That's true,' said Will. 'He was certainly interested in you. I put it down to your bewitching qualities. But he even seemed interested in Revill, which seemed pretty interesting in itself, seeing Revill was such an uninteresting sort of person.'

'What sort of interest?' Plant asked.

'Much like yours,' said Nell.

'Nosey,' said Will, 'is what she means.'

'What did he want to know?'

'He didn't say,' she said. 'He just used to ask about Revill. What he used to be like, who his friends were, what he talked about. He'd drop by once in a while and ask if we'd heard from him.'

'Had you?'

'You're joking.'

'Why did he come here?'

'For a drink, I'd imagine,' said Will.

'He claimed he was checking out the local settings of Dennis Wheatley novels,' said Nell. 'And thought he'd look in.'

'How did he know you knew Revill?'

Will scratched his head. 'Can't imagine. Maybe Revill told him to look up the wife when he came back, the way these lads do. "If you're looking for a good time, why don't you look up old Nell?" That sort of thing, I imagine.'

'I see,' said Plant.

'And now you're going to ask, "Did she?"'

'Did she what?'

'Give him a good time.'

Will looked expectantly from behind the bar. He looked like he was waiting for one wrong move from Plant, one misplaced word, one excuse for mayhem.

'What was his name?' Plant asked.

'Ford Prefect,' said Will. 'Or was it Morris Minor?'

'Archer Major?'

'Something like that. We might have one of his books somewhere, it would be on that. He tried to sell it me at a discount price. Bunch of cheapskates, these fellows. I said I'd wait till it was remaindered, but Nell might have bought it when I had my back turned.'

'I threw it out,' she said.

'Why was that?' Plant asked.

'It was rubbish. Useless,' she said.

'What, no spells to restore a husband's head of hair?'

311

Will asked.

'No spells. No charms. Waste of money. I could do better myself.'

'And she does,' said Will. 'She's not so good on the hair restoratives. But come the full moon, she's out there, flying round the cathedral tower.'

'Really?' said Plant.

'You'd better believe it,' said Will.

Nell gave her eldritch cackle.

'So who was getting the anonymous letters?' Will asked.

'Major,' said Plant.

'Major?'

'The fellow who wrote the book on magic.'

'Fancy that,' said Will. 'Writing his own fan mail, was he?'

# Thirty-Two

Plant sat in his room listening to the sounds of an Oxford night. Bells. More bells. Drunken revelry from drunken students. He sat there listening because there was no way to drown it out. No radio, no television, no CD player, no computer. It was as if he had been transported back a century or more. He stood at his window and looked at what he could see of it. The silent moonlight picking out the Gothic spires and towers and crenellations. The ancient quadrangle. The steep slate roof. Furled, gowned figures on the flagstone paths, their footsteps clattering and echoing till they were swallowed up by one of the archways or entered one of the staircases. One strode purposefully towards Plant's staircase and trod heavily up the wooden stairs. Then came the knocking at the door.

Plant opened it and Major stood there, gowned and pink cheeked.

'I want to talk to you,' Major said.

'Come in.'

'Not here,' said Major.

'Where then?'

'Follow me,' said Major.

They walked down the staircase and through the quadrangle, into another, beneath a tunnel-like archway and up a short flight of stone steps. Major took out his keys and opened an ancient, heavy, iron-studded door. The light from the tunnel revealed high ranks of dark wooden shelves reaching up towards the ceiling, forming a series of bays down each side of the room.

'Wait,' said Major.

He walked down the length of the library, looking into the bays each side of him. At the end he turned and came back, stopping halfway and switching on a reading light in one of the bays. It had an ancient metal shade and was fixed a foot above the desk.

'This should do,' he said.

He vanished into the bay and Plant heard the sound of chairs being moved.

'Well come on down,' Major snapped.

I should have stuffed a blunt object in my pocket, Plant reflected. A knuckleduster at least. He looked at the library shelves. Maybe one of the heavy tomes would do. Ancient folio volumes bound in ancient leather. If he could get one off the shelf surreptitiously and swing it with sufficient force, it should quell any opponent. But how to get it off the shelf? The bigger volumes must have weighed several kilograms. There was no chance to carry one unobserved. While the smaller ones would not have sufficient weight. Octavos and duodecimos. He remembered the terms from some ancient memory, savoured them, and the smell of old bindings, vellum and rag paper, lengthy commentaries on *Leviticus* and *Revelation*.

If Revill were right and Major had security connections, then not wanting to talk in a room that might be bugged might explain it all. And if he were on the security payroll they were probably bugging him routinely to make sure he was still on their side, and bugging any room he put a research assistant in. It could be as simple and sensible as that. And not a way of luring him to his doom. Not the body in the library episode. It was no doubt too late at night to walk through the Parks or the Meadows. And too cold. Not that it was warm in the library.

'Come on down, what are you up to?'

'Just finding my way,' Plant said.

He felt himself shivering. And then he remembered Revill's remarks on the chill of black magic, and shivered even more.

If Revill were right and Major had security connections and practised magic, then it would be only wise not to reveal that any of this was something Plant knew. Or suspected. It could be the sort of knowledge or suspicion that got you killed. In a cold library late at night, undiscovered until some dutiful undergraduate or fellow came in to study. And that could be a while.

He sneezed. The dust and the mustiness, the ancient aromas of ancient learning tickled his nostrils, irritated his sinuses. Or maybe they cleared his head. It was like a chapel, except it was books that were buried here rather than bodies. As far as Plant could tell. No tomb for the trysting lovers to lie on, swoon over, fall beside. No lovers.

'Where have you been?'

'It's a bit dark,' said Plant.

'The last couple of days.'

'I spent the weekend in the country.'

Major grunted.

'You heard about Revill.'

'Yes,' Plant said.

'Typical.'

'What happened?'

'Sudden death,' said Major.

'Do you know how?'

'Keeled over after dining at High Table. If I've told the bursar once I've told him a dozen times, those kitchens are unhygienic. Absolute death trap.'

'So it was food poisoning? Really?'

'No idea, to be honest, but I wouldn't be surprised.'

'Did you invite him to dine?'

'To give him food poisoning? Absolutely not. Not after his disgraceful performance when Lucy invited him home. Fellow couldn't hold his drink. Never could. Wouldn't want him embarrassing me in hall.'

'So who did invite him?'

'How should I know?' said Major.

The wisdom of the past surrounded them, ranked along the shelves, massively bound and forever untouched. Everything thought and known before the modern age. And now nobody was going to know anything. That was the one thing Plant knew without any doubt.

'Did he embarrass you?'

'Managed to keep well away from the chap.'

'How did he seem when he left?'

'Didn't notice. Like he always seemed, probably. Half pissed.'

'But not ill.'

'Not that I noticed.'

'What did he die of?'

'How should I know?' he said again.

'I thought you might have heard.'

'Not a peep,' said Major. 'You met him. You talked to him. Did he seem like a sick man to you?'

Plant hesitated.

'It's hard to tell,' he said.

'These chaps are so unfit,' said Major. 'Never exercise. Smoke and drink. They could keel over any moment.'

'I suppose so.'

'Take my word for it,' said Major. 'Revill's your evidence.'

'You think it could have been a heart attack or something?'

'Most likely,' said Major. 'Too much rich food, too much claret, too much port, not used to the high life, strain on the system. Unless he decided to end it all. Quite possible. Wise career move. You talked to him. Did he seem like he was on the way out?'

'It's hard to tell.'

'So you keep saying. What did he have to say for himself?'

'Not a lot.'

'You saw enough of him.'

'Two or three times.'

'And you got nothing out of him?'

'I wouldn't say nothing.'

'What would you say then?'

What would he say? Plant reflected. What did Major already know?

'Are you any good at this, Plant? Did I hire the right person?'

The reading lamp made a small pool of light in the dark library. It picked out bits of Major, his nose, his glasses.

'Why are we meeting in here?'

'Don't you like it?' said Major. 'Atmosphere. Give you a taste of the original Oxford before you go.'

Was that a threat? Plant wondered. It depended on how you interpreted going.

'Just doing my job,' said Major. 'Making sure everything's in order. All ship shape and Bristol fashion. Put out the lights and then put out the lights.'

He gleamed at Plant. His teeth and glasses sharp and bright in the enveloping night.

'Surgeon's rounds,' he said, and laughed. It echoed hollowly beneath the high arched roof.

'My responsibility to keep everything neat and tidy,' he said, fixing Plant with a piercing look. 'As fellow librarian,' he explained. 'Apart from making sure people don't try and order unnecessary rubbish I have to make sure there are no bodies lying around before I lock up for the night. So, kill two birds with one stone, as it were. Talk to you here while I check out the other corpses.'

*

'Wraps it all up, anyway.'

'Wraps what up?' Plant asked.

'The business of the notes, of course. He won't be sending any more, now.'

'If he was sending them.'

'Not a doubt.'

'No?'

'No,' said Major, firmly.

'What makes you think it was Revill?'

'Who else? He was here. He was resentful. He was evidently crazy. Balance of the mind disturbed. Motive, means and opportunity, Plant, motive, means and opportunity.'

'Possibly.'

'Did he say anything to you about sending them?' Major asked.

'No,' said Plant.

'Nothing at all?'

'Nothing at all.'

'But it was him. We can be sure of that.'

'I don't know.'

'I do,' said Major.

They stood there silent.

'What did he say about me?' he asked.

'Not a lot.'

'Not a lot,' said Major in tones of disgust. As if it were another mark of Revill's failure that Major had not featured largely in his conversation. Or of Plant's failure in that he had not elicited anything. 'You sure?'

'What would you expect him to have said?'

'How would I know? Who knows what went on in his paranoid imaginings?'

'You feel he was paranoid?'

'Of course he was paranoid. Always going on about blacklists and dark forces blocking his career. Career. What a joke. Always hinting I was behind it.'

'He didn't say any of that to me,' Plant said.

'Really?'

It seemed like a good time to know nothing. Act daft, as Revill's mother had put it.

'No.'

'Hard to believe.' He looked at Plant untrustingly. 'I never heard him do anything but whinge.'

'Oh, he whinged.'

'What about?'

'About his career, that's true. But not about you.'

'He didn't see me as the devil incarnate?'

'No.'

'Or some black beast in his path?'

'No. Why, should he have done?'

'What he should have done was get treatment. He was quite evidently bonkers. Anyone who thinks the government is paying chaps to go around casting magic spells onto the loony left is self-evidently loony.'

'Unless he was right,' said Plant.

Major gave Plant that old-fashioned look and fiddled with the little metal chain that served to switch the desk light on and off. He pulled it down and the light went out.

'You have to be joking.'

Plant forced out a tentative jokey laugh.

'You're sure you're not missing something?' Major asked.

'Not that I'm aware,' said Plant. 'It's possible I might have missed something, but I'm not conscious of it.'

'Not holding out on me?'

'Why would I do that?'

'Did he go on about magic?'

'Magic?'

They both waited there in the dark library. A slight tinge of moonlight came in through the high, narrow windows. There was a rustling that could have been mice or rats in the wainscoting. Or Major removing some lethal weapon from beneath his gown.

'He struck me as more of a scientific rationalist,' said Plant. 'Your old dialectical materialist rather than a new age thinker.'

'There's nothing new age about magic,' said Major.

'I suppose not.'

'The ancient wisdom,' said Major.

'I didn't get the impression that it was his thing,' said Plant.

Major clicked the light back on.

'Good,' he said.

He looked fixedly at Plant.

Plant looked back. He was good at being immobile.

'I think someone went through my room while I

was away at the weekend,' Plant said.

'Did they take anything?'

'No.'

'So how do you know?'

'There were drawers left open. Things tossed on the floor.'

'Sure you didn't do it yourself? Get home drunk, or something.'

'No.'

'Sounds rather clumsy.'

'I think whoever it was wanted me to know they'd made a search.'

'Well, it wasn't me,' Major said.

'And it can't have been Revill.'

'Why should it have been Revill?'

'If Revill had been sending the anonymous notes, he might have searched my rooms to see if I had written up a report, see if I suspected he'd sent them. He knew I was onto him. But since he's dead it can't have been him. So either he wasn't the person who sent the notes, or someone else did the searching.'

'Can't imagine who,' said Major.

'Ah, well,' said Plant.

'But I don't have any doubts it was Revill who'd been sending the notes.'

'Maybe.'

'No doubts at all,' said Major, decisively. 'You better believe it.'

# Thirty-Three

Lucy woke him. Plant was dreaming horrible death in the library dreams when she hammered on his door.

'Theysayhekilledhimselfbutthat'snonsense.Idon't believe it.'

'Who, Revill?'

'Is anybody else dead?' she asked. 'Yet?'

'Can you give me a minute while I just put some clothes on?' Plant asked.

'No,' she said. 'I can't stop. Just listen.'

He sat on the edge of the bed, shivering.

'Oh, just do it,' she said, 'Naked men are no mystery to me.'

He picked up his shirt and trousers from where they lay on the floor.

'They say it was some obscure poison. In small, controlled doses it's supposed to be hallucinogenic. Take too much and it kills you.'

'What's it called?'

'They wouldn't say.'

'That figures,' said Plant. 'So where did he get it from?'

'They say he looked it up on the internet. How to make it, what the ingredients were. They checked his computer and got his internet records.'

'Convenient,' said Plant. He pulled the shirt over his head.

'It's nonsense,' she said. 'He never used the internet.

He was too paranoid.'

'Is that so?'

'Yes. He told me.'

'Why?'

'Why what?'

'Why did he tell you?'

'No reason. I was telling him about something I'd done a search on. In the long lonely mornings, noons and nights of North Oxford. And he said to be careful. There's no privacy. Everything's logged. If you want to find out something just go to a library. Get the book from the shelves yourself. Read it there. Make notes. Don't photocopy, that can be logged too. Then put the book back on the shelf where you found it. Don't even put it on a trolley for returned books. Best no one ever knows it was ever looked at. Or you can go to a bookshop, look it up there. If you buy it just make sure you pay cash, don't leave a credit card trail. He went on about this sort of thing all the time. He would never have made an internet search. For a fucking drug? They've got to be joking.'

'Makes sense,' Plant agreed. 'From what I knew of him. Though if he was planning to commit suicide, he mightn't have been worried any more about being tracked on the internet.'

'He would,' said Lucy.

'Yes,' Plant agreed, 'he would.'

'Anyway,' said Lucy, 'he wasn't the sort of person to commit suicide.'

'So what was he doing?  Taking a trip that went

wrong? A flash back down memory lane. How very seventies.'

'No,' said Lucy. 'He didn't mess around with those sort of drugs. Not any more. He was too paranoid. Smoking the odd joint was as far as he went.'

'And quite often,' Plant suggested.

'Maybe,' she said. 'But this is nonsense. Someone else used his computer.'

'Any ideas who?'

'The murderer,' she said, as if there were no need to give the name, it was obvious to anyone who it was.

'Is that so?' said Plant.

'Yes,' she said.

He'd got his trousers on and was reaching his hands beneath the bed for his socks.

'I've got to go,' she said, 'I've got things to do.'

She gave him a peck on the cheek and rushed out.

Plant took off his shirt and trousers and went back to bed.

*

They came for Plant later in the morning. Discreetly. No kicking in the door, no loud hailers calling 'Put down your gun'. Just the tap on the door and the two of them standing there. Equal opportunity. Male and female.

He was still in bed. It seemed more comfortable in bed than not in England. In the chill mornings. They asked him if he minded having a few words with them. He did mind, but there was clearly no point in saying so. They waited politely while he dressed. Watching.

'It's about Mr Paul Revill,' they said.

'Uh-huh.'

'We hoped you might be able to fill in a few details.'

'I hardly knew him.'

'Well, in that case it shouldn't take long.'

They weren't into saying 'Sir'. None of the, 'Just step down to the station, Sir' business. They didn't seem like local coppers. They exuded a substantially more ruling class air than you would expect from local police. If Revill had been there he could no doubt have identified from their accent and stance the precise social fraction to which they belonged. The female person could have been one of those ladies that Major claimed made Lucy feel uneasy. He could understand that now. She made Plant feel uneasy. A classic English rose, all thorns and briars protecting a puckered up, pink cheeked face. He was used to police. He was familiar with the unease they projected. But this was something different. She flashed open a wallet with an insignia. Something special. They were always special. Special constables, special operations executive, special air service, special operations command, special branch. It was the name of a tree-lopping firm in Sydney, Special Branch. He wondered where these two had concealed their chain saws.

He waited to be escorted through the college and out to the car waiting on the double yellow lines, the rear door opened, the hand on top of his head, the firm push to shut him in. The doors centrally locked. The windows tinted. Tinted windows that you could see neither into nor out from. A screen between the driver and the back, like a taxicab. Tinted and opaque and no doubt bulletproof. Left to himself in the back. Is this where they gas me? He felt sympathetic to Revill's views on the secret state. It wouldn't be a long drive. When they stopped and opened the door for him, they would be inside a garage. No windows. Automatic door already closed. The one bare light globe lighting the brick walls and concrete floor. They would take him into the house. The blinds drawn. The furniture lonely and unused. Suburban Oxford safe house. You would think they would call it a special house. Spécialité de la maison: safety. It didn't seem the appropriate time to suggest it.

But they didn't take him anywhere. They just stood there.

If only a small percentage of what Revill had said were true, then it would be best to forget all of it. Who knew which percentage could get him killed? Get Plant killed. Revill was already dead. Plant considered it. He felt full and frank cooperation might not be the best idea. He decided to deny everything. Everything that Revill had said. Deny that Revill had said anything at all. After all, Revill was not there to argue about it. And keep it up until they produced the hypodermic and shot him up with the truth serum. But they wouldn't do that, would they?

Not unless they had already decided to kill him, so didn't care what he saw them do. But it was more likely they would avoid killing him if they didn't have to. Or maybe they would just slip something into his coffee. Or whatever they offered. But so far there was no suggestion of coffee. They seemed not to have brought a thermos flask. He wasn't going to start demanding it. Nor was he going to offer to make any. In the meantime, until he started feeling trippy, agree to everything and say nothing. And keep calm. Keep that cool, imperturbable, inscrutable catatonic mask that had unfitted him for most other forms of social interaction. Because without a doubt it was all being covertly recorded, ready for voice analysis to detect the slightest flicker of hesitation, maybe even a pinhole camera in a jacket lapel to note any flickering eye movement, Major's inauthenticity researches presumably contributing to the analytical tools.

'Yes,' he agreed, he had met Revill.

'Here?'

'Yes, here.'

'Australia?'

'Yes, Australia too.'

'Why?'

'This is confidential?' Plant asked.

They looked at him blankly.

Plant looked blankly back.

'Dr Major informs us you were doing some work for him.'

'Yes.'

'What sort of work would that have been?'

'His inauthenticity project.'

''Fraid not,' said the tall blond one with cold blue eyes. The male. He was the sort of blond whose eyebrows and eyelashes seemed almost invisible. Plant could imagine him doing unspeakable things to people. To people like Plant.

'I'm sorry,' said Plant.

'You will be if you try messing us around. We know why Dr Major hired you.'

Plant nodded.

'So?'

'As far as I understand, I'm on the books of the inauthenticity project.'

'Well, you might be. We'll come to that. But Dr Major mentioned anonymous notes.'

'Yes.'

'Which you were investigating.'

'I still am, as far as I know.'

'Well,' said the other one, the female person, 'you might be in for a surprise there.'

'Really? In what way?'

'We'll ask the questions,' said the blond man.

Plant nodded.

'What do you call yourself, Mr Plant?'

'Plant,' said Plant.

'I don't think you should play the smart guy.'

'I wouldn't,' seconded the English rose.

'We'll try it again,' said the blond man. 'You call yourself an investigator?'

'Research assistance, investigative reporting.'

'And in your country that means what?'

'Research assistance, investigative ...'

'Hit man?' said the English rose. 'Contract killing?'

'No.'

'Stand-over man?'

'No.'

'No?'

'Absolutely not.'

'Were you hired to tidy up a little problem? Find out who was sending these so-called anonymous notes and dispose of him?' said the blond.

'Or her,' said the English rose.

'No. I don't do that sort of thing.'

'You're quite sure of that?'

'Of course I'm sure.'

'Did you take on a contract to kill Mr Revill?'

'No. I don't kill people.'

'Dr Major approached you?'

'To find out who was sending him anonymous notes.'

'You found out who was sending these notes.'

'Not yet.'

'You found out who was sending these notes,' said the blond one again.

'No.'

'It's not a question.'

'Oh.'

'Dr Major told us the evidence pointed to Revill.'

'He might have thought so,' said Plant.

'But you don't.'

'No.'

'Why not?'

'There's no evidence. It's possible, but there's nothing firm to go on. Revill happened to be on leave here. Beyond that there's no reason to think it was him. There's no more reason to think it was Revill than Mrs Major.'

'You think it was Mrs Major.'

'No. No reason to think it's either of them.'

'Why mention her then?'

'The category of the equally unlikely,' said Plant.

'Or equally likely?'

'Well, if it's about Major having a bit on the side, she's as likely to object as anyone. Whereas Revill wouldn't know what he'd been up to in Oxford.'

'And you think it's about Dr Major having a bit on the side, as you put it.'

'Probably.'

'And not something else.'

'There's no suggestion it's about anything else. There's no suggestion it's about anything, for that matter. The notes I've seen were just vague threats.'

'Really.'

'As far as I could make out.'

'And Mr Revill could not have known any of this? About Dr Major's having a bit on the side?'

'I suppose he could. But he didn't give any indication he knew anything. Or had any interest.'

'You ask him?'

'Not directly.'

'Then how do you know?'

'You get a feeling. You let people talk.'

'Is that what you do? You let people talk?'

'Yes.'

'We should let you talk,' said the English rose.

'I am talking.'

'Only when we ask you questions.'

'Look,' said Plant. 'Dr Major hired me because he was worried about these notes he was getting. He jumped at the idea it was Revill because Revill had been in Australia when Dr Major was there, and then came over here on leave. But his wife was in both places too. Anyway, you don't need physically to be in a place to arrange for notes to be mailed. As far as I could see there was nothing to link Revill with the notes. Or his wife.'

'They've stopped now.'

'Have they? I haven't heard anything. They don't seem to have come at regular intervals, anyway.'

'Why are you so keen to put Revill out of the picture?'

Plant pondered.

'I just don't make him for it. Apart from which, if it was him then the notes will have stopped and I'm out of a job.'

'Does that worry you?'

'Not especially. Something always turns up.'

'Then it won't worry you if we tell you you're out of a job whether it was Revill or not?'

'Really?'

'Because you shouldn't have a job, should you? Not here. Not on your tourist visa. No work permit.'

'I imagine Dr Major took care of that,' Plant said.

'You might have imagined it, but he didn't.'

'He didn't?'

'He didn't.'

'But he said he'd put me on the books.'

'What books would those be?' asked the blond one.

'Well, I don't know. I guess it's a figure of speech.'

'There aren't any books.'

'Not even a few boxes of *Major Magic*?'

'No books and nothing about you being on any books,' said the blond man. 'But you might find yourself on a plane first thing tomorrow morning,'

'If not before,' said the English rose.

It seemed best to follow the never complain, never explain rule. Being deported might be an attractive option. It might turn out to be the best thing that could happen. In the circumstances. And the sooner the better.

'Tell us more about Mr Revill,' said the blond man. 'Tell us about your conversations with him.'

'What sort of things?' Plant asked.

'Did Mr Revill have any enemies?' asked the English rose.

'I don't think so.'

'You're sure?'

'No more than usual for an academic.'

'Go on.'

'They all have that sense of injured merit. Complain they lack advancement. Feel they've been blocked. But generally the hostility seems less against those who might have blocked them than a matter of envy of those who've got ahead.'

'And Mr Revill felt his career had been thwarted?'

'Oh, yes.'

'Why?'

'I think he felt because of his politics.'

'You think.'

'Well, I don't know,' said Plant. 'But that was what he said.'

'His politics.'

'Yes.'

'Which were?'

'Oh, utopian.'

'Subversive?'

'I don't know.'

'Don't you?'

'Not from what he said to me.'

'You're an expert on subversion, are you, Mr Plant?'

'No, not at all. I just don't know what his politics were.'

They looked at him coldly.

'They could have been subversive,' he conceded, throwing Revill to the wolves, but Revill was dead anyway, so what did it matter? 'It's not my area.'

'That's not what we understand,' said the English rose.

It seemed best to say nothing.

'And who did he think was blocking his career?'

'He didn't say. He just seemed to think that was what usually happened. Institutional practice, was what he said.'

'Institutional practice,' said the English rose. 'That has a familiar ring.'

Plant looked blank.

'One of the phrases known subversives use.'

'I don't know,' said Plant. 'It was just what he said.'

'You have a good memory for phrases?'

'Not especially.'

'How about names?'

'Names?'

'Did he name names?'

'What sort of names?'

'The name or names of those allegedly blocking his career.'

'No.'

'You're sure of that.'

'Yes.'

'Yes?'

'Absolutely.'

'Is there anything further you would like to tell us?'

'No.'

'You're sure of that?'

'Quite sure.'

'Right then,' said the blond man. 'Don't go talking about any of this with anyone.'

'Any of it?'

'Any of it.'

'Is this the Official Secrets Act?'

'Nobody said that.'

'Do I have to sign anything?'

'No. You don't have to sign anything and you don't have to say anything. To anyone.'

'So how do I know it's Official Secrets if I don't have to sign anything?'

'Nobody said it was.'

'So why is it not to be talked about?'

'We're telling you.'

'And that's all it needs?'

'That's all it needs.'

'If that's the way it is …' said Plant.

'That's the way it is. Make sure it stays that way.'

'And have your bags packed ready to catch your flight out,' said the English rose.

## Thirty-Four

As Plant walked into college the next day he noticed the flag flying at half-mast over the entrance. He went through the archway and a voice called out to him from the porters' lodge.

'Mr Plant, sir. A message for you.'

He didn't know they knew his name. But they did. And they were looking out for him.

It was a message from Lucy. She was in the Radcliffe, please call.

He couldn't imagine what she was doing in the library. And how could he call her there? It seemed very odd.

'The Radcliffe Camera?' he checked with the porter.

'No sir, the Radcliffe hospital. Tragic business, sir.'

\*

Lucy was looking radiantly convalescent. Her eyes were bright even if there were traces of darkness beneath them. And that could have been artfully applied make-up. Plant was suspicious of but inexpert in the wiles of womankind. A swathe of magazines covered the bed, *Vogue, Harpers, Elle.* A television fluttered with the sound off.

'Plant,' she said. 'How nice of you to come.'

He smiled his chivalrous smile. Like a knight from some old-fashioned book.

'How are you?' he asked.

'Desperate for a smoke. You wouldn't have one with you, would you?'

'Sorry.'

'Not even tobacco? I'm dying for a smoke.'

'Not even tobacco.'

She sighed.

'They're keeping me under observation,' she said. 'Whatever they mean by that.'

He didn't quite know how to begin. She saw that, and smiled in a contented sort of way.

'They say I'm lucky to be alive.'

'I would think so,' he said.

'Three cheers for addictive behaviour,' she said. 'Long live eating disorders.'

'Tell me,' said Plant.

'It seems,' she said, 'that I vomited most of it up and survived.'

'That was lucky. What was it, do they know?'

'Oh, some evil witch's brew Archer had found in some old book. One of those native poisons which slay in a split second and defy the skill of the analyst. Untraceable, of course.'

'Untraceable?'

'Yes. After long enough.'

'And it was long enough?'

'Well, there I was, vomiting my little guts out, as is often my wont. And there was Archer, out to the world. By the time I'd come round and found him it was all too late. For him, that is.'

'How did it happen?'

'Can't you just get the police report and read it?'

'No.'

'Won't they let you see it?'

'No.'

'I thought you were a private investigator.'

'Apparently not in this country. They think I'm an undesirable alien here. They're deporting me.'

'What a bummer,' she said.

'Maybe.'

'Oh well, here goes. You sure you want to hear it?'

'Yes.'

'I'm not sure I want to go through it again.'

'I'm sorry.'

'"I'm sorry but please go on," is what you mean.'

He smiled.

She smiled back.

'It seems,' she said, 'it seems, because there is no clear evidence, but it seems that Archer mixed up some poisonous brew from one of his ancient books of recipes. He had all the drugs there in his little medicine cabinet. Research tools, he called them.'

'You've seen them?'

She tapped the side of her nose in Major's insinuating gesture.

'Then he gave me a dose and self-administered the rest. Put it in the coffee, or the wine or something. He conked out in his study. I had a couple of furtive joints and the odd drink before I went to bed and chucked it all up. As per usual. But that was not something I had ever apprised poor Archer of. And he was never that observant. Not about me. So. Chucked it all up and flushed it all away. No traces. Went to bed. Heavy sleep. No sign of Archer in the morning. Nothing unusual about that. Assumed he'd been out tom-catting all night. Feel groggy, have breakfast, chuck it all up. Feel rotten. Go back to bed. Dinner-time arrives. No Archer. Phone the college. Not there. Look in his study just in case. There he is. Out cold. Phone doctor. Doctor comes. Takes pulse. No pulse to take. Doctor phones police. Police come. Doctor puts me in hospital for observation. And here we are.'

'What was it?'

'They wouldn't say. Probably the same stuff he used on Paul,' she said.

'How do you know Archer gave you the poison?'

'Oh, he left a little message on his computer. How he could face it no more. Sick of my adulteries. Paul was the last straw. So he decided to kill him. And me too.'

'Did he say he'd killed Paul Revill?'

'Oh, yes. Popped a potion in his port after High Table. But then he said he realised killing Revill wasn't the answer. It was his beloved wife who was the problem. So he fixed that. But having done it he felt the future was bleak and his chances of the chair were slim in the circumstances. Scandal and all that. So he was ending it all.'

'Are the police sure he wrote the note on the computer?'

340

She looked at him owlishly.

'It would've been better if it had been in his handwriting,' he added.

'Better for whom?'

'More persuasive.'

'What a suspicious mind you have.'

'It's my job.'

'How sad. You must be a very untrusting person. Anyway, I'm not sure you have a job any longer, now Archer's gone.'

'Are they certain?' he asked again.

'Well, no other prints were on the keys. And the timing was about right.'

'About right.'

'Within the time frame. The computer clock recorded it.'

'I see.'

'Of course,' she said, 'you could see them thinking through the possibility that I'd written the note and mixed up the brew and slipped it to poor Archer and taken just a teeny-weeny little bit myself. But they're being very nice about it. No third degree.'

'And did you?'

'What a terrible thing to ask. You do have a suspicious mind. Fortunately,' she said, 'because of Archer's secret work, the funnies came along.'

'The funnies?'

'His secret service friends.'

'And?'

'We had a little chat.'

'And what did you tell them?'

'Well, it's all Official Secrets Act stuff, so I'm not able to say.'

'Of course,' said Plant.

'But effectively I said I thought Archer had been worried about Revill sending those anonymous letters. So he'd bumped him off to keep him quiet. And then when he realised I knew, or suspected, what he'd done, he tried to bump me off.'

'And they accepted that?'

'Of course. Why shouldn't they?'

'I see.'

'Do you? The point was that whatever Archer was up to was all such hush-hush stuff, and if it ever came out then Archer would have been ruined. The secret services would have denied everything, naturally. So they could see his motivation. He would have been lucky if they didn't bump him off to keep it all under wraps. Come to think of it, maybe they did and faked the suicide note. What do you think? Anyway, they naturally didn't want any of this getting out. Especially if they did bump him off. So I think they had a discreet word to the local police.'

He wondered. Could some secret service operative have killed Revill and Major to keep it all under wraps? If there was something that needed keeping under wraps. Who would ever know? And wouldn't Lucy have been bumped off too? Or could Lucy have done it? Killed Major because he'd killed Revill, if it was Major who killed Revill. Or if she thought he had done. Or even killed Revill to frame Major, and then finished off Major and made it look like suicide. None of it seemed any less believable than the official story. Whatever the official story was.

'How did the funnies get into the act, anyway?' he asked.

'I called them,' she said.

'You called them? How? Why?'

'I thought they'd need to know. Archer gave me this number to call if ever something happened to him. And since something incontrovertibly had, I called it.'

'Incontrovertibly,' said Plant, half to himself.

'It's not often you get a chance to use a word like that, I know,' she said. 'So I took it.'

'What are you going to do now?' he asked.

'With Archer dead? Oh, sell up. I wouldn't want to stay here. I thought I might come home to Australia when they give me my passport back. Get back to a decent climate. Maybe we could have lunch some time. Share an illicit smoke. Catch up on unfinished business. Now your client's dead and the case is over we'll be able to do that, won't we? I've got your number. You never know, I might need to hire you at some point, depending on how things go.'

Plant smiled, wanly.

'You look wan,' she said. 'Oh, what can ail thee, knight at arms, alone and palely loitering?'

'I'll be all right,' he said. 'I just feel a bit fragile.'

'Oh, we're all a bit fragile,' she said. 'But we're all going to be all right. Aren't we, Plant? We just have to think positive, don't we?'

'Yes,' said Plant, 'yes, absolutely.'

'That's what Paul used to say. In his lectures on the novel, bless his memory. He used to say it was the essential thing.'

'What was?' Plant asked.

She smiled, the radiant image of womanhood, spelling it out for him.

'The positive ending.'

# MORE FINE FICTION FROM PRESS ON / ARCADIA

## Michael Wilding
## THE PRISONER OF MOUNT WARNING

What were the 60s & 70s really about? How authentic were those stoned revolutionaries? What if it was all a fraud?

'With a detective called Plant and a journey from Sydney to the dope fields of Byron Bay, the private eye novel has come a long way from Raymond Chandler ... the detective novel's move into an era of magic mushrooms and free love.' – *Sydney Morning Herald*

'This satirical odyssey from an Australian literary legend has his protagonist heading north to find himself, among other things. Charles Dorritt recovers from a breakdown by doing a writing course and decides to write of his torture and slavery at the hands of the security services. He's pursued by Plant, who's been hired to dissuade him from revealing all ... Wilding was at the forefront of a rebellious Australian literary movement in the '70s; in this book, he weaves a narrative of personal, literary and political dimensions into an entertaining yarn.' – Phil Brown, *Brisbane News*

## Peter Corris
## THE COLONIAL QUEEN

1886. Rosa Nightingale, prostitute, Lucas Ramsay, ex-soldier turned bandit, Stanley Stoneham, prizefighter, Alexander McPherson, alcoholic doctor, and Griffith Summerhill, police officer, are aboard the majestic Murray River paddleboat steamer *The Colonial Queen*. Rosa is fleeing her louche life and opium addiction and searching for her remittance man brother. Ramsay is on the run from the law after robbing a bank. Stoneham's fighting career is drawing to a close as he resorts to stopping off in the river towns for exhibition bouts. McPherson battles his demons and yearns for a life like that of his hero, fellow Scotsman Robert Louis Stevenson. Summerhill is on the trail of Ramsay. Their lives collide and intertwine as *The Colonial Queen* moves down the swift-flowing, ever-changing river.

'Authentic and unforced ... not divorced from the society and politics of the time. And part of the politics is to do with water, just as is the case now.' – Thomas Keneally

'Corris has successfully combined his considerable knowledge of the sport of boxing with his dramatic account of the nineteenth-century paddle steamers that serviced the third-longest navigable river in the world. The result is a cracking storyline with sharp dialogue and an original setting.' – John Dale

## Morris Lurie
## HERGESHEIMER HANGS IN

You are an unarmed man in the wilderness being hunted by men with guns and dogs. The ATM business? That number you pulled on the gullible art world? Those anonymous envelopes slipped under the door? Or deeper? Darker? A disappeared daughter? An absent son? Your name is Hergesheimer. This is your world. Deal with it.

'Lurie is a gifted impressionist; he arranges scraps of dialogue, reverie and observation in a volatile mixture that bubbles with life.' – *New York Times Book Review*

'Reading Morris Lurie's stories … is like having a brilliant, funny friend. It's not that he's always good for a laugh, which he is, but also that he's a help when the going gets tough. He faces sadness, even tragedy, with spirit.' – Bruce Grant, *Australian Book Review*

'Lurie has that kind of acute appreciation of social farce that tots up to a real observation of the styles of the culture.' – Malcolm Bradbury, *The Guardian*


## Ross Fitzgerald and Trevor L Jordan
## FOOLS' PARADISE: LIFE IN AN ALTERED STATE

'Wake up, Australia,' Grafton Everest exhorts viewers every morning on Australia-wide breakfast television. This doesn't please those he attacks like wily former premier Hoogstraden, whose biography Grafton is forced into writing. Grafton's day job as Professor of LifeSkills and Hospitality is under threat from the economically and sexually rapacious Vice-Chancellor Deirdre Morrow. And Lee Horton, head of Australia's newly privatised Secret Service (trading as Spyforce Australia) is worried too. He knows that Grafton has trouble lying. And nothing is more dangerous than a man who habitually tells the truth.

'Grafton Everest is a wonderful creation whom I would place without question in the ranks of Philip Roth's Portnoy and Kingsley Amis's Lucky Jim.' – Barry Humphries

'Conquering Everest.' – Howard Jacobson, *The Observer*

'*Fools' Paradise* is Grafton Everest's most over-the-top excursion – it has more sex than before, crazier politics, more pointless academic life, a tighter net of anxieties. Some might say the real world forced Ross Fitzgerald and Trevor Jordan's hands.' – Carl Harrison-Ford

Garry Disher
**PLAY ABANDONED**

Every summer, the country families load the roof racks and motor south to the Bon Accord hotel. They find order here, beside the sea. Constancy in a changeable world. But this time ladders and workmen choke the foyer. There's foreign muck on the menu, posters proclaiming a Summer Festival of Writing. And child abductors are lurking on the sun blasted streets, in the tricky dunes. There's smoke in the hot inland winds. Everything's different this time. This time Marian Parr is not complete. She knows she should not have come. As love fractures, and old certainties crumble, Marian leans grieving against a balcony post, meddling with the cosmos.

'A rare pleasure.' – *New York Times Book Review* on *Blood Moon*

'...grand and sweeping, full of action but also reflection, and deeply satisfying.'
– *Sydney Morning Herald* on *Past the Headlands*

'...Disher's masterpiece, an astonishingly told caper that's tough, tender, poignant and totally captivating.' – *The Age* on *The Dragon Man*

 ARCADIA *an imprint of* **australian scholarly publishing**